Christmas Revels III

THREE REGENCY NOVELLAS

Kate Parker

Anna D. Allen

Hannah Meredith

SS

Singing Spring Press

This is a work of fiction. All names, characters, and incidents are the product of the author's imagination. Any resemblance to actual occurrences or persons, living or dead, is coincidental. Historical events and personages are fictionalized.

CHRISTMAS REVELS III : THREE REGENCY NOVELLAS

ISBN: 978-1-942470-02-1 (Print)
ISBN: 978-1-942470-03-8 (E-book)

Published by Singing Spring Press

Table of Contents

Magdalena's Christmas Rake

by

Anna D. Allen

Magdalena's Christmas Rake

"GOOD GOD, MOTHER! NOT HER!" Thomas Eddington stood in Lady Eddington's sitting room and watched from the window as two more houseguests emerged from yet another snow-dusted carriage below. "How could you invite her, of all people?"

"Really, Thomas. Such language may be acceptable among your London acquaintances, but I will not tolerate it." Despite her even-toned admonishment, his mother joined him at the window to see of whom he spoke. She promptly asked with some surprise, "Surely you can't mean Miss Olivia Winslow? She's delightful."

"No, no. Not her. *Her.*" And he rudely pointed at the bespectacled lady accompanying the very lovely Miss Olivia up the steps to the house. "Her aunt. Mad Maddie."

"I've never understood why you call her that," Lady Eddington said moving away from the window. "Miss Maddie Winslow is quite the sanest person I know, which is rather amazing when one considers that mother of hers."

"It's the alliteration, my dear." Sir William Eddington spoke up from behind his paper as he sat reading beside the fire. "The sort of thing a seven-year-old would think quite clever."

"And I don't understand why you dislike her so," his wife continued speaking to their son as if never hearing her husband.

Thomas turned away from the window and shrugged dismissively. "I simply can't abide the woman. That's all. Besides, she looks like a perpetually mourning Madonna, and who wants that around to ruin all the fun?"

"That's all?" Sir William abruptly lowered his paper, and Thomas feared what was coming before his father spoke another word. He suddenly wished he'd stayed in London rather than coming home that morning for the Christmas season. "You haven't liked Miss Maddie since she caught you naked at the pond."

Lady Eddington let out a shriek. "Good Heavens! Another scandal?" Thomas knew, had he been half his height, she would have tanned his hide. "Why haven't I heard of this one?"

"I was five, Mother."

While that clarification calmed his mother's sudden burst of outrage, it did not stop his father from recounting the tale. "It was that party on the lawn. You remember, Sophia. The one where Aunt Charlotte pilfered the bottle of brandy—which I was saving for your next confinement—and Amelia somehow...."

"No, do not remind me. My children will be the death of me."

Thomas wished his father would relate the significantly more humorous tale of his toddler sister's discovery of an abandoned glass of brandy in the midst of company. "Shouldn't you go down to greet them, Mother?" he suggested in an effort to stave off his father and distract his mother.

"Certainly not," Lady Eddington replied, "Miss Olivia is barely out, and while the Winslows are good, respectable people of means, all this will be quite overwhelming to her—her first party, the first time to do anything without the scrutiny of her mother's constant gaze—and with Lord and Lady Bollingbrook here as well. No. Best to let Miss Olivia settle in, and I will convey my apologies when I greet them before dinner." She turned to her husband and said, "Pray, William, you were saying?"

Sir William continued as if he had never stopped. "Well while you were occupied with Aunt Charlotte and Amelia and trying to explain things to the vicar, Thomas decided to take off all his clothes and throw them in the pond."

"Chartreuse," Thomas grumbled, as if that explained his actions on a summer's day more than twenty years ago, "If Mother dressed you in chartreuse, you would do exactly the same."

Looking pained, Lady Eddington gave a sad, little gasp and for a brief moment, seemed at a rare loss for words. "It was such a lovely little outfit and you looked adorable in it. I always wondered how you managed to get it so filthy. It was completely spoilt." Thomas suddenly felt ashamed for hurting his mother by his actions as a five-year-old—but not enough to regret them.

"And there Miss Maddie was," Sir William continued, "all of ten years old..."

"Twelve. She was twelve, Father."

"She grabbed him by the hand and marched him right up the hill to me—in the midst of all our guests— naked as the day he was born. And she said, 'I believe this belongs to you, sir.'"

Both his parents burst out laughing.

"It was humiliating," Thomas mumbled.

"Well, you deserved every moment of it," his mother said, "Throwing away that lovely little suit. After I had it specially made."

Sir William raised his paper again but, from behind it, concluded, "And that, my boy, is the real reason you can't abide Miss Maddie Winslow."

Thomas felt a modicum of relief. Not because his father had finished recounting the first humiliation of Thomas's life but because he had left out the key fact that had started it all. So presumably, only he and Miss Maddie knew that detail.

"But I don't understand why *her*, Mother," Thomas said, "Why did you invite *her*, of all people?"

"Wrong question, Tom." His father piped up from

behind the paper. "Why *Miss Olivia* is more like it."

Thomas glanced from the newspaper hiding his father to his mother and feared the answer.

"Mother?" he tentatively queried.

"The most beautiful girl in the county. She's to have her first Season this Spring, and I...," Lady Eddington seemed to blush, "...I merely wanted you to have the... opportunity to meet her before all that. Besides, Alice wanted her to visit. No doubt by Twelfth Night, those two girls will have every day of their Season planned down to the minute."

Thomas nodded in understanding. "And Lady Caroline Forbes? Why did you invite her?"

"Same *opportunity*, son," his father said with a chuckle.

Lady Eddington shrugged and smiled, as if trying to look innocent of any attempted matchmaking. "I've wanted to invite Lord and Lady Bollingbrook for some time now. So naturally, I expected Lord Sutton and Lady Caroline to accompany their parents, it being Christmas and all."

"Naturally." Thomas folded his arms across his chest and nodded, knowing exactly what his mother was up to.

"John and Lord Sutton are such good friends, after all," his mother added, bringing Thomas's youngest brother into the equation.

"Oh, is that it?" Thomas feigned ignorance of his mother's machinations before saying, "Really, Mother, you're as transparent as the glass in the Orangery. Alice is to have Sutton, while John and I get to fight over Lady Caroline and Miss Olivia. Alice will be a viscountess and eventually a countess, while one of your sons gets Lady Caroline's ten-thousand and the other son gets next Season's incomparable as recompense for losing out on so much money. Bravo. Splendid plan."

Lady Eddington opened her mouth in horror—not, Thomas knew, because he suggested she possessed such pecuniary motives but because he dared to give voice to them.

"Only you've ruined all your mother's hard work in arranging this party," Sir William pointed out without the least rustle of his newspaper. Lady Eddington sent a glare in his direction.

"*I've* ruined it?" Thomas asked, completely baffled by the suggestion.

"Yes, Thomas," Lady Eddington said, "all my careful plans for this party ruined because you couldn't be bothered to write before..."

"Before what?"

"...*Before* bringing your friend home with you. Completely unannounced." Lady Eddington took a breath and attempted a more amiable tone. "I'm sure Mr. Matheson is a very decent and likable person...."

"But wherever did *you* manage to meet a man of the cloth, Tom?" Sir William chimed in with a laugh at his son's expense.

"You should have written, Thomas, to say you were

bringing a guest," his mother continued, getting a tad flustered, "then I could have had Miss Maddie bring the next Winslow girl, Miss... oh, what is her name, William?"

"Lucinda. Miss Lucinda Winslow," Sir William provided without the slightest difficulty.

"Yes, Miss Lucinda. She's not out yet, but this is an informal occasion with just family and friends..."

"And the Earl and Countess of Bollingbrook," Thomas drolly added.

"...and her behavior is well above her limited years, and her mother wouldn't have minded one bit, and Miss Maddie handles those girls so well... but no, no. It's all ruined now because my son couldn't even take the time to write to his mother." She abruptly turned toward her husband, her eyes brightening with a sudden idea. "William, do you think we could send for her—Miss Lucinda, that is—and have her here by tonight?"

"Unescorted?" Sir William dropped his newspaper and sounded horrified by the very suggestion. "No, no, my dear. Someone would have to return with her, and we'd still be in this quandary. Miss Maddie would have to go for her, and she can't very well leave Miss Olivia here alone. So Miss Olivia would have to leave as well. And who knows what this snow will do. None of them might make it back by tonight, and that really would ruin everything."

Lady Eddington let out a long sigh, her brow furrowing with resignation as she sat down. "Yes, you are right, of course."

Sir William put on a brave smile and added, "Perhaps tomorrow. We'll see how the weather is and decide then."

Lady Eddington brightened. "Then that just leaves dinner tonight."

Thomas could not take this any longer. "I'm sorry but I just don't understand why all the fuss."

"Can you seriously be that obtuse?" his mother asked. Apparently so, Thomas thought, as he could not see the problem that so vexed his mother and even perplexed his father. And then his mother said matter-of-factly, "We now have an odd number with too many gentlemen for the number of ladies."

"Oh, dear." Despite his words, Thomas wanted to laugh.

"You won't think it very funny when you discover for yourself the extent of the problem you've caused," his mother scolded.

"Explain it to him, Sophia."

"Three eligible gentlemen—you, your brother, and Lord Sutton. Three eligible ladies—your sister, Lady Caroline, and Miss Olivia. Walking out, dancing in the evening, going in to dinner. But you cannot very well go unchaperoned, now can you? Or has London life convinced you to do away with such quaint conventions?"

"No. Of course not, Mother." Thomas spoke the truth. He would not want his sister—or Lady Caroline and Miss Olivia for that matter—to go without a chaperone, especially while they were under the protection of his father's house.

"I will be entertaining Lady Bollingbrook. Thus we asked Miss Maddie to accompany Miss Olivia, so that someone would always be with the young ladies. Your Uncle George was already coming, so there was no need to invite an extra gentleman to escort Miss Maddie into dinner or to sit out the dancing with her."

"She is, after all," Sir William said, "a guest and not a nurse or governess to be ignored."

"Her sister-in-law will be glad to be rid of her for a few days, but have no doubt, Lady Winslow will find the running of Winslow House without Miss Maddie there a trial at best. Such a marvel, that Miss Maddie is. And she possesses that rare talent of being able to communicate with the lower orders. It's such a shame. If only she had a prettier face or a larger fortune...."

"Sophia."

"Ah, yes. Well, there it is. All my careful planning. Twelve at table. A perfect number. Not too many, not too few. With everyone having someone to talk to. No one too erudite. No one overly devout. No one to drone on about politics. All in all, a very amicable company."

"But now we have your Mr. Matheson," Sir William pointed out.

Thomas began to see the difficulty. "Thirteen for dinner."

"And it gets worse," Lady Eddington continued.

"Uncle George will not be walking out with all of you or participating in your amusements, given his gout. But Miss Maddie? An outing with an extra lady—particularly one acting as chaperone—is perfectly acceptable. And at any other time, she is happiest with a book and perfectly content to sit out of any frivolities, *but* with an ever watchful eye. There's never any need to entertain Miss Maddie. She does quite well on her own."

"And now I've ruined that?"

"With your Mr. Matheson, there are now *four* gentlemen and only *three* ladies, plus Miss Maddie. So all the gentleman will race to get one of the ladies, while the loser will be stuck with...."

"...Mad Maddie." Thomas groaned.

"Before, all you had to do was be polite and considerate with her. Now, one of you will have to walk with her and dance with her and call upon her to make up a fourth when we are all playing cards. One of you will be stuck with her when I intended for you and John to be stuck with Lady Caroline or Miss Olivia."

"Yes, Mother, I now see the difficulties," Thomas finally conceded, "But why Miss Maddie? She can sit with you and Lady Bollingbroke when we go walking, and Miss Bagley can accompany us instead," Thomas said, suggesting his sister's governess act as chaperone instead of the bane of his childhood.

Sir William started laughing. "Obtuse is right, Sophia."

"Did you not hear a word I said, Thomas?" his mother demanded. "It was the first thing I told you when you walked in to the house."

"He and Mr. Matheson were too busy admiring Lord Bollingbrook's cattle."

"Has something happened to Miss Bagley?" Thomas asked, suddenly fearing the worst. She had been with the family for nearly thirty years, and he loved her as if she were a dear, devoted aunt.

"Miss Bagley twisted her ankle," Lady Eddington explained, "Badly. The surgeon said it was the worst he'd ever seen where the bones were not broken."

"Is she all right?"

"Yes, yes, she's resting. But she will not be walking out anytime soon. So Miss Maddie will have to suffice."

Thomas shrugged. "Perhaps it will snow, and there will be no walking out."

Sir William snapped his newspaper and began reading again. "Oh, yes, Tom. Very bright of you. The countryside blanketed in snow and all the young people will decide to stay inside? I see that money for your time at Oxford was well-spent, indeed."

"Well, that's that," his mother said, "I wash my hands of this. It is your problem and you will have to deal with it, Thomas. But mind you."—She pointed her forefinger at him.—"You are to be kind to Miss Maddie. And make sure the others are as well. She is so very useful, and I wouldn't want a falling out with her."

"Run along, Tom," Sir William said, "Find something

for the gentlemen to do until it's time to dress for dinner. And be sure to stay out of my brandy."

"That was Aunt Charlotte and Amelia."

"Yes, I know. But accounts of your London exploits do reach our ears."

Thomas left his mother's sitting room in order to find Mr. Matheson, Lord Sutton, and John. But he had no doubt. He should have stayed in London.

Magdalena Winslow held no illusions about why Sir William and Lady Eddington had invited her to attend their house party for the Christmas season. Her niece's invitation made perfect sense; Olivia and Alice Eddington were close friends and would have their first season together this spring. And with two eligible Eddington sons as well as Viscount Sutton in attendance, Olivia's mother had no qualms about parting with her daughter at Christmastime. Olivia was so very pretty she could easily snag one of them with just a smile and a blush, if she so wished. Not that Olivia would do such a thing, Magdalena knew; Olivia had very particular requirements in a potential husband.

Magdalena, however, was not attending the Eddingtons' Christmas party to meet potentials suitors or for the dancing or for the festivities or even simply to add one more to the dinner table. No, she was invited to chaperone Olivia and Alice. And any other young ladies who might be in attendance. All so Lady Eddington could be with Lady Bollingbrook and her other guests without the distraction—and exhaustion—of managing husband-hunting females. No matter. Magdalena was accustomed to such things.

But she had her own reasons for accepting the invitation. Celebrating the holiday away from her brother Arthur's house would be a welcomed change. She loved her brother and his family dearly, but living with them in her late father's house—her childhood home—and having no real position there aside from spinster aunt often strained her nerves. Her sister-in-law's inability to deal civilly with servants only made matters worse and increased the tension. Old servants—employed since Magdalena's infancy—and new alike preferred dealing with the master's sister over his wife, which did not sit well with the current mistress of Winslow House. Under normal circumstances, Magdalena would have expected Harriet to nag her husband until he relented and found some other relation to take Magdalena in... except, given Harriet's frequent confinements and even more frequent megrims, having someone who could manage the household when the mistress was indisposed proved beneficial to all concerned. At least, for the time being.

Still, a pervasive sense lingered that Arthur would one day quietly suggest Magdalena enjoy an extended stay with one of their numerous relatives scattered about the country.

Of course, Magdalena would never want for

anything. With five brothers and two married sisters, she would always have a roof over her head, come what may. But she would always be the unwanted relation. Never the *poor* relation, as she had eight-hundred pounds a year. Never mind that she had received the income only upon her father's death, which she regarded as a very poor bargain, indeed.

She sometimes thought of removing to London— but even with eight-hundred pounds, she couldn't purchase a house, at least not in a respectable part of Town. And acquiring rooms... well, a gentleman could stay in rooms, but for a lone lady, that was unthinkable. The other possibility was to lease a cottage from one of her brothers. She could easily afford that, even a couple of servants. But if she did that, she really would be alone.

This Christmas, however, more importantly than escaping the tension of her brother's home, Magdalena would get to spend part of the time at Eddington Hall with her good friend, Julia Bagley. Despite seeing each other at least once a week on Sunday and exchanging frequent notes, they rarely got to spend more than an hour in each other's company at any given time. So spending Christmas together, even while chaperoning the younger ladies, was something to look forward to. Besides, ever since receiving word of Julia's accident, Magdalena had been especially anxious to see her.

Lady Eddington did not greet them upon their arrival, for which Magdalena was grateful. She was not in the mood for inconsequential pleasantries. Olivia's boundless energy and enthusiasm for the visit was tiring, and the sooner Olivia and her friend Alice Eddington were ensconced in some corner to share secrets and make plans, the better. It was only five miles from Winslow House to Eddington Hall, but the short journey had been slow due to the snow, Sir William's coachman being extra careful as they made their way across the wintery grey and white landscape. Magdalena arrived cold—peevish and peckish, too— with nary a thought beyond warming her hands and feet and longing for a cup of tea, followed shortly thereafter by a proper dinner, which she knew from long experience could be found at Lady Eddington's table.

Within minutes of reaching their room—Magdalena and Olivia were to share—Alice Eddington bounded in and whisked Olivia away to meet the oh-so-very fashionable Lady Caroline Forbes, daughter of the Earl and Countess of Bollingbrook. She was to have her first season this spring, as well, and her father knew Lord....

And Magdalena heard no more. They left her alone to unpack, until Lady Eddington's maid knocked and volunteered to finish the job. Grateful—and with the maid's assistance—Magdalena quickly changed out of her travelling clothes and managed to tidy up her generally uncooperative hair. The golden tresses of her childhood had long ago turned a dull brown, and she looked nothing like the lovely Olivia, who bore an uncanny resemblance to Magdalena's mother. The Webster women were famous—and occasionally infamous—for their great beauty, going all the way back to the Restoration. Magdalena, however, looked like her father. Worse, she had inherited his eyesight, requiring she wear spectacles, which, she noticed, did nothing to correct the problem permanently, despite the oculist's claims. Still, the spectacles presented one advantage; she could take them off and pretend to be blind as a bat when, in fact, she could see well enough, albeit with a blurred edge to everything. She could even still read, but only if she squinted.

Magdalena inquired with the maid as to the whereabouts of Miss Bagley. When informed that the governess had taken to resting in the new Orangery, she had to ask directions to the latest addition to the house, as she had not visited in well over a year.

She soon found herself approaching the glass doors that separated the great house from the man-made bit of the tropics, and already she could see the green foliage of the trees. She opened the door, immediately feeling the warmth, like a gentle summer day without the heavy heat of the sun, and she stepped inside the room. Only it wasn't really a *room*, but more of a long corridor made very, very wide, with high ceilings to accommodate the trees. Tall glass windows—some of them really doors—lined one wall, allowing in the southern light and revealing a view of the snowy grounds, while the opposite wall was solid and whitewashed to reflect that light. And it all smelled like oranges and watered earth. It only lacked the songs of birds and a stirring of the air found on a real summer's day.

Magdalena closed the door, moved past a stove, and weaved around the trees, until she saw Julia Bagley seated in an overstuffed chair, her injured foot propped up before her with a fire blazing in the hearth. As usual, her nose was in a book.

Like Magdalena, Julia was an old maid, but Magdalena was uncertain as to how old she was. Nearing fifty, she believed, making Julia about fifteen years older than Magdalena. The governess had been with the family for nearly thirty years, and now her last charge, Alice Eddington, was coming out. As yet, there were no granddaughters in the family, only a bevy of grandsons via the eldest daughters in York and Cornwall. So Julia would soon be forced to seek employment elsewhere. For her own selfish reasons, Magdalena dreaded the day that would happen. The mere thought of the impending loneliness left her stomach feeling hollow.

The older lady glanced up as Magdalena approached, and her face lit up with delight.

"Maddie!" she said, holding out her hand.

"Julia." Magdalena accepted the offered hand with a smile and leaned in to kiss her friend's cheek. She moved to take the matching armchair opposite her, but Julia stopped her.

"Ring for tea first."

Once that was done, Magdalena sat down and, with a sympathetic smile, asked, "How did you do it?" motioning to the foot nestled atop two cushions.

"I went half way down the stairs, remembered I'd forgotten something, and turned too quickly to go back up," Julia explained. "Next thing I knew, I slid down the stairs, and this..." She motioned to her foot. "...somehow happened."

"So now you hold court in this bit of paradise." Magdalena raised her eyebrows at the sight surrounding her.

"Lady Eddington has found it too bright in here, and the light bothers her eyes. So I am allowed to stay, and everyone knows where to find me. If I need anything, the gardener's boy is usually about. He even sleeps in here since the stoves need stoking during the night."

"The wonders of the modern world." It was a marvel, this warmth—and tropical fruit—but she pitied the poor boy.

After a short while, their tea arrived, along with some sandwiches and biscuits, and the two friends sat chatting about nothing, Magdalena learning all about the other guests, particularly all the gossip regarding Lord and Lady Bollingbrook.

But as Magdalena poured a second cup of tea, she heard the door to the Orangery open, followed by the click-clack sound of dainty footstep approaching. She rose to see Lady Eddington.

"Ah, Miss Maddie. There you are," the mistress of the house said, "I've been searching for you."

"My lady?"

"My imbecile of a son has brought home an extra guest," Lady Eddington said, "A perfectly respectable gentleman, I'm sure, but now we have thirteen for dinner."

"Oh!" That was Julia, quite horrified by the prospect.

The number boded ill, but *that* did not give Magdalena cause for alarm. It was the fact that Lady Eddington felt the need to find *her* about this matter.

"Really, it is quite unforgivable of Thomas," Lady Eddington continued, speaking to both ladies, "and I am left to clean up the mess." But then she fixed her gaze on Magdalena. "What I was wondering, Miss Maddie, is if you would mind dining tonight with Miss Bagley? After all, you are friends, and I'm certain you'd find that preferable to dining with all of us. It would solve the problem nicely—although, there will still be too many gentleman but we'll have to manage somehow. But do you mind?"

"Not at all. Glad to be of some help."

In truth, Magdalena really didn't mind dining with Julia at all. She would have liked to have dined with her every time she visited Eddington Hall, but governesses did not dine at table with their employers regardless of any affection felt. So the choice of company at dinner delighted her. It was the fact that Lady Eddington thought of her that gnawed her. Magdalena was not a priority at this event. She was the lowest. She understood why perfectly well, but that did not mean she had to like it. She was never anyone's priority. In fact, she was the one person no one had a problem with making wait. When her turn in the queue came, there was always something more pressing—*Miss Maddie? She can wait. She won't mind. She never minds.*

"Oh, excellent!" Lady Eddington clasped her hands together. "Thank you, Miss Maddie. That really is kind of you."

"Think nothing of it." Magdalena pasted on a smile, all the while realizing Lady Eddington's sense of relief came in the knowledge that Magdalena would be absent from the table.

"We'll make better arrangements tomorrow," Lady Eddington added before heading off to deal with the new dinner arrangements.

When Magdalena turned to Julia, the governess gave her a reassuring smile and said softly, "We'll enjoy ourselves."

"I know we will," Magdalena replied, believing every word she said, but still she saw a shadow in Julia's eyes, and she knew there was one person who understood how she felt.

She had only just resumed her seat when another set of feet—younger, livelier, and heavier—came hurrying over the stone floor.

"Miss Bagley!" a male voice called out with great joy. Magdalena looked up to see Thomas Eddington. She quickly looked down at her cup of tea and tucked a stray lock of hair behind her ear, her finger barely touching the cold metal of her spectacles.

No man should be so handsome. It simply wasn't fair to the rest of humanity. He could at least be spotty or have thinning hair. But no, Thomas Eddington possessed a physical perfection usually found only in the sculpted works of ancient masters, except he was flesh and blood, with thick black hair and piercing blue eyes framed by long dark lashes the envy of every female he encountered. Magdalena had known him practically all his life, but they'd rarely spoken more than polite greetings... although, she recalled an incident when he was a very small child..., but she preferred not to think of that day.

Otherwise, Mr. Eddington always left her with the impression that he disliked her immensely, which she simply could not understand given their limited contact. She viewed it as typical of his kind, those beautiful people who inhabited the *beau monde* and disdained females like her—plain, dull, unattractive even.

"Thomas! Home at last."

Magdalena peered over the rims of her spectacles and saw Mr. Eddington take Julia's outstretched hand and plant a kiss on her knuckles. The governess seemed uncomfortable with this display, although she did not discourage him. And as he released her hand, he laughed. And then he kissed her cheek and called her *Dearest Miss Bagley*, like some swain come a-courting.

Julia told him that was enough, and the farce ended. But something about it sickened Magdalena, as if affection were a matter of frivolity, to be teased and laughed about, at the expense of an aging woman who would soon find herself without a position. The feigning of affection was a kind of false witness and as damnable because it harmed a fellow human being. He did not seem aware that Julia, despite her age, was still a woman and still capable of feeling.

Only when Mr. Eddington reached for a nearby garden chair did he show any notice of Magdalena.

"Oh, Miss Winslow," he said, standing up straight. He barely glanced at her but said, "I didn't see you there."

"Mr. Eddington," she replied with a nod and said nothing more as his focus—and charm—returned to Julia.

Magdalena imagined being a beautiful man was much like being a beautiful woman; otherwise she doubted Mr. Eddington could get away with so much. He simply did as he did now and charmed his way out of difficulties, with his parents, with his lovers, with whomever might object to his behavior. Magdalena had seen much the same from her mother and sisters and many of her female relatives throughout her life. Beautiful women could get away with anything. They could be dumb or intelligent, dull or clever, cruel or kind, and men would forgive them anything. But an unattractive women... Magdalena found people looked for a reason to dismiss an unattractive woman. The slightest bit of anger, an outburst of distress, a moment of madness, and an unattractive woman was condemned as difficult.

Magdalena had to work to appear cheerful and pleasant. As long as she was deemed useful, her presence would be tolerated. And being here at Eddington Hall was no different in that regard. But at a party such as this, as much as possible, she found it best to go unnoticed. That was her plan for this Christmas party—be useful and try to remain unnoticed as much as possible.

Keeping her eyes lowered, Magdalena rose. Mr. Eddington stood as well.

"Please excuse me," Magdalena said, "There are matters to which I must attend, and I'm sure you have much to discuss."

She hurried away, trying to figure out where exactly she was going. And then she remembered Olivia would be dining without her that night. She needed to make sure her niece was properly prepared. Olivia had to be on her best behavior; she mustn't follow Alice's lead on any foolishness. Not that Magdalena expected Alice or Olivia to do anything beyond reproach, but one never knew what silly girls might do.

A heavy snow fell throughout the night, and the household rose to a world blanketed white, with dark grey skies heralding more to come.

Thomas woke at half-past ten—early for him—but then, he had retired long before midnight—again, early for him—only to lie wide awake for several hours. He'd forgotten these country hours. And then the evening had ended so early, without dancing or cards, everyone claiming fatigue from the long day of travel. Dinner had been uneventful, and to his surprise, his mother managed to seat twelve rather than the thirteen he'd unwittingly forced upon her. But when he glanced about the table, everyone seemed in their place. Only after counting again and silently reciting the guest list twice did he realize who was absent—*Mad Maddie*—like a servant to be dismissed when no one required her presence rather than a guest in their home. He felt a pang of regret over that; if anyone had been left out of the gathering, it should have been him.

Seeing Mad Maddie—he must remember to call her *Miss Winslow*, although, as he recollected, no one else did—had been something of a shock...not her arrival, but when he paid his respects to Miss Bagley. In his memory, Miss Winslow was tall with a strength of iron, and even though he had seen her numerous times over the years, that memory remained his mind's vision of her. But when he saw her there in the Orangery, she had seemed so small, so quiet, as if fearing notice. And had he not watched her leave, he never would have discerned her departure. She was nothing like the termagant of his imagination. He did not see her again after that; nor did he think further on the matter.

Despite the number of guests, the house was still and quiet, and Thomas did not encounter a soul as he made his way downstairs. But as he crossed the hall toward the dining room, his mother emerged from the sitting room.

"Really, Thomas," she said, "Half the day's gone."

"I couldn't sleep." It was the truth. But his mother gave him an incredulous look. He knew what she was thinking. The hours he kept in London *were* scandalous, as was the company he kept, with the exception of Matheson.

"Well, there's still some coffee in the dining room, but as for anything else you might want, you'll just have to wait until luncheon."

Thomas could see Lady Bollingbrook and Uncle George talking in the sitting room, but he asked his mother, "Where is everyone?"

"Reverend Dixon came to see Uncle George, and Miss Dixon and Fred tagged along. Poor Miss Dixon... a beautiful face won't go far without a dowry. No doubt she hopes to accompany Alice to London this spring. Fred brought his sled to go coasting down our hill, and your friend, that Mr. Matheson, decided they should all make a party of it. You should go join them."

Thomas grumbled. Spending the day in the cold and trying to amuse girls barely out of the schoolroom simply did not interest him. He wondered why he'd even decided to come home for Christmas, when he remembered Matheson had suggested that as well.

"You'll enjoy it," his mother said, and then added with a pointed look, "And no need for pairing off."

After a quick but lukewarm cup of coffee, Thomas bundled up against the cold and headed outside to find this coasting party Matheson had organized. He found it on the west side of the house, where the wide, level lawn suddenly dropped into a long, gentle slope leading down to the half-frozen pond and meadows. The pond was easily avoidable, as, Thomas noted, the partiers had discovered, just by pushing off to the right.

As Thomas expected, the coasting party consisted of the younger houseguests, with the addition of the Dixons from the village. Garden chairs had been set up around a brazier burning with a good fire. Miss Winslow sat in one of the garden chairs, reclining as if some invalid, her feet propped up and blankets tucked about her. She held a slim volume and seemed unaware of her frigid surroundings. Thomas settled into one of the garden chairs by the brazier.

He hoped John had alerted the others to the existence of the stump, now hidden under snow. Fred kept running and diving onto his sled in an effort, Thomas knew, to build up speed. But it also appeared to Thomas that the boy aimed for the hidden tree stump— if he hit it just right, he could go sailing through the air, and Thomas suspected that was his goal. Matheson, John, and Lord Sutton seemed to be having a grand time taking turns coasting with Lady Caroline and Miss Dixon. As for Alice and Miss Olivia, those two girls kept to themselves, oblivious to the others, with giggles being their primary means of communication.

And as Thomas watched them all, and in particular the young ladies his mother wanted him to get *stuck* with, it occurred to him that he didn't want to get *stuck* with any of them. It was like watching children. Miss Dixon was the eldest at twenty, and even that felt so very young to him, despite an age difference of only seven years.

"I'm getting old," he grumbled and shook his head.

"Nonsense."

The sound of Miss Winslow's voice surprised him. He didn't realize he had spoken so loudly.

"You're what?" she continued, peering at him over the rims of her spectacles, "Twenty-seven, I believe." He nodded. "Then you've yet to reach your prime," she said before sighing and quietly adding, "And of course, you're a man."

How truly odd. "What does that have to do with it?" he asked, curious to know her meaning.

She laid the book, still open, face down on her lap, and tucked her mitten-clad hands underneath the blanket. "Unlike women, men are still deemed of value regardless of age. Even in your dotage, some addle-brained female will willing take you on." Miss Winslow paused for a moment, glanced skyward, as if contemplating her own words, and appeared to reach a new conclusion. "Of course, she would love you only for your pocket book. But then, you'd love her only for her pretty face and luscious curves. So it all evens out in the end."

Thomas was shocked. Not by her words but by the fact that he could not recall hearing her ever say so much. However, he said, "That is harsh."

"But true. I recommend you marry sooner rather than later."

Thomas's face must have betrayed his amazement. He managed to say, "How did you...?" before she interrupted.

"Everyone knows Lady Eddington is trying to find brides for you and your brother."

He wanted to laugh. Instead, he moved his chair closer to her. He leaned in and, with a grin, asked in a conspiratorial fashion, "Then who do you suggest I pick?" and he glanced toward the coasting party.

He expected her to choose her own flesh and blood, Miss Olivia, but instead, without any hesitation, Miss Winslow replied, "Lady Caroline is pretty enough, and she comes with ten-thousand a year—which more than amply makes up for any aesthetic flaws you might find in her."

"Ah, but I don't need ten-thousand a year."

"Whereas Mr. Matheson does, and you note how he dotes on her. Yes. Best leave him to his fate. I say pick Miss Dixon."

"Miss Dixon?"

"Bound to be next Season's incomparable." Miss Winslow picked up her book again. "Snatch her up while you can. Otherwise some inbred duke will get her. Or worse."

"Worse?"

"Prinny will make her his mistress and accidently crush her."

Thomas's jaw dropped. Of course, he frequently heard significantly more shocking things at his club, usually sprinkled with the coarsest of vulgarities that could send a groomsman blushing. He simply couldn't believe the prim Miss Winslow had said such a thing, and in such a droll tone. He had known many ladies in London who could quite readily converse in an irreverent manner, but they were women of experience, sophisticated and assertive denizens of the Ton— nothing like Miss Winslow. She looked the very picture of a maiden aunt, drab and dreary, made more so by her white and grey surroundings.

"She is very small," Miss Winslow continued, glancing toward the vicar's daughter. Then she looked back at Thomas and must have seen his expression of disbelief. "What? I'm not supposed to know such things? I may be old but I am not ignorant."

She was hardly *old*, he thought. If he recalled correctly, she was about thirty-four, and he could not spot a single grey hair or fine line. Recovering from his shock, Thomas asked, "And what about your own Miss Olivia?"

"Afraid not. Wasting your time with that one, my dear."

"Wasting my time? But she is very pretty and has a nice little dowry. Whatever is wrong with her?"

"I have it on good authority—being her aunt and all—that she has sworn to marry a ginger-haired boy... and you just don't pass muster with those raven locks of yours."

"You're jesting?"

"Not at all."

"Well how silly is that? Rejecting a poor man for the color of his hair?"

She frowned, looking sympathetic, and nodded with understanding. "Almost as silly as rejecting a woman for the prettiness of her face... or more accurately, the lack thereof." He felt her sting with that one. Her feigned demeanor changed. "But there you have it. Love makes fools of us all."

"I doubt love has anything to do with it."

She raised one eyebrow, the corner of her mouth turning upward at the same time, and she gave him a knowing look. "I suspect you're right."

"I suppose you want Lord Sutton for Miss Olivia. He is ginger, of a sort." Thomas glanced over at the young lord throwing a snowball at Fred. "When the light hits him right. And he will be the next Earl of Bollingbrook."

"Oh no. I don't of approve of that."

"*That?*"

"Being a wife and mother is difficult enough without having to deal with the position of countess. But if that is where her heart and reason lead her, there is little I can do to dissuade her."

Thomas sat back, baffled by his companion before the brazier. She appeared a creature more suitable for a rectory than for a country house party attended by the aristocracy. For such as Miss Winslow, the village was the world, and venturing beyond this hill or that stream was too far afield for good, decent folks to travel. But she spoke with an intelligence and awareness usually reserved for those with a lifetime of experience—in complete contradiction with the dour vision in grey.

As the sun broke free of the clouds, Miss Winslow set aside her book and began unraveling the bundle of blankets about her. "I need a cup of tea." She stood up—Thomas standing as well—and she called out to Miss Olivia. Her niece and Alice, with some difficulty, came running up the hill. But when Miss Winslow suggested they go inside to warm up for a while, Miss Olivia protested.

"Not yet." And she gave a pretty pout that Thomas knew would doom many a suitor. He, however, would not be counted among them. The girl's face then lit up with an idea. "One more time down the hill," she suggested, "and then we'll go in to warm up. But this time, you go down with us!"

Thomas fully expected Miss Winslow to refuse the very notion as too indecorous, but to his surprise, she quickly agreed and climbed onto the nearest sled, Alice and Miss Olivia taking up position behind her.

"Give us a push, Tom," Alice insisted.

With a grin, Thomas did as he was told... only, just as he pushed them off, his boot slipped in the snow, thereby changing ever-so-slightly the course the sled sped down the hill, and now it headed right toward the hidden stump.

"Jump off!" Thomas shouted and ran after them. "Jump off!"

Alice seemed to hear him, and she was soon tumbling free of the sled. But it was too late for Miss Olivia and Miss Winslow. They hit the stump, Miss Olivia falling off the back of the sled, while Miss Winslow flew up and landed in a heap several feet away.

Oh God! I've killed the chaperone!

However would he explain this to his mother?

Lord Sutton managed to reach Alice first—*at least that would please Mother*—while John hurried over to Miss Olivia, unscathed and laughing, and pulled her to her feet. But Thomas ran past them, to where Miss Winslow lay prone, face down in the snow. He feared the worst, but as he neared her, she stirred and struggled to right herself.

Only with the relief that she was alive did he notice how her skirts had become twisted about her, leaving her legs exposed. He stopped in mid-step, suddenly absorbed by the sight before him.

How could such a dull creature possess such exquisite legs?

While grey stockings covered her delicate ankles and shapely calves, the material stopped just above the knees, leaving her thighs bare for several inches before her skirts hid the rest. Thomas felt like he gazed at some tantalizing map encouraging him to travel just a bit further north to discover a rare treasure. And for a moment, he wished they were elsewhere, London, his rooms, that he might push those skirts up further and know....

"Oh! Ow!" Miss Winslow quietly cried out, turning herself over just as Thomas reached her.

"Miss Winslow!" He knelt beside her. "Are you injured?" His hand, as if of its own accord, went to her skirts and pulled them down to cover her legs.

"I lost a mitten," she said holding up her bare hand and looking about her. She seemed stunned, but then she peered at him and said, "Mr. Eddington. That was exhilarating... well, until it stopped." And she gave a little laugh. She looked different, Thomas thought. Her cheeks were flush, and some of the pins had fallen from her hair so that several long, lustrous locks now tumbled down, strangely streaked gold and copper in the sunlight. And he had never noticed her eyes before, like green tidal pools on a warm summer day, with blonde eyelashes he never would have seen if not so close to her... only, she had the gaze of a well-satisfied woman on waking in the morning after a night of relentless passion. Then he realized... her spectacles were missing.

"Are you all right?" He brushed back a loose lock of hair from her face, only to discover blood over her eyebrow. "You're bleeding." He pulled out his handkerchief and gently pressed it to the wound. "It's not bad."

She raised her hand to touch it but suddenly stopped. "Where are my spectacles?"

Thomas glanced around in the snow, and found the twisted bit of metal, the glass gone from one eyepiece and cracked in the other. He handed the ruined spectacles to her.

"The glass is probably what cut your brow," he said.

"Oh dear." And she shivered.

"Here. Let's get you back to the house before you freeze," Thomas said, and he lifted her up into his arms—a gasp escaping from Miss Winslow as he did—and he began carrying her back up the hill to the house.

As he trudged through the snow, the weight in his arms surprisingly light, his mind strayed to thoughts of warm fires and rumpled sheets and those exquisite naked legs parting at his touch. He inhaled deeply, thankful for the cold air, only to breathe in the intoxicating scent of her, faintly reminiscent of oranges. She turned her face away from his, casting her gaze over his shoulder, her small hands clutching his coat, but he felt the beat of her heart against him, the heat of her breath on his neck.

And in that instant, he knew.

He had to have her.

The sooner, the better.

Magdalena shivered. When she crashed, snow had gone down her half-boots, up her sleeves, down her neck, and even into her remaining mitten. And now, it was all melting. But that wasn't the only reason she shivered. She had never been held by a man. Even when she was small, she could not remember her father or her brothers ever lifting her up.

And now, the oh-so-very handsome Mr. Eddington carried her with such ease and gentleness, one hand beneath her knees, the other pressed against her ribs, and despite the layers of material, she felt the imprint of him searing into her. She couldn't help but tremble with his touch, so alien a sensation in her limited experience. She draped her arms over his shoulders and looked away, trying to steady her nerves, but even the smell of him, clean and freshly bathed, left her shaken.

She didn't like this, this effect he had on her, and she wanted nothing more than to get away from him, away from this raw masculine strength. She scolded herself for even speaking to him. She was supposed to go unnoticed at this party. She should have left him muttering to himself. The things she said! Such brazen bluntness! And to jest about Miss Dixon being mistress to the Prince of Wales! *Good Lord in Heaven*, what he must think of her!

"I wish I'd thought of that."

Magdalena clearly heard Lady Caroline speaking to Alice as they passed the girls on the way up the hill. Mr. Eddington undoubtedly heard it as well, as if she had crashed on purpose, all in order to attract male attention. She'd be the laughing stock of the village—the old maid throwing herself at the London rake. How humiliating!

"I can walk," Magdalena quietly said to her rescuer.

"I'm sure you can," came his only response, and he kept on walking.

The nearest door into the house took them directly into the Orangery, a wave of heat welcoming them as they entered. Magdalena expected Julia to be there— perhaps Mr. Eddington did as well—but she was nowhere to be seen... although, as Mr. Eddington set Magdalena down by the fire, she noted her friend's belongings remained, as if she had only just exited the room.

Mr. Eddington pulled off his gloves and removed his coat and knelt before her. He tugged off her wet mitten before moving on to the buttons of her coat. He soon helped her out of the garment, but he did not stop there. His hands moved to her throat, where he untied and unraveled her scarf, his fingertips lightly brushing against her skin. And then to her surprise, he hooked his finger beneath her chin and tilted her head up to face him. She had a difficult time meeting his gaze, those dark blue eyes boring into her with an intensity she found disturbing. And she felt strange without her spectacles, as if they provided her some kind of protection. He moved a lock of hair away from her face.

"The bleeding's stopped," he said, and sat back on

his heels. She thought he was done—*undressing her*—when he took hold of her ankle and began to work her half-boot off. She never realized the sensation of a man's hand encircling her ankle could be so... oh, it was scandalous. She opened her mouth to breathe properly. And then he moved to her other ankle.

She should have stopped him. She should have said something. But she couldn't think clearly. And then he cradled one wet foot in his hands and looked up at her.

"You need to take off these wet stockings," and like a scoundrel, he added, "and if you won't, I will." The sudden vision of him reaching under her skirts and slowly rolling down a single stocking filled her mind... and brought her to her senses. She suddenly felt angry for some inexplicable reason.

"Mr. Eddington." She jerked her foot from his grasp and tucked her feet—cold and wet—neatly underneath her skirts and out of view before standing up. "You needn't ply your charms with me." He stood up and stepped away from Magdalena.

"I beg your pardon?" He looked sincerely confused.

"This—whatever it is that you're doing—that you do with women. Like you did with Miss Bagley last night."

"Miss Bagley?"

"Flirting." She felt flustered. "Only it's worse than flirting." She took a deep breath and tried to calm herself. It didn't help much. "You tease old women."

Mr. Eddington appeared baffled by her words. His

confusion gave her a moment to collect her thoughts.

"The attention you showered on her, that you've showered on me, as if we were young girls you were courting. It amuses you, this feigned infatuation. It provides you with a moment's laugh, but at the expense of another. It never occurs to you that Miss Bagley was once a girl, too, and that she still is that girl in many ways, just trapped in an aging body... as if that makes her immune to masculine attention. You come in, looking like you do, and pretend to be the pretty boy who wants to dance with her, but it's just a joke." Mr. Eddington opened his mouth to speak, but Magdalena did not give him the chance. "She has spent her life raising other people's children—*your* sisters—but she was never blessed with her own. Do you really think that's what she wanted from life? But you would never notice that. When not completely ignored, she is an object of pity... or scorn. And should some gentleman take notice of her, he'll be some widower with a dozen children and in need of someone to care for those children. He won't want her for herself. And now she finds herself in this predicament."

"What predicament?"

"Oh. Of course *you* wouldn't know. When Alice goes to London, Miss Bagley's employment here will no longer be needed. After nearly thirty years in this house, she is to lose her position and her income."

"I didn't realize...."

"What did you think? That she'd live here forever?"

And Magdalena stopped abruptly, realizing she was practically yelling at the poor boy for no reason of his making. She saw the intense look on his face—anger, fear, disgust, she couldn't tell what he was thinking, but it could only be ill.

Good God!

This was the Miss Maddie Winslow of his memory— fiery and passionate and only in need of a spark to set her ablaze. And oh how he wanted to burn with her! Preferably on cool sheets, but anywhere would do, even the stone floor here. But on further consideration, and with a glance at the floor, no. He wanted time to linger with her, long and slow, not some mad frenzy finished in a rush.

He clinched his fist, fighting his baser urges, and watched as her demeanor suddenly changed, her face softening.

"I'm so sorry," she said. Once again, the quiet Miss Winslow returned. She looked down and seemed to disappear into herself, as if, yet again, she wanted nothing more than to go unnoticed.

"No, no." He spoke calmly, trying to reassure her. "Think nothing of it. As you surmised, I was unaware of Miss Bagley's situation. Thank you for informing me." He gave her a polite nod. "But you do me an injustice, Miss Winslow. I have the highest regard for Miss Bagley. She has been a constant in my life, and regardless of what my parents plan, I will see to it that she never wants for material necessities. She will always have a roof over her head. That much I can do for her."

Without looking at him, she quietly said, "Thank you, Mr. Eddington."

Thomas stepped away from her as if to leave, but stopped, despite knowing he should just walk away. She had had her say. He would have his.

"I appreciate your honesty. Allow me to be honest with you as well."

Miss Winslow jerked her head up, a look of apprehension in those green eyes. It didn't prevent Thomas from continuing. After all, a gentleman should always declare his intentions.

"I think you and I should become lovers."

Apprehension turned to shock.

"Is this some kind of joke?" she demanded. At least she didn't act as if she hadn't heard him. "A wager between you and Lord Sutton? Let's *torment* the old maid?"

"Not at all." Thomas took a step toward her and resisted the urge to reach out and take her hand. "I never joke about whom I want lying naked in my bed."

Shock quickly turned to anger, Miss Winslow's jaw tightening. When she spoke, her voice was cold and calm. "If I were a man, I'd call you out."

"If you were a man, there'd be no cause."

He could see the fire building in her, her eyes blazing, her breath quickening. He awaited the expected verbal lashing. But instead, she abruptly moved to leave.

He grabbed her wrist and stopped her from storming out.

"No. I'll go. You stay. Take off your stockings and warm yourself." He leaned in without letting her go and added, "Consider what I've said. I can assure you, you would enjoy it immensely. I'd see to that."

And with that, he let go of her wrist, picked up his coat and gloves, and casually strolled to the glass doors leading out of the Orangery. He stopped and looked back. Miss Winslow stood defiant among the trees and watched him. He grinned, went inside the house, and shook his head. *Mad Maddie. Of all people!* Well, he supposed he shouldn't be surprised, given their history.

Magdalena sat there stunned, her now bare feet stretched out before the fire, the stockings draped over a garden chair to dry. Never in her life had anyone ever said such a thing to her. *Lovers!* Her and Thomas Eddington! She could readily imagine him speaking in such a manner to some fashionable lady of the Ton—his reputation did precede him, even to their remote village—but not her, a spinster aunt so far on the shelf she was positively dusty. No man had ever even looked at her, and now, the most rakish of rakes wanted to bed her! She was old enough to be his... his... well, his older sister. Such an age difference was not unheard of, but sadly, that was the least shocking thing about the whole matter.

The most shocking part of it all, however, was how

very tempting it was, how very tempting *he* was—not that she would ever consent. No, of course not. But the idea... such a man, with those blue eyes that pierced her soul and made her want to break commandments... and to be held again in those arms that carried her with such ease up the hill. Only, this time, in his bed. *Naked.* She knew she should be ashamed of herself for even imagining such things.... Well, she supposed it was the shock of his suggestion; she wasn't thinking clearly.

She could hear her family—*Maddie, a lover? Nonsense. Who would have her?* Mr. Eddington, apparently. Oh, she wanted to laugh. And if it were someone other than herself, it would be hilarious.

She should have slapped him for his audacity, but she wasn't the kind of woman to think such things in the moment. Someone wanted her—if only for a brief, physical moment to relieve his temporary ache. And the way he looked at her, that intense gaze... she could understand how newly out girls could succumb to such attention. She, of course, would not be one of them. For one thing, she was hardly a girl. For another, she had no desire for a broken heart, and Mr. Eddington would, most definitely, break her heart.

He would gaze into her eyes with such sincerity, and she would believe anything and everything he said down to her very core... and then he'd be done with her and leave her without a backward glance. All the kindness he had shown her this day, the desire in his eyes, would turn to disdain when he finished with her.

After all, he was a rake. Using and discarding women was their stock and trade.

"Maddie?"

Magdalena looked up to see Julia hobbling on her crutch into the Orangery. "Maddie, are you all right? Thomas said you'd taken a tumble."

Of course, he did. "I'm fine, Julia," Magdalena assured the governess.

But when Julia took her seat before the fire, her expression of concern transformed to confusion. "Are you sure you're all right?" she asked, "You look different."

"How so?"

Julia studied her for a moment and then said, "Your eyes."

"I broke my spectacles."

Julia shook her head. "That's not it." She leaned forward and said with some surprise, "And you're flushed," before lowering her voice and asking, "Has something happened? Other than the accident?"

Magdalena looked around as if someone might be hiding among the trees, even though she knew they were alone. Then she leaned forward. "Can we discuss... shocking..., scandalous things? Things you and I are *supposed* to be ignorant of but aren't?"

Julia sat back. "We can discuss anything."

Magdalena hesitated then quickly asked, "Have you ever had a lover?"

The question did not seem unexpected. One side of

Julia's mouth twisted in a half-smile. She blushed a bit and replied, "No."

"If you had, would you tell me?"

"Probably not." She appeared to consider it further. "Well, maybe… if he'd been a good lover. Why do you ask?"

Magdalena took a deep breath. "A gentleman has made me a proposition."

"Thomas?"

"Yes." Magdalena sat back, feeling disappointed that Julia guessed the matter with such little information. She undoubtedly knew the man all too well. "Given Mr. Eddington's reputation, I suppose he does this sort of thing frequently."

"In London, yes, I imagine so. But to my knowledge, *never* here."

For some bizarre reason she couldn't fathom, Magdalena felt some relief about that particular fact. Not that it changed anything, of course.

"What I can't understand," Magdalena said, "is what does he want with someone like me?"

"Given the nature of his proposition, that should be obvious." Julia smiled. Really, Magdalena thought the governess found this all too amusing.

"No." Magdalena felt herself blush. "I mean why me? How did I become the object of that gaze?"

Julia turned serious and sat pensive before replying, a hint of sadness in her voice, "I don't know, Maddie. I've never understood why men recklessly pursue some ladies while ignoring those considerably more worthy of their affection. So why one would suddenly turn his attention on a lady so deserving of love...." She shook her head.

Magdalena suddenly felt like they no longer discussed Mr. Eddington or his proposition. "Julia, was there someone, once upon a time, someone you loved?"

"No. I never had the opportunity, not really." She gave a little sigh. "I went from the schoolroom to here, a governess at eighteen, well aware that if I did not live up to my employer's expectations, I would be turned out and probably end up destitute. Anything else wouldn't have been deemed appropriate, and Lady Eddington was very punctual about producing daughters, so I've always had plenty to occupy my time."

Magdalena reached out and covered Julia's hand with her own. "I'm sorry."

"Well, no matter. I would've had to possess a great fortune for a gentleman to pause long enough to consider me." It saddened Magdalena to hear her friend speak so, but she felt much the same. Neither of them were beauties, and it would be charitable to call them plain. Even her own eight hundred pounds was not enough incentive to entice a second glance—thus Magdalena's great confusion regarding Mr. Eddington's designs on her.

Julia was not finished. "I've seen unattractive women happily married, and truth be told, I don't understand how they managed to find husbands. I've seen beautiful but cruel women married to men who adore them, yet those husbands don't have the good sense to realize their wives make them miserable."

"But would you have such a man?" Magdalena asked.

"I would have had any man who treated me well…" She inhaled deeply before wistfully adding, "…and still would." She turned her gaze to the fire. "A life unshared is not worth the living."

Magdalena felt the pain of Julia's words, as the governess gave voice to her own thoughts and feelings from time to time. And she saw Julia wipe a tear from her eye. Magdalena smiled and said, "I don't think unshared is a word."

"It should be." Julia returned Magdalena's smile with one her own. Then she took a deep breath and said, "We are overlooked. Everyone passes us by, never noticing us. We have experienced filial love and platonic love, but never erotic love. *Love* alone should be enough, but it's not. We were made for something more." She leaned toward Magdalena and asked, "Is it so terrible that Thomas has seen something in you that others have overlooked?"

"But as someone *bonny* and *blithe* in his bed? He's not seeking the love of a good woman."

"Perhaps that's all a man can ever truly give of himself. The physical, and nothing more."

"You don't really believe that, do you?"

"I don't want to, but I don't know. I have as much experience in these matters as you do."

This conversation was not going the way Magdalena expected. Julia should be stunned and shocked, as she was, outraged that Mr. Eddington would suggest such a thing. Instead, Julia acted as if this were all perfectly acceptable behavior.

"What would you do?" Magdalena cautiously ventured to ask.

"Oh, I don't know." But then Julia sat there, quiet for a moment, before exhaling and admitting, "No, that's not true." She smiled and almost laughed. "I would succumb in a heartbeat. But I am older. It's not like he could get me with child. It's not as if I have a family that would be ruined by the scandal that might follow any discovery. And I have suffered enough disappointments to expect his eventual desertion. I could live with that—just to have known such happiness for however brief a time we have. But you? Could your heart endure such a betrayal?"

Magdalena found it difficult to believe what she was hearing. Not that Julia would succumb to a man like Mr. Eddington. Strangely, she understood that. It was something within Julia's words that Magdalena thought she was hearing. Just to be certain, she asked, "Are you encouraging me to accept him?"

"No. Not at all. I'm simply saying, *if you did…* I know what it's like to look back over my life and to see so little or to think on the future and be afraid. So if you seek solace in the arms of a handsome gentleman, if only for a moment, I will not condemn you." She shook her head. "Don't accept him out of fear of loneliness, but don't reject him because you fear what the neighbors might think. Find a better reason than that." She gave Magdalena a weak smile.

This conversation disturbed Magdalena in ways she never imagined. When she broached the subject with the governess, she expected sympathy, a laugh or two, but not a suggestion to seriously consider becoming Mr. Eddington's lover. The idea of him wanting her was shocking enough—but to accept? Preposterous. Magdalena simply wasn't the sort. Yet now, Julia had put all these thoughts swimming in her head. Worse, Magdalena was now thinking... oh, it was all too outrageous.

Thankfully, Julia changed the subject. "Luncheon should be laid out by now. Could you fetch me a plate?"

"Of course." Magdalena picked up her stockings, tucked them under her arm, and made her way—barefoot—across the cold, stone floor.

But then she heard Julia add, "I promise I won't be so maudlin when you return."

Magdalena turned back and smiled—what else could she do? Instead of comforted and reassured, she left more confused than ever, now fearful she might actually consider becoming Mr. Eddington's lover.

By the time the revelers returned to the house, they

discovered luncheon already laid out on the sideboard in the dining room. Thomas, however, could take only so much giggling from the gaggle of girls and their circle of suitors. Famished from his lack of breakfast, he piled his plate with roasted pork and potatoes smothered in gravy and wedges of bread slathered in butter, before retreating to the solace of his father's library... especially since his father preferred the sitting room. A bottle of port also awaited him there, and he dined in relative peace and quiet before the fire, until Matheson sought him out in the dark, masculine room. Likewise, the man of the cloth carried a plate.

"I doubt your mother planned for port to accompany this meal," Matheson said as he helped himself to a glass.

"Well, it won't be the first of her plans to go awry this Christmas."

"Such as her matrimonial plans for you and your brother?"

"And Alice, too."

Matheson took the armchair opposite Thomas and draped a serviette decorously over his lap before settling his plate there. After a couple of bites, he observed aloud to his companion, "I've never seen you so ardently avoid females. Usually, you sniff out the prettiest bird and pounce before anyone else can get a shot off, but this time, you left the field to us lesser mortals." Thomas caught his wry grin.

"If I had known my mother was in a scheming

mood, I never would have come home." Thomas took a sip of port and remembered Matheson's enthusiasm for a country Christmas. The man had practically dragged him out of White's at the prospect. "This could be construed as all your fault. Why ever did you want to come?"

Matheson shrugged. "It sounded like fun. Christmas away from London. Home with the family. Carols and dancing. Goose and...."

"If you mention chestnuts or mistletoe, I will call you out."

Matheson chuckled, then fell silent and resumed eating. But when trills of laughter from the dining room trickled in, Matheson suddenly asked, "Do you honestly expect me to believe that none of the ladies strikes your fancy?"

"Yes. I do. They're all lovely, but it feels like they're..."

"They're what?"

"...children." Most people recognized Thomas had a habit of pursuing certain ladies of the Ton, but in truth, he simply preferred older women. They knew their own minds—and spoke them. There was a confidence and a self-awareness in them that he never found in debutantes. He saw the same thing in Maddie Winslow, and as usual, it lured him like a Siren's song... well, that and those exquisite legs. "So you are welcome to pursue Lady Caroline to your heart's content."

Even in the cinnabar glow of firelight, Thomas saw

Matheson blanch. He opened his mouth—to protest, Thomas expected—but then said nothing, looked down at his plate, and returned to eating. Thomas struggled to keep from laughing.

"And what about that chaperone?" Matheson asked a moment later without looking up from his plate. Thomas easily caught the mirth in his tone. But that didn't sour his mood. The appellation *chaperone* did that, as if Miss Winslow were nothing more.

"What about Miss Winslow?" He ground out the words, all the while trying to hide the anger now rising up in him, to his utter bewilderment.

"What did you say to her?"

"Why do you ask?"

"She was getting a plate for the governess, and she just looks... different. Different from this morning when I was introduced to her."

"She broke her spectacles."

"That's not it." Matheson studied his plate for a while and then added, "And she seemed rather flustered." He raised his head and looked directly at Thomas. "*You* tend to have that effect on women. Except she didn't smile. Your conquests always smile. Which leads me to believe she wouldn't...."

"Nothing happened." Thomas hoped his tone would lay the matter to rest, but Matheson continued to glare at him. So he added in the most nonchalant manner he could muster, "If you must know, I merely suggested to Miss Winslow that we become lovers. That's all."

"That's all?" The tenor of Matheson's voice so startled the two men that both glanced around in fear they might attract attention from a further room. Determining they hadn't, Matheson lowered his voice and leaned closer to Thomas... only to scold. "The same woman whom, only yesterday, you called 'Our Lady of Perpetual Sorrow?' She's the chaperone, a guest in your parents' house. She is no bored London matron or some wanton widow seeking a randy rake to plough her field."

The crude description of his typical bedmate struck Thomas most peculiarly. He felt... *insulted*, despite it being a very apt portrayal of his amorous adventures. And while guilt over his past pursuits played no part in his thinking, the insinuations disturbed him for some reason.

"You know me too well," Thomas replied, trying to sound blasé.

"Well enough to know that Miss Winslow is not the sort you associate with, which leads me to wonder why her, of all people?"

"I've simply seen her in a different light." It was the truth, after all, quite literally, the sunlight still shimmering off her tumbled tresses in his mind's eye. "And I find she has numerous qualities in keeping with my former paramours—intelligent, witty, with a fire...." He exhaled, long and slow, trying not to imagine her in bed, those legs wrapped around him.

Matheson pursed his lips and nodded. "That may

be, but I suspect she has little experience with men."

"Oh, I do not doubt her virginal state." Thomas took a sip from his glass of port before continuing with a tangential thought. "Although, these days, one can never really tell until the deed in done... and sometimes, probably not even then." He set the glass down and raised his forefinger in a declarative manner. "But Alice told me Miss Winslow spent four months in London several years ago. Alone."

"Alone?"

Thomas shrugged. "Except for the servants."

"Well that just demonstrates her virtue. No one believed her capable of... uh... straying. After all, she is now the chaperone here."

"Trust me. No woman, no matter how plain faced, can remain in London for long without some milksop pursuing her. I can even see an upright vicar-to-be calling upon her." Thomas raised his eyebrows at his companion. "She would make an excellent vicar's wife."

"Very funny." But then Matheson gave him a long, hard look and quietly added, "Just be careful. She may have many of the qualities you admire in your London ladies but she is not one of them."

With a single nod, Thomas replied, "Point taken." He lifted his fork, only to have a second, worrying thought. "Matheson. You are a man of God, and you are not to repeat what I've confided to you. Seal of the confessional and all that."

"Have no fear. However, she might."

That gave Thomas pause. His *London ladies*, as Matheson so succinctly put it, valued discretion or already possessed such ruined reputations that a bit more would do no harm. Yet here, where a single look or lost handkerchief could send the whole village atwitter with rumors of romance or claims of domestic discord? Propositioning the village spinster at a Christmas party would set the gossips off for decades. Worse, his father would be furious and there would be no end of it from his mother.

But no, as Thomas considered it further, he did not think Miss Winslow would say a word to anyone. And that disturbed him even more. While part of him breathed a silent sigh of relief that he would not have to face his parents' wrath, another part realized Miss Winslow had no one to turn to, no one to protect her from men who might prey upon her. Oh, Thomas may have propositioned her, but that was hardly the same thing. It was a game, a bit of sport, and he understood perfectly well the word *no*. Yet he recognized there were those who didn't, and Miss Winslow would be helpless against one of them should they take notice of her. That thought, more than anything, frightened Thomas.

Miss Dixon stayed for dinner. As a result, there were now fourteen for dinner, and no one suggested Magdalena dine with Miss Bagley again. This also presented an even number of ladies to gentleman, which undoubtedly pleased Lady Eddington, who could maneuver the potential couples to her heart's content. Magdalena also knew Uncle George would escort her in to dinner. She didn't mind. After all, that was the plan. And Uncle George was a dear, elderly gentleman, full of politeness, and then largely silent, making for an excellent companion at a large gathering.

So when Magdalena entered the drawing room before dinner, she expected Uncle George to toddle over to her and ask for the honor of escorting her in. Once seated together, their conversation would never extend beyond the excellence of the pheasant or the quality of the pudding, thus leaving Magdalena free to listen and watch, largely unobserved, requiring nothing more of her than an occasional *Please*, or *No, thank you*, or perhaps even *They are all quite well* when pressed.

But that did not happen.

Before she even had a chance to take the room in fully—a slow perusal due to the unaccustomed absence of her spectacles—she found Mr. Eddington standing at her side. To her surprise, rather than feeling flustered under his intense gaze, she felt instant annoyance. The man's image and words had lingered far too long in her mind that afternoon. She did not wish to spend the evening with the living flesh as well. All politeness went out the door.

"What do you want?" she demanded in a rushed whisper, but upon seeing the sudden mischievous spark in his eyes, she immediately said, "No! Do not answer that."

"As long as we understand each other."

"Hardly."

"You know, I do believe you are right. We should rectify that and come to some *mutual* understanding."

She glared at him and said, "Really, Mr. Eddington, you lack a moral compass."

"I happen to have a very strong moral compass. I just don't follow it very often."

Magdalena decided to ignore him—or was it a snub? She wasn't quite sure—and glanced about for Uncle George. But just as she turned away, Mr. Eddington gave her a slight bow and offered her his arm. She then realized everyone was going in to dinner. Mr. Eddington's eyes softened, no longer that intense gaze that disturbed her so. Instead, his blue eyes conveyed an unspoken message to have no fear. It was only his arm. It was only dinner. And Magdalena felt her resolve dissipate... which only made her more annoyed—with herself this time, because she wanted to be angry with him. But with a mere look, she had succumbed to his wishes, as if she had no say in the matter.

Someone had rearranged the place cards. Magdalena saw Lady Eddington trying to contain her fury—quite successfully—as she silently sought out the culprit, her eyes eventually settling on her eldest son, who audaciously winked in reply. Nothing could be done now, and Magdalena found herself seated between

Mr. Eddington and his friend, Mr. Matheson, rather than alongside Uncle George down at the far end of the table.

When Mr. Eddington took his seat beside her, Magdalena experienced a sudden surge of fear. Not from anything he did, but, out of the blue, she remembered stories told by her sisters regarding licentious suitors and their antics at table. One had placed his hand on Katherine's knee for the entire meal while another had removed his shoe and stroked Isabella's leg. Magdalena sat in dread, expecting much the same from Mr. Eddington.

Instead, as a dinner companion, he behaved in keeping with Uncle George, quiet with the rare bit of conversation amounting to little beyond *More Claret, Miss Winslow?* Whatever other qualities Mr. Eddington possessed, his table manners were immaculate.

How strange, sitting there next to him. Save for his indecent suggestion that they become lovers, he seemed a perfectly respectable man, courteous and polite, nothing like the rakehell she knew him to be. And when Sir William spoke at the head of the table and all eyes turned toward their host, it afforded Magdalena the chance to study Mr. Eddington, however briefly, in perfect profile—his straight nose, that strong jaw, and those high cheekbones. Magdalena easily saw how women succumbed to one so beautiful. Even she had to admit, if only to herself, that she found him very appealing, and in this state—quiet and still—he made some part of her heart flutter. In fact, she realized, it made her feel much the same as when he carried her that morning. She didn't like it. She much preferred the contained anger she felt when verbally confronting him. At least now he wasn't looking at her. *That* unnerved her to no end.

After dinner, while the older gentlemen lingered over their port and the ladies ostensibly adjourned to the drawing room for tea, John Eddington and Lord Sutton rolled up the carpet in the hall and carried in the pianoforte for dancing. Magdalena's one saving grace: she lacked all musical talent, and no one expected her to play for the dancers. That honor went to Miss Dixon.

Due to a draft, Magdalena retrieved her wrap—as well as her book... and a magnifying glass—and settled herself out of the way near the fire in the hall. The music commenced, and the steps of the dancers soon reverberated through the floorboards. Magdalena, meanwhile, retreated from her troubling thoughts into another world between the pages of her book.

"You're not dancing."

Heaven above! Would she have no peace? Magdalena looked up to see Mr. Eddington claiming the seat beside her on the settee.

"What keen powers of observation you have, Mr. Eddington," Magdalena coldly replied.

"May I have the honor?"

"How extraordinary. I never expected you to know that word." She returned her attention to her book, yet felt strangely guilty for treating him so rudely. "Find some other lady to stand up with you."

"You are the only lady here not dancing."

She glanced over at the dancers, quickly counted, and realized he was right. With Miss Dixon playing, the gentlemen outnumbered the ladies yet again. Magdalena suddenly wished she could play.

She returned her gaze to her book and said, "No, Mr. Eddington, I will not be dancing tonight."

"Pity."

They sat without a word for a while, and Magdalena managed to finish a paragraph, all the while hoping he would eventually seek out more amicable company. But that was not to be.

Without taking his eyes from the dancers, he leaned slightly toward her and asked in a low voice, "Have you given any further thought to my proposition?"

In an exasperated sigh—and without lowering her book—she replied, "In all honesty, Mr. Eddington, I haven't given it a second thought." It was a boldfaced lie, and she feared he knew that as well. In truth, she could think of little else. And that disturbed her as much as his proposition did. One could easily decline the offer of cake when asked; but to have a decadent slice laid out on a plate before oneself, especially as hunger gnawed the stomach? Virtue without temptation was nothing, merely lack of opportunity. *Avoiding* temptation in the knowledge that one would always succumb was one thing. But to have temptation sitting there, all smiles and laughter, with those eyes gazing intently, beckoning one to submit....

"Allow me, then, to liven the pot." He practically purred.

"Please don't."

"Did you enjoy London?"

That caught her off guard, her feigned indifference momentarily slipping. "I beg your pardon?" She turned to look at him but he was watching the dancers.

"London? I understand you spent some time there." Then those blue eyes turned on her. "Do you like London?"

"I like the anonymity of London."

He smiled. "A house, then. Somewhere quiet in Mayfair, and you as my mistress."

"Your mistress?" Her earlier anger began bubbling up inside her. As tempting as he might be, his suggestions were not.

"Yes. Not a mere tryst but something more, where we can both indulge our passion until we are both completely satiated. Away from prying eyes." Magdalena followed his gaze and saw a slightly blurred vision of his mother entering the hall.

Magdalena spoke in the most pleasant tone she could manage. "And I suppose you would pay for this house?"

"Of course."

"And you'd bring me all manner of trinkets and set up accounts for me in the finest shops so I could spend your money to my heart's content?"

"We would work something out, but essentially, yes." He appeared so very pleased with the direction he undoubtedly believed this conversation progressed.

Magdalena stopped smiling. "Reports of your charm are greatly exaggerated."

Mr. Eddington's face fell and his forehead creased with confusion. "I beg your pardon?"

"Rather than expecting me to behave like some trollop, you now expect me to behave like a seasoned courtesan?"

Mr. Eddington's eyes widened, and he pulled back from her slightly. Magdalena could not tell if her choice of words offended him or if her accusation hit the mark. Neither possibility stopped her from continuing.

"Never mistake my inexperience for ignorance," she said, "You may think we live in the middle of nowhere and, therefore, are unaware of your exploits, but we hear plenty."

"They're not exploits." He shrugged, one side of his mouth turning upward. "Just a bit of fun."

"Was it fun or an exploit when you and Lady Beaufort were caught naked at the Serpentine?"

Mr. Eddington shook his head. "We were not naked. *She* was naked. I still had my breeches on."

"A married woman old enough to be your mother."

"Then she would have been a scandalously young mother," he pointed out, "But she enjoyed it. And I am certain I am not the first person she enjoyed it with. Nor the last."

"And her husband? Would it have been fun if he'd shot you?"

He turned sober, all laughter disappearing from his eyes.

"Miss Winslow, perhaps my reputation...."

But Magdalena didn't want to hear his excuses. She was too angry. Made more so by the fact that she knew it wasn't Mr. Eddington that so upset her. It was herself. It was the part of her that wished to submit to the temptation of him.

"I know what you're about, Mr. Eddington," she said. "You can't very well seduce one of the pretty young ladies here." She motioned to the dancers. "And rather than go without for a while, you've set your sights on the old maid in the belief she will be grateful for a taste of masculine attention." He opened his mouth, undoubtedly to object, but she didn't give him the chance. "Should I happen to succumb to the temptation, it's not as if I would be ruined as no man would ever have me, so on a technical level, you're not ruining me for another man or destroying my chances for marriage. But should I protest, should I raise a fuss? Well, who would believe a man such as yourself would ever even look at someone like me? And if they did believe it, they would laugh over it, knowing it was some practical joke played by you and your friends."

When she finished speaking, Magdalena felt exhausted, her heart pounding with her anger. She could barely believe she'd spoken so bluntly to the man, but she'd had enough. Mr. Eddington sat there, his gaze never wavering from her face, but she could not read his expression.

When he spoke, his voice was low, strangely soft, and almost tender. "You have a very low opinion of yourself, Miss Winslow."

His tone failed to pacify her."No, Mr. Eddington. I am fully aware of my limitations." Given all she'd said, there seemed little point in lying to him now. "But more importantly, I am aware that you are without limits."

Magdalena rose abruptly, Mr. Eddington quickly following suit. She tried not to look at him, but she still saw the sympathy in his face. That was worse than his desire.

"Goodnight, Mr. Eddington." She moved away from him and sought out their hostess to bid her goodnight as well, before hurrying up to her room. But Mr. Eddington soon bounded up the stairs after her and stopped her in the corridor. He reached out and gently grasped her hand, her heart pounding as he did. She could have pulled away at any time and yet did not, her fingers strangely comfortable in his clasp. He seemed to study her for a moment, and when he spoke, an alluring warmth replaced his former cockiness and arrogant certainty.

"You want me," he whispered, those blue eyes piercing her, "I can see that. I can feel your pulse racing in your wrist. Your breathing is irregular. And you are parting your lips to breath. It is most beguiling."

A shudder went through Magdalena. Not because she feared him or what he could do but because she knew he was right. He could see through her. But this was not what she wanted, not really. She wanted something genuine, not this semblance of love he so craved.

"Do not mistake a physical response for real desire," she said, just as quietly. She suddenly felt sorry for him. She tilted her head to one side and asked with all sincerity, "What did you think? That I would be flattered that you wish to bed me?"

He shrugged. "I thought you would enjoy it. That we'd both enjoy it."

Magdalena nodded in understanding. "You're probably right."

He smiled, his eyes pleading with her. "Then why not say yes?"

"Because I have no desire to be used like a handkerchief." And with that, she pulled her hand out of his grasp and continued on to her room, very much alone but realizing with every step the masked loneliness of the man she left behind.

Thomas struggled to sleep that night. Bouts of tossing and turning gave way to false respites of feverish dreams, followed in turn by wakeful moments of perfect clarity with Miss Winslow's words echoing in his head.

How could she think no man would have her?

Especially as he so obviously would, in a heartbeat.

Each time he saw her, she appeared lovelier than the last. Throughout dinner, he kept wanting to touch her, lightly, just her arm, nothing lurid. And when she declined to dance with him, he felt such disappointment that it surprised him. He never expected that. All the while, their conversations stirred him to no end. Fire burned beneath that ice of hers and blazed white hot every time they spoke.

Despite all her cold reproofs, she never actually refused his proposition. Given everything else she had said, he found it impossible to believe she wouldn't simply say no. That gave him hope. He did not believe for one moment she played a game with him, as some ladies of the Ton might do, toying with him and stringing him along as part of a protracted negotiation. Miss Winslow was no coy female skilled in the mercenary arts of love. Perhaps she disliked the manner of his pursuit; his upfront, even aggressive tactics failed with her. She was too skittish and required a gentler hand to win her trust.

It pained him, though, that she knew so much about his life in London, as much as he tried to laugh it off. Lord Beaufort could have easily called him out—and probably would have killed him—if not for the intervention of friends. For all Lady Beaufort's indiscretions, her husband still *loved her*. Thomas had never been ashamed of his antics, but now... doubt crept in.

And poor Miss Bagley. He should have been aware of her situation. *That* made him feel ashamed. But he had told Miss Winslow the truth. He did love Miss Bagley, and he felt responsible for her, just as he would with any member of his family, but he wished there were something more he could do to assure her happiness.

Thomas eventually rose as the first streaks of light penetrated his room. It felt early, but dawn came late on these winter days, and much of the house was already awake, including some of the guests. And tonight was Christmas Eve.

At breakfast, Thomas encountered Miss Winslow, but with so many others about, nothing passed between them beyond mundane pleasantries. That changed later that morning when Matheson organized a party to gather greenery. The man's enthusiasm grated on Thomas to no end. Trudging through deep snow and cutting smelly, sticky, sappy pine branches to go with prickly holly and poisonous mistletoe did not strike Thomas as fun. He could think of better ways to spend a wintery day.

Yet when a groom brought the sleigh around and Thomas saw his siblings—John and Alice—and their guests—Lady Caroline, Lord Sutton, Miss Olivia Winslow, and Matheson—all on horseback, he silently blessed the future vicar. Thomas would be *stuck* with the chaperone in the sleigh. He tried not to grin too much.

When Miss Winslow—book in hand—emerged from the house, she looked none too happy with the arrangements. Uncertainty filled her face. For a moment, he expected her to beat a hasty retreat back inside. But instead, she raised her chin and proceeded to the sleigh like a duchess. Only when Thomas held out his hand to assist her did she hesitate.

"Please," he whispered, "it's just my hand. I promise I won't mention the other matter. Everything will be most appropriate."

She stood perfectly still, as if considering the situation. Then, as the others drew closer, Miss Winslow lowered her eyes, placed her hand within Thomas's, and climbed into the sleigh. He tucked the lap rugs and blankets about her—for a moment surprised that she let him—and positioned the hot bricks to her advantage. He climbed in beside her, and they were off, gliding through the snow toward the forest.

Miss Winslow said nothing. She sat silent, like she often did in company, and as much as Thomas enjoyed the mere presence of her beside him, he also missed the indignant, fiery woman dwelling inside her. It made him wonder—who was the real Miss Winslow: the quiet creature desperately wishing to go unnoticed or the lively spirit materializing whenever they spoke, confident and intelligent, full of wit, and strangely wise.

As they passed into the forest, the branches overhead laden with heavy snow, Thomas attempted conversation and asked, "Are you warm enough?"

"Yes, thank you."

And then he asked a question he had been pondering since her arrival at Eddington Hall.

"Why does everyone call you Miss Maddie and not Miss Winslow?"

She looked over at him and took a deep breath. "You didn't know my elder sister, Cecilia," she said, "She died about the time you were born. She was Miss Winslow, I was Miss Maddie, and my mother never saw fit to allow me the courtesy of being the eldest daughter." Thomas did not remember much about the late Lady Winslow, but he recalled his mother's dismissive tone regarding the woman. Miss Winslow—Miss Maddie, he supposed—looked away and said nothing more for a long time. He thought she had finished, but then she added, her voice sad, "One often hears people lament 'but that would be like having to choose which of my children I love the most.' But we know that's not really true. Parents may love all their children equally, but everyone knows who their favorite is, because they *like* some of their children more than the others." She shrugged and looked over at him again. "I understand *now*. My mother was grieving, for her first born, for the person she loved most in the world."

Despite the ache he felt for her, Thomas thought Miss Winslow perfectly amazing. He had no idea what had occurred between mother and daughter except it had caused long-lasting pain, but even now, she defended her mother. "But knowing that doesn't make it any less difficult, does it?"

Miss Winslow raised her eyebrows and twisted her mouth before saying, "I don't think she liked being reminded that she had produced such a child as me. She was, after all, a Webster, and the women in that family have always been noted for being great beauties. And here I was, pimply-faced, fat, wearing spectacles."

With any other lady, Thomas would have suspected she was fishing for a compliment, but to his great horror, he feared Miss Winslow actually believed her own words. He had known her all his life, and he could not recall her ever being 'pimply-faced.' But then, he hadn't noticed her eyes until the crash, so what else had he failed to notice? Besides, spots plagued everyone at some point. As for being fat, whoever convinced her of that clearly thought females should have figures like emaciated boys. Nothing about Miss Winslow suggested fat, and the little he'd seen was shapely and alluring. Her clothing hid much, and he imagined once he got her undressed, he would discover her all luscious curves and soft valleys.

But in regard to those Webster women and their great beauty, he had known a few of them in London; they were also known for their great vanity.

He gave her a reassuring smile. "Well, since breaking your spectacles, none of that is true." When she failed to reply, he continued, "But they say you were your father's favorite."

"If that were true, he could have reduced my sisters'

dowries—after all, neither ever lacked for suitors—and I could have had a larger portion. Then I might have had a husband... but then, Isabella might not have caught herself an earl, and that just would not suit Mother."

It occurred to Thomas that he had no business judging the late Lady Winslow. After all, he had viewed Miss Winslow as a drab, dreary female of little consequence until he saw her legs. He had never really looked at her before then... well, at least not since his childhood.

But regardless of what he now thought of her, he knew it would take lots of time to convince her of how truly lovely she was. It was if she'd been *taught* how to be unattractive. She kept her eyes lowered. She dressed like a widow. She wore her hair so severely. But there were moments when she lifted her chin and raised her eyebrows—her eyes would widen, and she looked amazingly different, as if all that passion on the inside suddenly surfaced.

Up ahead, in a clearing, he saw the head gardener and several other men waiting with the sledge. While the party would do all the gathering, the men would do the heavy lifting and take it all back to the house. Thomas pulled to a stop.

"Tell me," he said, "What is your Christian name anyway? Matilda?"

"Magdalena."

He never expected that. The name conjured up sensual visions of luxurious long hair and naked limbs, blended with selfless devotion and sincere repentance for past sins.

"That's beautiful!"

"You think so? I think it sounds like I should be a nun, spending my life at my devotionals and nursing lepers, all while wearing a hair shirt. Isabella is a name for a heroine of a novel, and Catherine is a name that could lead troops into battle."

Yes, he had his work cut out for him. He would have to teach her brand new lessons.

The others dismounted and, in a swirl of laughter, set about gathering the greenery. Thomas, however, stayed in the sleigh with Miss Winslow. She returned to her quiet self, and he fully expected her to open her book and start reading. Instead, she simply watched the others. He thought, perhaps, she wished to join them, but then he heard her speak, her voice barely audible, although wistful, as if she spoke to herself.

"How do they manage it?"

"Manage what?" he asked.

She turned and gave him a quick smile. How he wished she would smile more. "Oh, nothing," she said.

"No, tell me. Please."

"Look at them." She gestured toward Alice, Miss Olivia, and Lady Caroline ostensibly clipping sprigs of holly nearby. "Immaculate." Miss Winslow shook her head. "How do they get those pretty wisps of hair to fall just so like that?"

"I thought it occurred naturally?"

"Heavens, no! *That* is hours of calculated work after years of practice. *And* they have ladies' maids to help them."

"I had no idea."

"Why do you think it takes them so long to *dress*? Any lady who is ready in less than half an hour is either unnaturally beautiful and in league with the devil or she is unattractive and knows it's just not worth the effort."

Thomas sat there mystified and watched the three girls. They giggled and simpered and, in a manner he found disturbingly familiar, managed to get their male companions to do much of the work while they stood around and chatted. But Miss Winslow was right. They looked immaculate. Even though they wore riding habits—scarlet, green, and black—they appeared ready for a ball, perfectly coiffed, plumed and feathered, as if waiting for a cup of punch and the promise of the supper dance.

"Are you telling me that Lady Caroline's beautiful eyes...?"

"She blackens her lashes with lamp black and uses rouge to create those rosy cheeks." Miss Winslow squinted at the threesome before adding, "Although, today, with this cold, some of that might be natural."

While deemed no great beauty, Lady Caroline was considered quite attractive... although, her ten-thousand pounds provided additional appeal. And if Miss Winslow spoke the truth—he had no doubt she did—then Lady Caroline had been taught how to be attractive.

The lady in question suddenly laughed, and her voice carried across the clearing. "Isn't Lady Hurst her sister? One would think with a connection like Lord Hurst, she could have snagged a husband."

Thomas stiffened at the unkind words. He glanced over to see Miss Winslow lower her eyes and retreat further into herself.

"I'm sorry you had to hear that," he said.

"Why?" She turned to face him. "It is the truth. Isabella was so beautiful and Catherine so lively that gentleman flocked to them. One would have thought I could have snagged one of their castoffs. But I was never clever enough to do even that."

"You don't have much tolerance for beautiful people?"

"Why should I? The *beau monde* has no place for the likes of me. Except to serve as a chaperone." She raised her eyebrows. "Or as one's mistress. Hidden away. *Somewhere quiet*, I believe you said. You wouldn't parade me around. No trips to the theatre. No strolls in the parks. You wouldn't introduce your respectable friends to me."

He didn't like the direction of this conversation, so he replied, quite drolly, "I don't have any respectable friends."

"Mr. Matheson?"

"Well, *one* respectable friend." Then Thomas shook his head. "I thought we weren't going to mention the other matter?"

"I never said that."

But Thomas, for some reason he didn't understand, wanted nothing more than to avoid that topic. And he did not want to explore the possible reasons for his sudden reluctance.

So instead, he asked, "When were you in London?"

"During the Treaty of Amiens. Isabella went to Paris on her wedding journey, and Lord Hurst had just purchased a house in town. My mother sent me to ready it for their return."

"By yourself?"

"Scandalous, isn't it?" Mischief filled her eyes. "Of course, Lord Hurst had people for that, and while they treated me very well, I had little to do." She smiled. "All of London was mine to explore."

"So you attended every ball, every musicale, the assemblies, Vauxhall Gardens...."

"I *never* went out after dark." She said it as if the mere idea were indecent.

"Why ever not?" In his experience, most of the town didn't wake until dark. Then the real fun began.

"I was alone. I didn't have an escort."

Thomas gave a single nod in understanding. A lone female could never go about unattended at night. During daylight, she could get away with it, or perhaps Miss Winslow took a maid with her. Society viewed a maid trailing after a lady as perfectly acceptable... but not at a ball.

"Wherever did you go?"

Her face lit up. "The Tower, the Menagerie, the art exhibitions, the antiquity museums, Westminster Abbey, Hatchard's." Clearly, her London possessed little in common with the London he knew. She did not stop. She continued on about all the sites she had visited and all the things she wished she could have experienced— sit in the gallery during a session of the House of Commons, go boating on the Thames, see the illuminations at Vauxhall Gardens, attend the theatre— during her four months in town.

And as they spoke of the excitements of town, Thomas realized, when left to her own devices, without anyone to answer to, she did the most extraordinary things, all by herself, with no one ever to see or share them with her. And he remembered that twelve-year-old girl—before spectacles hid her green eyes—who took him fishing down at the pond so long ago. His assessment of her then matched his assessment now. And why not? Children often knew the real truth of a person's character.

Miss Winslow—Magdalena—was simply marvelous.

Lord in Heaven! He must think her an absolute fool.

When they set out, Magdalena intended to read her book quietly and watch the girls. She had never expected Mr. Eddington to remain in the sleigh with her. And then she had rattled on about her mother and sisters, all the while revealing thoughts and feelings she never told anyone. She sounded so pathetic, as if her life amounted to nothing more than some dreary Banbury tale—*how mortifying!*—only to follow it up with a boring recount of her pedestrian exploration of London, the very place he called home. He had simply gazed at her, a small smile on his lips, and indulged her as one would a prattling child.

Then, just as she began to realize how truly asinine she sounded, the others signaled their readiness to return to Eddington Hall and promises of hot drinks. In no time, they headed back through the forest. As the sleigh emerged from among the trees, Magdalena saw someone in the distance arriving at the house—a lone man on horseback.

"It's Mr. Yarborough." Mr. Matheson spoke up from where he rode close behind the sleigh.

"No, that's not Yarborough," Mr. Eddington replied over his shoulder.

"Who is Mr. Yarborough?" Magdalena asked.

"A friend. Charles Yarborough. Son of a cit," he explained to her. Then he grinned. "We would have brought him home, too, but he was too drunk to get out of bed."

"No," Mr. Matheson said, "Not Charles. His father. Mr. *Alexander* Yarborough."

Nothing further passed between the two men on the subject, but Magdalena noticed Mr. Eddington's brow creased with concern. By the time they reached the doorstep, Mr. Yarborough had long since entered the house, and Mr. Eddington had returned to his normal, lighthearted self. Magdalena put it out of her mind. The hot bricks had cooled, and while she remained comfortable enough, she longed for a cup of tea. Thankfully, once inside, they discovered luncheon laid out in the dining room.

Instead of fixing herself a plate right away, Magdalena went to see if Julia needed anything. As expected, no one had thought to bring the governess luncheon. However, as Magdalena left to go get plates for both her friend and herself, Julia requested she first find another book for her to read from the library.

Magdalena readily agreed and soon found herself in the dark, masculine library, the pocket doors to Sir William's study slightly ajar. Julia required something cheerful, Magdalena thought, and perused a shelf of novels. Perhaps something by the lady authoress. Or Mrs. Radcliff.

But as she considered the possible works, a commotion in the study intruded on her search.

"Really, Thomas!" That was Sir William's voice, uncharacteristically loud. And angry. "A thousand pounds?" The door slammed. "I can't believe you've been gambling for such high stakes." Magdalena felt her heart plummet. She could not understand Mr. Eddington. He could be so charming, kind even, and then he would turn into such a naughty boy. It was the same when he was a child; he had been so kind and friendly, and then a moment later, he tore off his clothes and threw them into the pond."

"That's over the course of nearly a year, Father."

"You shouldn't have let it get out of hand like that. You have a responsibility. Good God, Thomas, do you have any idea how much money that is? Do you have any idea how hard people have to *work* to make that much money?"

"By my calculation, Miss Bagley would have to work for us for another five years to have made that much. Frightfully little, given all she has done for us."

"Don't be impertinent."

Magdalena wished to retreat from the library, but she knew she could not slip past the partially opened pocket doors without notice. With a forgotten book still in hand, she stood unmoving, perfectly quiet. But her heart pounded fiercely out of fear of discovery.

Only when another voice spoke did she realize others had entered the room with Sir William and Mr. Eddington.

"I just want this matter resolved, Sir William." Magdalena didn't recognize the gravelly voice and assumed it was Mr. Alexander Yarborough.

"I should expect so, given you came all this way on Christmas Eve."

"A thousand pounds, Mr. Eddington." That was Mr. Yarborough.

"Really," Mr. Eddington replied, "this isn't necessary. I will forgive the...."

"I don't want my son indebted to you," Mr. Yarborough said, "so take it."

For a moment, Magdalena was confused. Then she realized this Charles Yarborough *owed* Mr. Eddington the thousand pounds, not the reverse. Strangely, she felt some relief over that fact but agreed with Sir William; it was most irresponsible of Mr. Eddington to allow his friend to get so deeply into debt, especially by way of gambling.

No one spoke for a moment, and then Magdalena heard Sir William say, "I guarantee Thomas will have nothing more to do with your son."

"No need. Charles is now bound for the East Indies on one of my ships. Time for him to make something of his life."

"Poor Charles." That was Mr. Matheson.

"Not the brightest of my boys. Thankfully I have four more with better sense."

Mr. Eddington spoke, his voice accusatory. "Did you have something to do with this, Matheson?"

No one spoke for a moment. Even Magdalena could feel the tension. Then she heard Mr. Yarborough's voice.

"I asked Matheson to make sure you weren't in town when I came to fetch Charles," he said. "You have too much influence on the boy. I didn't know how he'd react if you were there."

Silence fell over the group again, until Mr. Eddington spoke.

"I understand," he said, but Magdalena thought she

heard pain in his voice, a kind of grim acceptance.

"No hard feelings?" Mr. Matheson asked.

"No," Mr. Eddington replied, "Now I know why you were so enthusiastic to come to Eddington Hall."

"My *enthusiasm* had nothing to do with Charles." His cheerfulness assured Magdalena all was well.

"Now then," Sir William said, "if that is all settled, Mr. Yarborough, do us the honor of staying for Christmas. It's two days to Bristol, a miserable journey even in the best of weather, and you'd never get home in time for Christmas."

"Thank you, yes, I'd be grateful," Mr. Yarborough said, "I planned to spend Christmas with my eldest's family."

Magdalena hoped they would soon finish and go in to have luncheon, but instead, they lingered, and she feared they might decide to move into the library where they'd discover her. Additional, inconsequential bits of conversation passed among the gentlemen. Then, she heard Mr. Eddington's voice.

"Mr. Yarborough," he said, "I understand from Charles that you are currently in search of a wife. Is that true?"

"Yes—but what an addlebrained generation we have coming out these days. I require little more than companionship and *some* conversation, but these empty-headed debutants can barely string two words together." He paused for a moment, and when he resumed, his tone had changed. "However, that's no concern of yours."

"Please forgive my intrusion on your private life, but have you found anyone?"

"No," Mr. Yarborough grumbled, sounding disappointed.

"Well then," Mr. Eddington continued, "there is someone here I'd like to introduce you to." It occurred to Magdalena that he was playing matchmaker, a very odd occupation that she never imagined him doing.

"I have no interest in any *woman* you might...."

"No, sir. She's a respectable lady." Magdalena heard someone open the study door. She soon realized the gentlemen were finally leaving. "My father can recommend her, as well. I can arrange an introduction—if you are amiable to a lady closer to your own age and no longer of the first water."

Oh, Heavens. No. She remembered all her words that morning in regard to her failure to find a husband. She couldn't believe her lack of discretion. Normally, she was such a quiet person, but around Mr. Eddington, she simply couldn't hold her tongue and prattled on like the village gossip.

"As long as she doesn't mind an irascible old fool like me."

Magdalena heard no more, the voices trailing out of the study and drifting down the hall, toward the dining room she suspected.

She simply couldn't understand Mr. Eddington. One moment, he wanted her to go to bed with him, the next he played matchmaker for her. She didn't know whether to be insulted by the latter or appreciate the effort he made on her behalf. After all, no one else had ever thought to introduce her to any potential suitors. But given Mr. Eddington's reputation, she could not help but wonder if something nefarious were afoot. Perhaps it wasn't for her sake he thought Mr. Yarborough might do but for his own sake. What better way to hide any evidence leftover after an affair ends? A man with as many sons as Mr. Yarborough might not notice another in his nest, even a cuckoo.

The more Magdalena contemplated the matter, the angrier she became. Mr. Eddington had no business planning her life. Enough was enough. It was time she gave him a thorough piece of her mind once and for all. The nerve of the man, toying with her as if she were some kind of... of... toy! *Oh, splendid*. Perhaps she should calm down first. Her piece of mind should at least make sense. And preferably sound intelligent. Well-reasoned would be nice, too.

She stood in the hall and considered her options. For one thing, she realized she could not hear the gentlemen in the dining room; so now she was uncertain which way they went. For another—and more importantly—she could not face Mr. Eddington on an empty stomach. Maybe a cup of tea would help to calm her, she assured herself. And some cake.

She also realized she still held the book she had selected for Julia. That decided her course of action:

Julia first, then tea and cake—and anything else laid out in the dining room—as well as a plate for the governess, and only after that would Magdalena face Mr. Eddington. A most practical plan.

But as she entered the Orangery and heard male voices—very *recognizable* male voices—her heart leaped up in a most disconcerting way, and she felt quite ill. For there in the midst of the orange trees and tropical flora sat Mr. Eddington and Mr. Yarborough with Julia. Magdalena hesitated—a tad too long, it turned out—and as she turned to withdraw, Mr. Eddington spotted her and stood up.

"Miss Winslow," he said, all smiles and cheerfulness... when she wanted to throttle him.

"Mr. Eddington." She forced a smile and moved toward the little party gathered about the fire. Mr. Yarborough stood up upon seeing her. He seemed a gruff sort of man, about fifty, with fading blond hair and kind blue eyes. He sported a greying beard, neatly trimmed, the way his class sometimes did.

"Miss Winslow," Mr. Eddington said, "may I present to you Mr. Alexander Yarborough of Bristol."

A polite exchange of greetings, a curtsy, and a bow followed, and Magdalena thought, yes, had he come a-courting on his own, she wouldn't have been disappointed by first impressions. But she simply refused to tolerate Mr. Eddington's selfish machinations.

Magdalena handed Julia the book—Miss

Edgeworth's *Castle Rackrent*—before accepting the chair offered to her by Mr. Yarborough. But the moment she settled herself in and the conversation resumed, Magdalena had the most peculiar feeling. This, sitting here in company, with a suitor come to call, felt so familiar... and no wonder, given the number of gentlemen who had pursued her sisters.

And then Magdalena realized—barely containing the little gasp threatening to escape from her. Mr. Yarborough was calling upon Miss Julia Bagley! Mr. Eddington was playing matchmaker for the governess! He even looked like a managing mama—nervous but hopeful and trying to subtly encourage the potential couple by directing the conversation in constructive ways.

Relief washed over Magdalena and mixed with a growing hope for Julia. No, Magdalena did not expect this to turn into a blossoming romance, but Julia could always use another friend, especially a respected ship builder in Bristol.

And then, as the conversation continued, Magdalena contributing little, she began to realize how severely she had misjudged Mr. Eddington—at least, in this matter. She interpreted his kindness toward Julia as a nefarious act directed at herself, all based on a private exchange never intended for her ears.

The others suddenly stood—or it seemed sudden to Magdalena—including Julia, with the help of her stick and Mr. Yarborough's arm. Magdalena stood as well and discovered the party planned to luncheon in the dining room. *Yes*, Magdalena liked Mr. Yarborough! Anyone who could maneuver the Eddingtons into allowing Julia the privilege of dining with the family deserved high praise.

"Are you sure?" Magdalena instinctively reached out to help, concerned the walk to the dining room would pain her friend to excess.

"Yes, yes." Miss Bagley waved off her assistance with a smile. "I can hobble along well enough."

The pair—Mr. Yarborough and Miss Bagley—toddled toward the glass doors, Magdalena watching them. As soon as they were out of sight, Mr. Eddington turned to Magdalena.

"Are you all right?" he asked, his voice full of concern, "You look shaken."

Magdalena faltered, unaware of her transparency. She wanted to assure him she was fine, but then she could see no reason to start lying to him now.

"I'm sorry," she said.

"Whatever for?"

"I was angry. With you. I thought...." She shook her head and lowered her eyes. "I was in the library. I heard your conversation with Mr. Yarborough. I thought that you meant...." She felt so embarrassed.

Mr. Eddington's face brightened in comprehension of what she couldn't articulate. "No, no. You misunderstood."

"I see that now."

He grinned, his blues eyes twinkling as they did when he attempted to charm her. "Am I forgiven?"

She nodded her head, slowly, but on further consideration, she abruptly said, "No."

"No?"

"You've brought a handsome gentleman here in the belief that he might court her, when, most likely, nothing will come of it, and Miss Bagley will have yet another reminder of all she did not have in life."

"Handsome? You think Mr. Yarborough is handsome?"

"Quite so."

"But he's fat."

"Only the bit in the middle. It will happen to you, as well, when you reach forty. No more boyish good looks." She wanted to laugh, but instead, Magdalena took a deep breath and turned pensive. "Mr. Yarborough has a spark in his eyes. A kindness resides there. A lady could not ask for better." She smiled to reassure him. "It was very thoughtful of you."

"I'm not as thick as my parents believe."

"Thick? Hardly." She raised her eyebrows. "A licentious libertine living in London, yes. But I'd *never* call you thick."

"How very kind of you." He matched her jovial tone, but then he turned serious. "I'm pretty useless, aren't I? That's what everyone thinks. Thus why my father will not trust me to do anything."

"There are a thousand things that need doing on

this estate. Find something and do it."

"Such as?"

"I don't know. Muck out the stables." It was the first thing that came to her. Mr. Eddington looked none too happy with the suggestion.

"I beg your pardon?"

"Why do you need your father to tell you what to do?" She did not mean to speak so adamantly. It simply came out that way, forceful, insistent. And she couldn't stop herself. "Any house has dozens of things that need doing at any given moment. Find one and do it. You are a grown man. And men take responsibility for themselves and for anything and anyone who come within their sphere. So go muck out the stables. And when you've done that, find some other way to make yourself useful in this world."

When she finished, nearly out of breath, she realized Mr. Eddington stared at her, his gaze most peculiar.

Oh, Heavens! Not again!

She always talked too much in his company! But surely this time, she had gone much too far. She braced herself for his reaction.

Where did such passion come from? Thomas still found it hard to believe this quiet lady, so desperate to go unnoticed, contained such fire within her. It burst forth at the most unexpected moments, and he kept wondering what would happen if that passion were wielded for some better, more pleasurable purpose.

Her face was flushed from her admonishment of him, her mauve lips slightly parted to ease her breathing. Her breast rose and fell noticeably. He took a step toward her.

"I will... consider... your suggestion." He spoke slowly, his voice low, his eyes focusing on those lips.

And then in the space of a heartbeat—and none too gently—he pulled her into his arms and brought his mouth down on hers. At last, those enthralling lips belonged to him. She made a little sound. He ignored it, pulling her closer, tighter against his body. Vaguely, he sensed her clutching his lapels, and she seemed heavy in arms. He shifted his mouth, capturing her upper lip, and, still holding her about the waist with one arm, he raised his free hand to her caress her cheek... only to discover it wet with tears.

He released her lips and looked down at her. She opened her red-rimmed eyes, the green transformed from tidal pools to a deep, inescapable forest, the blonde lashes now made black with moisture. And in that moment, as she gazed up at him and looked so frightened, he realized no one had ever kissed her. Despite Thomas's previous belief otherwise, no doe-eyed milksop ever paid court to her in London or fancied Mother might think her acceptable.

Miss Winslow lowered her head and tried to pull away from him, but he refused to release her. Instead, he held her close, and she buried her face against his chest, her body trembling. Filled with tenderness, he kissed her forehead and rested his cheek against her head.

Matheson was right. Miss Winslow possessed the intelligence and wit Thomas found so attractive in the older women he pursued, only she had no more experience than a schoolgirl, a contradiction he found impossible to fathom. Until now.

"I'm sorry," he whispered.

She gave a little gasp that sounded something akin to a laugh. "When you kiss someone, you don't apologize." She sniffled. "Unless she slaps you."

He gave a small laugh of his own. However, he wasn't apologizing for the kiss. He wouldn't change that—although, he should not have been so abrupt with her. No, he apologized because no one had ever thought to kiss her. He apologized because no one had ever bothered to love her, and it felt like a kind of death to him.

Miss Winslow was so like the many women he had known—intimately known—intelligent, confident, commanding, capable. And yet she was a complete innocent, untouched, unloved. And for all her strength, she seemed the most vulnerable woman he'd ever encountered, and she drew to the surface every protective instinct he had.

And then Thomas realized... he was the first man ever to kiss her. The only man.

This time when she pulled away, he let her go,

slowly, holding on to her for as long as he could. She stepped back, but before she could leave, he pressed a handkerchief into her hand.

"I'll join you shortly in the dining room," he said.

She simply nodded and walked away.

For a long while after she left, Thomas stood there, his thoughts racing in a thousand different directions. He looked outside at the snow-covered landscape, so contradictory from the tropical world inside and the heat he endured. He could just make out the corner of the stable block from these windows. And he suddenly decided that, *yes*, perhaps he should take the advice of Miss Winslow—Magdalena.

Magdalena did not go to the dining room—not directly, at least. She made a detour to her room to make sure she looked all right. Not that it really mattered; she just did not want anyone noticing any tears remaining in her eyes. And over such a silly thing. Because a man had kissed her. Well, not exactly because of the kiss, but because of all the feelings that came with it and how frightening those feelings were, all mixed with the knowledge that Thomas desired her.

Thomas made her feel... nauseous... no, not nauseous. He made her feel *something*... and she did not like feeling *something*.

Oh, who was she fooling—certainly not herself. She knew exactly what she felt. She had known the moment she had opened her eyes and seen those dark blue eyes gazing down at her and piercing her very soul. Her heart had cried out for him, and her body had happily joined in, aching for him, and she knew if she did not remain strong, she would easily succumb to him, body and soul. She hated this feeling. She wanted it to go away. Nothing could be more ridiculous than the love of an old maid.

After washing her face with cold water, Magdalena hurried to the dining room. To her surprise, Mr. Eddington was absent from the small gathering. Julia sat with Mr. Yarborough, as well as Uncle George and Sir William, the younger people now busy decorating the house for Christmas. In a further room, someone played the pianoforte, none too well. Magdalena suspected it was one of the boys, as all the girls played splendidly.

No one really noticed Magdalena's arrival enough to say anything beyond a greeting before resuming their own conversations and meals. Julia, the one person who would have realized something was amiss, sat engrossed with Mr. Yarborough, for which Magdalena was grateful, for her own sake as well as that of her friend.

Quite famished, Magdalena piled up her plate— only, with her nerves on edge, her stomach kept turning somersaults… made even worse by the anticipated arrival of Mr. Eddington at any moment. How did one interact with a gentleman after being thoroughly kissed by him, Magdalena wondered. Thankfully, a cup of tea helped to calm her. Well, two cups. Maybe a third wouldn't hurt, either.

Still, Mr. Eddington did not join them in the dining room. Magdalena ate, the meal a cold luncheon, so the delay did not hamper the quality of it, and she soon discovered she was eating an excessive amount of cake. *Oh dear.* Perhaps she really just needed to rest for a while.

But then Lady Eddington rushed in, looking quite perplexed. She went to the window and looked out, then moved to the next window before moving on to another window.

"Whatever are you doing?" Sir William asked his wife.

"You can see better from the window on the back stairs," she replied.

"See what?"

She turned and gave her husband an exasperated look. "Your son."

With a grumble, Sir William rose. "What has Tom done now?" Magdalena felt all her nausea return in an instant.

"That's what I'm trying to see," Lady Eddington said.

Sir William joined his wife at the window.

"If you stand here," she explained, "and lean this way a bit, you can just make him out by the stables."

The stables? Magdalena never expected that. She nearly jumped up and rushed over to the window but managed to contain herself.

"Can you see him?" Lady Eddington asked her

husband.

After a long pause, Sir William replied, "Unbelievable. He's mucking out the stables." He gave a short, quick laugh. "Some lady assigned him a Herculean task? Perhaps your plan is working, my dear."

Magdalena felt herself blush and doubted Sir William and Lady Eddington would approve of the lady in question. Why Mr. Eddington decided to do as she suggested Magdalena couldn't imagine, but it made her feel giddy, quite foolishly. She tried to dismiss it. No, it couldn't have anything to do with her, not really. Still, she smiled, strangely pleased.

She excused herself and returned to her room. She hoped she might be able to see Mr. Eddington from her window, but she could only make out the corner of the stable block.

Someone wanted her... and all she had to do was give in to his wishes and she would know what it was to be loved, thoroughly, exquisitely, by this beautiful man.

Oh, how she wished she could just give in to him. To love without fear, if only for an hour. How easy it would be. How delightful. To indulge herself without a thought for her family or for the consequences. Only, she didn't know how to be that selfish.

But it wasn't real love that Mr. Eddington offered, just a vain mockery of love. At least on his part. Real love would respect her, admire her, protect her, even from his own desires. Love would never use her.

It would mean something to her. To him, it would

be nothing more than physical gratification. To her, so much more, and when he left her, it would break her heart, despite all her pragmatism.

Julia had told her not to reject Thomas's proposition because she feared what the neighbors might think but to give it some thought, and if she did reject him, to find a good reason to do so. Well, she had her reason. There was something worse than loneliness, worse than living life unloved. It was to be loved and then abandoned. Discarded. As if none of it had ever happened. And Magdalena did not want to learn how to survive that. She doubted she *could* survive that.

But the persistence of Mr. Eddington troubled her. Despite her disinterest—or did she feign it?—she feared he would persevere. And at some point, her strength and determination would falter. She would willingly succumb, and he would take complete possession of her.

Until he tired of her.

She had to find a way to get him to leave her alone, once and for all. And a thought occurred to her. Growing up, she had cultivated the art of invisibility in order to avoid her mother's displeasure. All these years of knowing Mr. Eddington, he had never really spoken to her, never noticed her. Until she spoke to him. Quite disgracefully, at that. She had pulled the curtain back, just a bit, and he had glimpsed something of the real woman.

Perhaps he needed more than just a glimpse.

Perhaps it was time to draw attention to herself.

Perhaps she should just give Mr. Eddington what he wanted.

That evening—Christmas Eve—as music and laughter drifted up from the hall below, Thomas paced back and forth on the first landing of the stairs. He had not seen Magdalena since kissing her in the Orangery that afternoon. When she never made an appearance in the drawing room before dinner, he feared his mother, yet again, had requested she dine with Miss Bagley in order for the number at table to be just so. But Miss Bagley dined with the family tonight, along with Mr. Yarborough. Reverend Dixon and his family joined them as well.

Only when Thomas had asked Miss Olivia about her aunt did he learn Magdalena requested dinner in her room but would come down later for the dancing before they all went to Midnight Service. Miss Olivia also mysteriously added with a cheeky grin that Magdalena had inquired after the assistance of Lady Bollingbrook's maid.

He did not like her absent from his sight— Magdalena—as if she were already his. Despite spending the afternoon hard at work with the grooms and stable boys, Thomas desperately wanted to be with her, sitting somewhere quietly in the house, just to be near her. And now he felt sore in places he never knew he had, even worse than going a round with Gentleman

Jackson. But because of his efforts, they had finished earlier than usual, which made for a merrier Christmas Eve for everyone.

A movement out of the corner of his eye brought Thomas to a halt, and he looked up to see Miss Olivia standing atop the stairs and clothed in a diaphanous white evening gown clinging to her curves and revealing a fair amount of cleavage. Only..., Miss Olivia, for all her beauty, lacked this lady's voluptuousness, and while Miss Olivia's hair shimmered golden in every light, this lady's Grecian coif....

And then Thomas realized.

It was Magdalena.

He gazed up at her, marvelous to behold, like some grand lady at a London ball. The high-waisted gown made her seem tall and left her arms completely bare. Her hair, light brown by candlelight, was piled up in coils and curls with soft ringlets framing her face and those lips so red, those eyes so mesmerizing. He wanted her even more now than when he had seen her bare legs. And if she had already said yes, he would have forgone the merriment below and found a private place for some merriment all their own.

And then, as his eyes swept over her, he realized why his thoughts turned so prurient, his amazement over her beauty quickly turning to anger. He took the stairs two at a time and, reaching her, grabbed her roughly by the upper arm.

"What the hell are you doing?" he demanded.

"Whatever do you mean, Mr. Eddington?" Her calm demeanor angered him even more.

"I can see your nipples."

"Oh, that." She had the audacity to smile. "I watered down my gown. They say it's all the fashion in Paris. I thought you'd like it."

"I most certainly do not! And you don't have any underclothes on."

Magdalena shrugged. "Makes things so much easier. Don't you agree?"

Without another word, he marched her back down the corridor to her room. Only once alone there with the door securely closed behind them did he release her arm. Now bathed in firelight, she appeared even more desirable, and he tried not to contemplate the flimsy material barely covering her. At least no one else had seen her.

"Really, Mr. Eddington," she said, "when did you become such a prude? Half of London saw your last paramour completely naked, and *now* you object to a bit of damp cloth and décolletage?"

"You will change into something appropriate." He glanced about for something—a shawl or such—to wrap about her. For while the gown tantalized him with its glimpses of soft flesh, it left him desperately wanting to see much more of her. He picked up a blue Indian shawl and stepped toward her, their eyes meeting. And he noticed the rest of her *ensemble*; she had painted her face... lampblack on her lashes, powder on her skin, rouge on her cheeks, and he had no idea what on her nearly blood-red lips. "And wash your face!"

"My face?"

"You look like a common whore."

"But that's what you wanted, Mr. Eddington... for me to be *your* whore." She purred and then glanced toward the bed. "Come now. Why waste a bed? We can be done with it in a minute. No one will even note our absence from the party."

Thomas stepped away from her, horrified she would ever suggest such a thing. He didn't recognize this woman. She wasn't the quiet creature simmering with contained passion who had captured his imagination. She was something else, someone he didn't want to know. But then he caught a glimpse of something hidden beneath this stranger's façade. Despite her words, Thomas saw fear in her eyes. Somehow, *that* calmed him.

"What are you doing?" he asked, his voice soft.

"I'm just submitting to your wishes. This is, after all, what you said you wanted."

"But this isn't you."

"No, it's not. But it is you. It's what you want." She tilted her head slightly. "Isn't it?"

Thomas didn't know what to think anymore. He swallowed hard and held out the shawl to her. To his surprise, she took it and wrapped it about herself. There. He saw her. Beneath the paint and the trappings of a worldly woman, he saw his Magdalena return. And he felt an overwhelming sense of relief.

"I'll wait outside," he said and quietly slipped out. He went to his own room and splashed cold water on his face. Then he returned and waited, sentry-like, outside her door, while his mind tried to unravel all his thoughts and feelings.

Good God Almighty! What just happened? He was concerned about her reputation! He'd never been concerned about anyone's reputation before, not even his own.

Oh, he was also furious with her. Part of him wanted to accept that invitation and drive himself into her and make her cry out... but in ecstasy and desire. Not this. He wanted to love her, thoroughly and properly, all night long and then some... not in a frenzied dash, over in a minute, followed by a hasty return to public company, all the while fearing discovery.

And he wanted to protect her, to protect her reputation, to protect her virtue—from himself even—and to protect her from the eyes of other men. In that moment he saw her on the stairs, she had been beautiful. Her eyes, always so lovely, now entranced him, while her mouth desperately needed a kiss. But then he saw the dark of her nipples pert against the wet fabric, and for the first time in his life, Thomas felt the mad rush of jealousy. He didn't want anyone else to see her—not merely because of her outrageous attire. He didn't want another man to feel that desire he felt for her, now made stronger than ever.

And then, as he waited for her, a thought occurred to him, a strange and unique—in his experience—thought.

He loved her.

It came as no surprise. After all, given everything that had happened so long ago, he supposed he had always loved her. His Mad Maddie.

He waited a long time, to the point of worry. He kept wondering if he should listen at the door—she could be in there crying, deeply distraught over all this—but he didn't wish to invade her privacy. And just as he feared she might never emerge, the door slowly opened. Magdalena stood there in a dark blue dress, the sleeves long, the neck high, with the Indian shawl draped about her. Her hair remained the same, soft about her face, but the rouge and powder were gone. She looked like herself once again... but no less desirable in his eyes.

"Better?" she shyly asked.

Thomas nodded and smiled. "Much better. Thank you." He offered her his hand, and when she accepted it, he bowed over her hand. He noticed the lampblack remained; he found he liked it. But he noticed something else.

"You cut your hair."

"Just around my face. To hide my forehead."

"I like your forehead."

She lowered her eyes, and he thought she blushed.

After all that had proceeded, she could still blush! *But of course.* None of it was real. Just a performance for his sake. Thomas shook his head. She could have tread the boards.

"You did this on purpose," he said.

"Yes."

He suddenly felt deeply ashamed of himself, that his pursuit of her led her to this extreme. He had treated her as an object of lust, when she deserved nothing less than love. This lady, who wished nothing more than to go unnoticed, had endured his unwanted attention.

"Are you all right?" he asked.

She gave him a small but reassuring smile. "I'm fine."

He shook his head again. "But what if I had taken up your offer?"

"I knew you wouldn't."

"How could you know that?"

Magdalena took a deep breath. "You do scandalous things *in London*, but never *here*, not in your father's house. Besides, I knew you'd be appalled by the suggestion."

"You did?" That baffled him. He knew it was the only time in his life he'd turned down such an invitation.

She nodded. "It's not what you really want."

He supposed she spoke the truth. And only now did he begin to comprehend what he truly wanted. However, all this time, he had been concerned with his wants... but never hers. So he asked with all sincerity,

"What do you want?"

The question seemed to surprise her, and her expression subtly changed, softening with sorrow. "I want to be cherished."

Thomas lowered his eyes and thought, yes, he could do that, if given the chance.

He took her hand and tucked it into the crook of his arm. "Let's enjoy ourselves," he said, "as if none of this ever happened. As if I never suggested we become lovers. As if we are old friends and neighbors celebrating Christmas together with all our family and friends."

Magdalena nodded, and they descended the stairs to the first landing. There, she stopped, looked him in the eyes, and said, "If it's any consolation, Mr. Eddington, you make me wish I were a different kind of lady. But wishing doesn't make it so. My answer will always be no."

"Even though you want to say yes?"

"Especially then."

Without another word passing between them, they continued down the stairs and joined the Christmas Eve celebration in the hall.

Christmas morning. Thomas woke full of anticipation. Bright, glorious sunlight poured through the room and reflected his mood. He knew what he wanted; he just had to convince others to see things his way.

He could hear activity outside. Horses, he thought; someone going for a morning ride, perhaps. Fearing what he might have already missed—and eager to see Magdalena—Thomas shaved and dressed. The hour surprised him, only mid-morning, when he and Magdalena had been up until two o'clock. He had danced nearly every dance with her, despite the whispers that anything more than two dances with the same lady was quite scandalous. He had sat beside her on the way to Midnight Service, then together in the same pew, and then again, side by side, on the return to Eddington Hall.

He was blissfully happy.

The house, however, seemed unusually quiet, especially for Christmas morning. As he descended the stairs and made his way to the dining room, he assumed that most of the guests were still abed. The few servants he encountered quickly scurried away. He entered the dining room in the full expectation of finding some of the guests and his family eating breakfast. Instead, he discovered the room empty, breakfast waiting on the sideboard. Only, he then noticed his mother standing at the window, her arms folded across her chest as she stared outside into the wintery world.

"Good morning," Thomas said.

His mother turned on him and said, "How could you, Thomas?"

Leave it to his mother to ruin his mood. "How could I *what*?" he asked, truly baffled. On any other occasion in his life, he most certainly deserved any number of accusations, but for once, he had done nothing wrong.

"It's all the talk below stairs!"

"What is?" He began to worry.

His mother let out an exasperated sigh and said, "You... and Miss Maddie... in this house! Your antics in town are bad enough, but really Thomas, you've gone too far this time."

For once, he had virtue on his side. "Anything being said below stairs is not true."

"Are you denying that you were in her room?"

He shook his head and managed to come up with a believable explanation. After all, he had plenty of practice. "She tore her gown last night while coming down the stairs. I simply helped her back to her room so she could change. That's all."

"That's all? After all the attention you showered on her last night? And I suppose the gardener's boy never saw you kissing her in the Orangery."

He couldn't deny that—he would never deny that moment with the woman he loved—but Magdalena's reputation was at stake here, so he would never admit to it. Instead, he said, "Where's Miss Winslow? She'll tell you this is all a misunderstanding."

"I'm afraid she's gone, along with poor Miss Olivia. It's really most unfair to her but she couldn't very well stay here by herself."

"Gone?" Outrage boiled up inside him.

"Yes," his mother said, "the moment I learned what

you've been up to, I asked her to leave. She behaved most decorously considering everything."

"She did nothing wrong!"

"So you say. Now eat your breakfast, and not a word of this to anyone else. They will all know but we will say nothing."

"Eat my breakfast? That's all you have to say to me? No scolding? No reprimand? You're not going to send me to my room without any supper?"

His mother should rail against him—he was the one who'd behaved disgracefully—but instead, she shrugged it off. "It's Christmas. Besides, boys will...."

"...Be boys. Yes, yes, always the excuse for a gentleman's bad behavior. But you have no qualms about condemning an innocent lady."

His mother gave him a patronizing—or what it matronizing?—smile. "Thomas, my dear boy, no female will remain *innocent* for long with you pursuing her." She motioned to the sideboard. "Now, no more discussion. Have some coffee."

"You're wrong, Mother." She opened her mouth to protest but he didn't give her a chance. "Miss Winslow is the most virtuous woman I've ever known. She has no artifice about her. She doesn't flatter or simper. She speaks her mind, truthfully, telling me what I need to hear, not what I wish to hear." He barely paused before rushing on. "And while I have, in fact, been *pursuing* her, as you put it, my intentions are honorable." So it was a lie of omission. His mother didn't need to know his intentions began as anything but honorable.

Lady Eddington looked incredulous, her mouth opening and closing twice before she finally responded. "Are you telling me you are seriously interested in Miss *Maddie* Winslow?"

"Completely."

She shook her head. "Well, the moment she learns of your interest in her, she will change at the prospect of snagging such a rich and handsome gentleman."

"With all due respect, Mother, she already has me, body and soul. I am the one who has yet to prove myself worthy of her regard."

"But she's old enough to be your...."

"She's old enough to be your daughter," Thomas said, "and as far as I am concerned, her age is ideal. She's not some empty-headed child thrust onto the marriage mart by some managing mama. She has a mind all her own."

Lady Eddington plopped down, most unladylike, in the nearest chair and shook her head, muttering, "Unbelievable."

"Now, when did they leave?" Thomas demanded.

She looked up at him, her brow creasing as she seemed to ponder the question. "Uh, twenty minutes ago, I think."

Thomas turned to leave.

"You're going after them?" his mother asked.

"Of course I am," he replied, "And I'm bringing them back. Before this malicious gossip reaches the village. I will not have my reputation as a womanizer ruin a virtuous lady who has done no wrong."

Magdalena sat in the travelling coach rocking this way and that as they made their way home. *How humiliating!* Olivia would barely speak to her. But given all the accusations Lady Eddington leveled against her, they had no choice but to leave. Mr. Eddington *had* pursued her. He *had* kissed her in the Orangery. And he *had* been in her room last night. Never mind the truth. Any claims of innocence meant nothing. Only appearances counted in this world.

Worst of all, she dreaded the moment her family learned of this. Arthur and Harriet would be furious. They might even ask her to leave. So much for fearing she might become the laughing stock of the village; now everyone would believe she had allowed a rake to bed her. If she were to be condemned for such a sin, she thought, surely she should have gotten the chance to commit the sin. Maybe then she might have learned what all the fuss was about. Part of her kept wondering what she would have done last night had Mr. Eddington accepted her feigned invitation. She doubted she would have had the fortitude to deny him anything.

Her only consolation was her eight-hundred pounds. She might be falsely ruined, but she would never be poor.

She wondered if it were wrong to pray that the carriage might break down, forcing them to seek shelter in a stable or with a farmer and his family. She did not want to go home, not merely because of the prospect that awaited her there but also because she so wanted to spend Christmas with Mr. Eddington.

They were nearly to the village, the way made slow and difficult due to the deep snow. Another three miles of travel awaited them to Winslow House. Magdalena—and undoubtedly, Olivia as well—was cold. In the rush to depart Eddington Hall, no one thought to put hot bricks in the carriage, thus forcing the two ladies to huddle together beneath lap rugs. Olivia rested her head on Magdalena's shoulder and seemed to sleep.

Just as the village church steeple came into view, Magdalena thought she heard shouting. Then, quite abruptly, the carriage halted. Olivia sat up.

"Have we become mired in the snow?" she asked.

Oh, God, please, make it so.

But then Magdalena saw someone ride past. She lowered the window and looked out... only to see Mr. Eddington on horseback speaking to the coachman.

"Mr. Eddington!" The happiness she felt at the sight of him threatened to overwhelm her. She longed to jump out of the carriage and rush to him, but she forced herself to remain calm.

He turned and smiled at her, but merely said, "One moment, Miss Winslow."

Magdalena closed the window and sat back. Then she felt the carriage turning around. A moment later, Mr. Eddington climbed in and sat down opposite the two ladies. He was out of breath, and a raven lock fell over one eye. He swept it back, and as the carriage began moving again—this time back the way they had just come—he smiled.

"I've explained everything to Mother," he said.

"You did?"

"How you tore your gown and I escorted you back to your room."

"See, Maddie." Olivia beamed with delight. "I knew there was some mistake. It's completely absurd to think you and Mr. Eddington...."

"Yes, quite," Magdalena replied through clenched teeth. A look passed between her and Mr. Eddington, an understanding, his face softening with a touch of sadness.

"So now there is no need for you to leave," Mr. Eddington said, "and we can all spend Christmas together as planned."

It occurred to Magdalena that, with just word from him, she was saved from ruination. Her word was not enough. The word of rake, though, had value. Still, he didn't have to do it. He had, after all, lied to his mother, for which Magdalena was very grateful.

"Thank you, Mr. Eddington."

He nodded his head, just once, by way of a bow, and replied, "It is the least I could do, Miss Winslow."

The journey back to Eddington Hall seemed to take longer. Thankfully, Mr. Eddington chatted and kept Olivia entertained with stories of life during the Season.

Magdalena sat quiet, mainly because of the cold. Had they been alone—she and Mr. Eddington—she would not have hesitated to seek out his warm embrace and rest her head against his shoulder. But they had come to an understanding last night, and now, such a thing would be impossible, even if they were alone.

At last, they made it back, and after Olivia bounded out—*Where did the young find such energy?*—Mr. Eddington kindly lifted Magdalena out of the carriage. Once inside, Lady Eddington greeted her with a half-hearted apology over the *misunderstanding*. Still, Magdalena sensed the lady of the house doubted the veracity of her son's version of events. No matter. In truth, Magdalena really didn't care. All she wanted was a warm fire and a cup of tea—preferably a pot—both of which she found in the Orangery in the company of Julia and Mr. Yarborough, where Mr. Eddington soon joined them.

Despite her enjoyment of the company and conversation, Magdalena didn't know what to make of Mr. Eddington now. His behavior seemed most peculiar to her, and she kept wondering what went on in his mind. He seemed so pensive, and she often caught him watching her. Knowing looks would pass between them—they shared secrets, after all—but they spoke few words, other than the polite necessities of social intercourse. She tried to dismiss it as regret on his part for all that had happened, but she knew something more occupied his thoughts.

Morning came and went. The afternoon slowly crept. And as the minutes and hours of Christmas Day passed, the house grew livelier with more guests arriving. Reverend Dixon and his children came again, and the music from a pianoforte echoed through the house. The smells of roasting meat drifted from the kitchen and mingled with the scents of pine boughs and the cinnamon of the wassail bowl.

The time came at last to change for dinner. Magdalena dressed in her respectable blue gown from the previous evening and managed to reproduce a reasonable facsimile of the Grecian coif. She did not attempt to darken her lashes with lampblack again. Washing it off—in the middle of the night—made a mess of her eyes, her basin, the cloth, and the towel.

Mr. Eddington greeted her in the drawing room. Though he spoke little, he did not leave her side. And when everyone finally went into the dining room, he escorted her in.

However, once there, Magdalena found herself seated across from Julia—seated alongside Mr. Yarborough—and next to Uncle George, practically on the opposite end from Mr. Eddington. She knew she shouldn't be surprised. Everything had returned to the way it was supposed to be, much to her disappointment.

In the midst of the soup course, Magdalena saw the butler whisper something to Lady Eddington, who, in turn, did little to hide her frustration. Something amiss in the kitchen, Magdalena suspected. A few words passed between Mr. Eddington and his mother. And then Mr. Eddington rose and, with a smile, looked over the large gathering of friends and family.

"There has been a slight delay with the goose," he said, "So this seems a good time to say a few words."

"Thomas," his mother interrupted, "this isn't really necessary."

"Yes, it is, Mother."

Magdalena plainly heard the tension in Mr. Eddington's voice. His mother looked none too pleased with him. Magdalena glanced at Sir William, who looked confused by the preceding at the opposite end of his table.

"First of all," Mr. Eddington said, "I want to thank Miss Winslow for returning, despite the misunderstanding." He looked down the length of the table, all heads turning with his gaze, at Magdalena. "As my mother now knows, and as I want everyone to know, Miss Winslow tore her dress, and I simply escorted her back to her room so she might change."

"Completely understandable, my boy," Sir William said.

"Of course, Thomas," Lady Eddington added, "No one seriously thought anything untoward occurred between you and Miss Maddie."

Smiles and a few small laughs followed around the table. But Magdalena saw Mr. Eddington clinch his jaw, while Julia gave her a sympathetic glance. Even with their unspoken support, Magdalena wanted to slink away, unseen, unnoticed, but thankfully, Mr. Eddington lingered no longer on that topic.

"Secondly," he said, "I've come to a decision. I will not be returning to my life in London." That captured the attention of Sir William. "That is to say, I won't be going back to town except in the company of my family, current or future. Instead, I've decided to stay here and learn every aspect of running this estate." Sir William looked very pleased. "If you don't mind, Father. And I would like to make the old rectory my home. It will need some work, but I think I'd be very happy there."

"The old rectory?" Lady Eddington asked. "You wouldn't rather be here at home? With your family?"

Mr. Eddington glanced down, a hint of a smile on his lips. He took a deep breath and said, "That brings me to the final thing I wish to say." He slowly surveyed the table but then looked at no one in particular. "In truth, I have been pursuing Miss Winslow."

Oh, dear Lord! Magdalena felt her stomach turn while her heart leaped up into her throat. *What was he doing?* Lady Eddington was right; this wasn't necessary. Magdalena watched in horror as confusion covered the faces of her dinner companions, many looking toward her. But then some realization occurred to each of them in turn, accompanied by knowing smiles and a few whispers. Now they looked toward Olivia several places down from her. Only Julia failed to regard the younger lady. Her eyes never wavered from Magdalena.

Mr. Eddington continued. "But knowing my

reputation, she rejected my suit. Rightfully so, if you ask me. I've been quite the scoundrel. Still, nothing deterred me, and she endured my unwanted and very unwelcomed attention." His gaze once again returned to Magdalena, and she looked down to stare at the last dregs of soup in her bowl. "Her virtue is impeccable, and anyone who suggests otherwise will have to answer to me. And rather than flee this house or raise a fuss, Miss Winslow put up with me. I suspect she feared spoiling everyone's Christmas, particularly Mother's, Alice's, and Miss Olivia's."

Sir William spoke up. "I'm confused, Tom. Of whom are you speaking?" Magdalena looked about her to see the same confusion reflected in almost everyone's face.

"Miss Winslow, of course." Thomas gazed directly at her. Sir William glanced at her in disbelief then returned his attention to his son.

"You mean Miss *Olivia* Winslow," he said.

Anger edged Mr. Eddington's succinct reply. "I mean Miss *Magdalena* Winslow." That set the table abuzz. Shocked expressions, raised eyebrows, and hushed comments passed amongst everyone.

"Magdalena?" someone whispered with a hint of disgust.

"The chaperone?" another voice said.

A few, furtive looks turned Magdalena's way, but then, as if ignoring her, everyone focused on Mr. Eddington.

"In return for my constant attention," he said, "I've

had the great fortune to discover a side to Miss Winslow few, if any, know. I have grown to respect and admire her as I never thought possible. In truth..." He turned toward Magdalena and spoke directly to her, his voice soft with emotion. "...I do not deserve her. But I live in fear that some other man will realize her worth and I might lose her to him."

Everyone looked at her, and Magdalena felt her face flush. Her heart raced, and breathing required a conscious effort on her part. And still, Mr. Eddington was not finished.

"Forgive me, Miss Winslow... Magdalena. I know how you abhor attention, but given my reputation, I know no other way to be about this, but... I love you." Someone gasped. It sounded like Lady Eddington, but it did not stop her son. "Here, before this company on this most holy of days, I declare my intention—to court you and to marry you and to be a faithful and devoted husband to you all the days of my life."

Magdalena could bear it no more. Without another word, she rose and ran from the room. Somehow, she ended up in the drawing room. She just needed to get away from all the stares and catch her breath. She needed to think and a chance to unravel her own feelings. And then she discovered her eyes wet with tears.

"Magdalena?"

She turned to see Mr. Eddington standing in the doorway. He moved toward her. Tall and handsome, with those piercing blue eyes and raven locks, like some chiseled block of marble come to life, he was everything a lady could want. Magdalena couldn't help loving him. She had no doubt of her love. As for his feelings....

Courtship and engagements were meant to be public matters to prevent unscrupulous men from ensnaring young girls. But she was not a young girl, and if Mr. Eddington intended to ensnare her, well, he already tried seduction and had failed. Even after her performance last night, when given the chance to satisfy his lust with a blatant invitation—albeit feigned—he had walked away. That alone demonstrated he cared for her on some level. But now this. There was no reason on Earth for him to declare himself—at Christmas dinner, no less—unless he truly meant it. He loved her.

"Mr. Eddington...."

"Please, call me Thomas." He stood before her. "I'm sorry to have put you through that, but I knew you'd never believe me if I said it in private. In such matters, you have no reason to trust me." He reached down and took her hand. "You said your answer would always be no, and I completely understand if you still say no to this new proposal, but I had to tell you how I felt and what I really want. Because I want you in my life, now until death separates us. Not just as my bedmate but as my wife."

"I don't understand. How can you...? You don't really know me."

"I've known you all my life. And this is hardly

sudden." He grinned, mischief sparking in his eyes. "After all, this isn't the first time I've declared my intentions to you."

"I beg your pardon?"

His grinned faded. "You don't remember?" When she shook her head, he added, "The day I took off all my clothes and threw them in the pond?"

Magdalena slowly nodded, wishing she never remembered that day again. "I remember that. I don't remember any *declaration*."

"We were down at the pond. I wanted to go fishing, and you were helping me with the worm and the hook."

"I don't remember that," she said. She simply remembered being by the pond, the Eddington children and a couple of her younger siblings playing nearby while all the adults had their party on the lawn by the house.

"I didn't know girls could do such things," Thomas continued. "I thought it marvelous, and right then and there, I said I wanted to marry you."

Magdalena smiled at the prospect and thought it so endearing. "And what did I say?"

"You laughed."

"Oh." All merriment vanished. "Oh, dear."

"Yes."

"And that's when you tore off all your clothes...."

"And threw them in the pond. Exactly."

"I'm so sorry."

"I admit I was devastated. But now I know you were

just laughing over the antics of an adorable child." He paused and cocked his head to one side. "I was adorable, wasn't I?"

"Yes, very much so. Until you threw that little tantrum. Then I wanted to bend you over my knee."

"Well, if you ever feel the need again, I am happy to oblige you."

"Oh, stop it," she playfully scolded, but then she turned wistful, recalling the rest of that day so long ago. "Strange the things we remember."

"How so?"

"What I remember of that day was my mother and yours pressing me into service and making me responsible for you, your siblings, and my younger siblings while they enjoyed the party. So while you remember me laughing over your proposal of marriage, I remember the thorough dressing-down I got the moment we returned home."

"Because of me?"

"And because Amelia wandered away from me and found that glass of brandy."

"I'm so sorry."

Magdalena shook her head. "You weren't responsible. You were a child."

"So were you." Thomas raised her hand to his lips and kissed her knuckles. "You've been responsible for other people all your life. Please, allow me the privilege of being responsible for you."

Magdalena felt tears well up in her eyes again.

Thomas cupped her cheek and wiped away a tear with his thumb. She needed no further encouragement, and she stepped into his waiting embrace.

"I love you, too," she said against his chest.

He simply held her for a long time, his cheek resting atop her head. Then he quietly asked, "Shall I obtain a special license?"

She pulled back, her arms still about him, and looked up at him. "Oh no. I want the banns read. I want to hear our names spoken before the whole church every Sunday for three weeks."

Thomas nodded. Then she saw that spark of mischief again.

"And *then* you will be mine?"

She replied with the one word she knew he longed to hear from her.

"Yes."

About Anna

Anna D. Allen is essentially half-Finnish and half-Southern, which means she has no sense of humor and will shoot you for wearing white shoes after Labor Day... unless you are attending a wedding and happen to be the bride. She holds a Bachelor of Science and a Master of Arts in Language and Literature. She is a recipient of the Writers of the Future award and a member of Science Fiction and Fantasy Writers of America, but she also has a great passion for Regency Romances. It is generally acknowledged that she spends way too much time with the dead and her mind got lost somewhere in the 19th Century. Case in point, her website: http://beket1.wix.com/annadallen

Along with her contributions to the Regency anthologies, *Christmas Revels* and *Christmas Revels II*, her available works include two collections: *Mrs. Hewitt's Barbeque: Seven Eclectic Tales of Food, Humor, and Love* and *Lake People and Other Speculative Tales*; the novel *Charles Waverly and the Deadly African Safari*; the Regency Romance novelette "A Christmas Wager;"

the Regency Romance novel *Miss Pritchard's Happy, Wanton Christmas (and the Consequences Thereof)*, as well as some boring scholarly stuff about dead people. Rumor has it she has run off with the Doctor—picking up Matthew Brady along the way—and was last seen in 1858 in a hoop skirt and running shoes, but she doesn't believe it.

In the virtual world, she can be found on Facebook: https://www.facebook.com/pages/Anna-D-Allen/366546213501993

Christmas Promise

by

Kate Parker

Chapter One

Eve Franklin gently propelled herself onto the ice as she became re-accustomed to the gliding motion she loved. She sailed across the smooth surface of Farnleigh Park's pond on metal blades carefully tied to her half-boots. The cold rains of fall had only recently given way to the icy blasts of dry air from the north. Yesterday, the men had doubted the ice was strong enough to hold the weight of the skaters. Today, most thought it safe. Four inches of ice appeared to cover the surface of the pond. Eve and several others, armed with ropes just in case, were eager to try it out.

It wasn't Christmas to Eve until she'd flown across the pond on her skates, and the calendar said Christmas was nearly there.

Closely watched by their nannies, the children set foot along the edge of the pond. Most of them promptly fell down. Eve glanced back at her niece, pudgy cheeks red from the cold, as she fell and rose again. That was how Eve had learned.

Eve was one of eight brave souls skimming along the ice. In previous years, her sister Ann had always skated with her, but Ann was increasing again, and they hoped for an heir this time.

Eve had promised to go once across the pond for Ann.

The skaters stayed close to shore for a few minutes until they'd grown used to the push and glide movement the ice demanded. Then they ventured farther out. All seemed to be well.

As the swish of her metal blades increased, the breeze tugged at her bonnet. That was one of the promises of Christmas she remembered from childhood, the feeling of freedom. The feeling of no longer being bound to the earth.

"I'm going to go straight across the middle," Eve called out. "Keep an eye out for me just in case."

She started out, heading away from Farnleigh Park House toward the lane and the woods beyond. The ice was smooth, and she was beginning to develop a long-paced rhythm as she reached the middle of the pond.

Then she heard the crack.

The ice directly in front of her disappeared under the water. All the practice and warnings she'd had as a child in Scotland set her feet in motion before her brain told them to act. She shuffled backward on the soggy ice while turning to the right where the shore was closer.

Her racing heartbeat pounding in her ears nearly

blocked the sound of voices shouting, "Look out!" She heard skates scrape cautiously behind her. No doubt rescuers armed with ropes.

By the time the stable lads, Vince and Wally, reached her, Eve was shaking. At least the ice closer to shore was holding all three without cracking. She sent up a silent prayer of thanksgiving.

"Come on, miss, we'll help you back," Vince said, putting a hand on her shoulder.

Wally said, "That was quick thinking. You can see waves coming over the ice in the center where you were. Any slower and you woulda gone right in."

"You had a close call, miss," Vince said. "But it's solid enough here. I guess they'll have to give it another two days."

She was trembling too much to do more than say, "Thank you." Her legs weakened, unable to keep her balanced on her blades. The tip of one caught on the ice, and down she went, flat on her face.

"Here, let me give you a hand," Vince said, but Eve was staring at the ice. Rather, through the ice, where a face looked back at her.

George Mattingly.

"V-V-Vince, Wally, look." She was on her hands and knees now, pointing at the ice.

The two men bent down to look. With a gasp, Wally skated a few feet backward, wobbling on his metal blades.

Vince put his hands on Eve's shoulders and tried to

turn her away. "Oh, dear heavens. We'll need to cut the ice to get him out. Wally, go get his lordship."

Wally raced toward the house. The nannies, having seen something was amiss, were packing up their charges and heading indoors.

Vince helped her up. "Are you all right, miss?"

Now that the shock had passed, Eve caught her breath. Death didn't frighten her. She'd helped her physician father care for his patients before she cared for him during his final illness. But this was wrong. George Mattingly was supposed to have returned to London. "Yes, I'm fine. Unlike poor Mr. Mattingly."

"Mr. Mattingly? But his lordship saw him off four days ago. Where's his driver, horses, and carriage?" He stared at the ice under his feet in horror.

"Don't worry, Vince. It's too shallow here for the horses and carriage to be submerged. I'm sure they're somewhere safe. We'll need to find out where. And I'm going to stay while you pull him out."

Vince jerked away from her. "Why, miss?"

"Because I don't think he ended up under the ice by mere chance. There's something suspicious about this, Vince. Why did he return?"

She hadn't seen much of Mr. Mattingly during his stay at Farnleigh Park. He was too busy flirting with the giggling young ladies, and she was too busy to waste her time on someone who wouldn't notice her.

None of this explained why he had returned.

Wally walked onto the ice a few minutes later with

the Marquess of Farnleigh and his son Robert, the Earl of Stonehill, Ann's husband. They were well bundled up as if they expected to be out on the ice for some time.

"Yes, it's Mattingly, all right. I threw him out, but what is he doing here? I saw him into his carriage and away from my house days ago. When did he come back? And how?" His lordship glanced toward Wally. "Get a crew and some ice saws. We need to get him out. It's a good thing the magistrate is here already."

As if summoned by the marquess's words, Sir Isaiah Truwell, the magistrate from the market town of Thudding Mill, appeared at the pond's edge. At least it was his voice that emanated from the huge pile of furs and woolens trundling toward them. "We'll need to get him out, milord."

"Yes, yes. I've sent for men to do that." Then more to himself, he said, "Why did he return? And how?"

A crew of estate workers arrived with saws and picks and ropes, and they made fast work of getting George Mattingly out of his watery grave. "Take him to the cold larder to be examined," the marquess ordered.

Eve followed at the back of the procession past the house to the cold larder. They moved all the foodstuffs to one side and placed the body on a table on the other. Sir Isaiah glanced over at the block of ice frozen to the body and shuddered. "We'll have to wait for an examination. In the meantime, Miss Eve, would you mind taking charge of the body and letting us know when all is ready?"

She nodded. Her father had taught her all he'd learned in medical school and in practice, and she'd assisted him for four years before his death. Before she had no choice but to join Ann here at Farnleigh Park House.

Sir Isaiah was one of the few of the better class who recognized, and accepted, her skill in dealing with the human body, dead or alive. The poorer classes willingly came to her with all their ailments and injuries. Willing, perhaps, because she didn't charge them for her time. "I will, Sir Isaiah."

When the others left, she set basins under the table to catch the runoff as George, as she now thought of him, thawed and the ice around him melted. She made careful note of the thickness of the ice. From four to five inches. When the melting was underway, she'd be able to tell how far into the ice George was embedded and then judge when he'd gone into the pond.

Sir Isaiah would use her examination for his own determination. He was a kind man, but he had an abhorrence of cadavers. He fulfilled his obligation by paying her to do his prodding and measuring, knowing she would never tell. They kept their agreement secret so no one would question his fitness as magistrate and coroner—or her suitability for her work or for earning her fee. The arrangement suited them both.

When she returned to the house, one of the maids told her Ann wanted to see her. Eve went upstairs, where she found her sister in the nursery.

Ann looked up from where she sat cocooned in a chair with her daughter. Her eyes looked small in her puffy face. "What's happened?"

"Frances will make a fine skater," Eve said, ruffling her niece's hair.

"Eve. What is going on?"

Eve smiled at the command in her sister's voice, and then worded the story carefully. Everything drove Ann to tears these days, but then, the babe was due soon and Ann hadn't been well for months. "The center of the ice isn't strong enough for skating, but the sides are well frozen. We made a find near the shore under the ice. George Mattingly."

Ann's lower lip quivered. "That poor man."

"I was surprised. I thought he left here four days ago, once the roads had frozen hard, to head back to London."

"Yes. We all saw him off. I think Lord Farnleigh was angry with him. You know how he gets very quiet and directs the servants with gestures when he's angry because someone has questioned his authority as marquess and landowner."

Eve had seen the marquess act that way before. This time, however, she had been at a tenant's cottage dealing with a young child with a fever and had missed seeing Mattingly leave. "What had Mr. Mattingly said that made his lordship so angry?"

"I don't know, and no one will tell me."

No one would tell her because everything upset her,

and no one wanted the mother of the soon-to-arrive heir of the Earl of Stonehill to be upset. "I'll see if I can find out, and I'll let you know if it's important."

"It's bound to be important." Ann shifted her swollen body in her chair. "Lord Farnleigh doesn't throw people out of Farnleigh Park House unless they've threatened him or the family in some way."

"Threatened him? That's pretty strong." Eve wanted to keep Ann from worrying no matter what. The child she carried was important to everyone at Farnleigh Park. After the death of Robert's two older brothers, he was the only heir left. He had to have a son. So far, he only had Frances.

"Everyone is coddling my feelings because of this baby. Don't you do it, too," Ann snapped at her.

"Someone must know the cause of the argument. I'll find out. Now, don't worry."

Ann nodded and cuddled the dozing Frances closer.

Eve made her way downstairs, worrying about her sister. She'd been pale and cold nearly the entire time she carried this child, just as she had been with Frances. This time she'd also swollen up. Frances's birth had not gone smoothly despite the best efforts of the midwife and Eve. Another delivery like the last could kill Ann.

Shivering as she pushed her thoughts away, Eve went in search of Adolphus Beck, the marquess's cousin. When she knocked and opened the door, she found him as usual in his laboratory, pouring over his ledger. His white mane hung shaggily into his eyes as he leaned close to the paper on the desk.

"Cousin Adolphus," Eve called out.

He looked up and removed his spectacles as he smiled vaguely at her. "Ah, Miss Eve. What brings you to this corner of our castle?"

"I have need of all your meteorological information from the last five days." She knew he kept meticulous records of the weather, the stars, the plants, and the animals at Farnleigh Park.

"Does this have to do with the poor unfortunate who fell through the ice?"

"It does."

"Ah." He shuffled several ledgers. "You probably need the summary book. Pressure and wind direction might not be necessary for you in this situation."

He handed her the book, and she flipped back to the day before George Mattingly left. The weather, already chilly, had turned bitter, matching the temperature at the dinner table. "What caused the falling out between his lordship and Mr. Mattingly?"

"I wish I knew. It was unlike Cornelius to allow himself to be goaded by such an unimportant person."

Eve bit back a smile. Only Cousin Adolphus would dare call the marquess by his Christian name. "Then their quarrel must have been serious."

"Very serious. And it must have started well before dinner. I'm surprised he waited until the next day to throw that young man out."

Eve looked at Cousin Adolphus's summary book. "It

snowed an inch that night, so the clouds were thick and there was no light. Perhaps the Lord Farnleigh decided to wait until morning so Mattingly's driver could find his way."

"Perhaps, but I don't think Cornelius had made up his mind. Their argument the next morning after breakfast ended in Mattingly shouting threats at my cousin."

"I wasn't here. I was nursing a sick child." At a cottage where there was a great deal less shouting. "Tell me what he said."

"When he came out of the marquess's study, Mattingly shouted something about 'you'll be sorry.' Or 'the truth will come out and you'll be sorry then.' The usual things people shout in novels. There was one odd comment, though. Mattingly said, 'You owe me.' Maybe this was about some business dealing that failed."

"Possibly." But then how did this business disagreement end so badly? "Was it snowing when he left?"

"No, it was quite cold, but it didn't start snowing until afternoon. Two inches of powdery snow, in fact." Adolphus read his spidery handwriting over Eve's shoulder.

"And we've not had any sort of a thaw since then?"

"None at all."

She handed him back his ledger. "What time did Mr. Mattingly leave?"

"About noon. The footman who was acting as his

valet took that long to get him packed. Ann, sweet child, asked him if he'd stay for luncheon before leaving. Cornelius looked like he'd have apoplexy, but he didn't say a word to her. Mattingly told her he had pressing business in London and couldn't linger and it looked like it might snow. He was really quite kind to her, which only made her worry more and made Cornelius angrier."

Eve bit back a smile. Cousin Adolphus tended to give more detail to every answer than anyone wanted to listen to. This time, she was grateful for his rambling reply. He was observant about more than just the weather.

"After that afternoon, the next snowfall was—?"

"The next morning?" Adolphus peered closely at the ledger. "Yes. Nine o'clock. And then it snowed all of that day and night, giving us another six inches of light snow. And then no more after that."

Curiosity made her ask, "Why doesn't the snow stay piled up on the pond like it does on the land?"

"There are various factors at work. The water is warmer than the air, so the snow tends to melt on the ice. Sunlight reflects off the ice, making the snow on top of it melt. And the land there is flat and open. The wind blows the snow off the ice and the surrounding lawn. In the summer, the area around the pond is cooler than the rest of the gardens because of the breeze. That same breeze occurs all year long and blows the snow away from that area."

Well, she'd asked. Eve thanked Cousin Adolphus, gave him a curtsy, and hurried away before she made the mistake of asking any more questions. At least she knew no human hand had swept the snow away ahead of their skating party. No one could have discovered George Mattingly before she did.

That had been her fate.

She reached the central staircase, deep in thought about what she'd learned when she heard Ann's voice downstairs by the front door. Changing direction, she walked downstairs to find Ann and her husband, Robert, Earl of Stonehill, greeting a stranger.

For an instant, she remembered the last stranger to arrive in the front hall. Now drowned and frozen in the cold larder.

"My sister, Miss Eve Franklin," Ann said, and Eve gave the man a curtsy, "found Mr. Mattingly's body under the ice."

The stranger scowled. Eve got the impression he did that often, but whether because he was angry or considering new information, she couldn't tell. He was too rough—his face too hard angled, his nose too obviously broken in combat, his eyes too shrewd, his lips too thin—for Ann to consider him handsome. But he had a look of resiliency, of practicality, that drew Eve.

Belatedly, the stranger said, "That must have upset you."

Surprised, Eve answered honestly. "Not particularly."

He blinked. "Are you accustomed to seeing drowned men?"

"As much as any other type of cadaver."

He stared at her in silence as Robert, never thrilled with her outspokenness, said, "Eve is a healer. She deals with injuries and accidents so she sees more than most of us." By now most of the Christmas house party had assembled in the front hall to discover the pedigree of the guest and greet him accordingly.

The stranger eyed her for a moment. "Not a skilled healer if she's accustomed to seeing death."

"Skilled enough to recognize death when I see it. And I don't flinch at the sight of what man becomes." Eve stared back, wondering who this blunt-spoken man was.

"That's good, because I need to find out what happened to George Mattingly."

"Why?" As far as she knew, that would be the job of Sir Isaiah.

Robert cleared his throat, telling Eve he was displeased with her outspokenness again. "Eve, this is Lord Adam Downing. A solicitor and investigator. And second son of the Duke of Northbrook."

Which didn't tell her why the second son of a duke was riding around the countryside in nasty weather right before Christmas. Or why he had an interest in the dead man she'd found. His arrival was decidedly odd. Nevertheless, she gave Lord Adam a polite smile. "Then I suspect we'll be working together."

"I work alone."

"Then you're a fool."

Blast. She spoke her thoughts aloud again. Everyone who had assembled in the front hall gasped. Eve stood her ground, waiting for an order from the marquess to leave them. Surprisingly, this second son of a duke didn't seem perturbed as he studied Eve. "I assure you, I'm not a fool."

"Then I'm certain we'll work together well."

"If you don't mind, milady, would you direct me to Mr. Mattingly?"

Eve heard the sarcasm he put on 'milady.' "If you'll wait for me to fetch my cloak, I'll take you to him now."

"Oh, Eve, I'm sure Lord Adam must be tired from his cold ride," Ann said.

"Not at all, my lady. The sooner I can bring this matter to a close, the sooner you can have a happy Christmas unimpeded by my presence." He then nodded to Eve. "I'll wait here for you."

Eve nodded back, reached out to squeeze Ann's hand, and hurried to get her cloak and needed supplies. In a few minutes, she led the way along the swept walk to the cold larder. Lord Adam followed, trailed by an unwilling maid. He shut the door behind them as Eve lit a lantern.

She took off her cloak and slipped on her butcher's apron to cover her gown. The maid glanced at the body and stayed near the door, shivering, and Eve gave her a sympathetic smile. Then she removed her warm knit gloves and put on long riding gloves that covered her sleeves yet gave her fingers freedom to explore the body lying in front of her.

"You've done this before." His voice was flat, expressionless, but his eyes appeared to take in everything.

"Yes." She pulled out a small notebook and pencil and then the ruler. "The ice has melted an inch since Mr. Mattingly was brought in here. If you crouch down, you can see he was barely embedded in the ice. Most of him was in the water beneath the ice."

"What do you make of that?"

"He went in when the ice was too thin to hold his weight. He sank. When gases formed in his body, he rose to the surface, except by then the ice was thicker and his body remained directly below the ice."

"How did he die?"

"We'll have to wait until he thaws to learn that."

"Had he been a guest here?"

"Yes, but he left several days ago." She wondered why he was questioning her while she was trying to examine the body and learn just how much of Mr. Mattingly was within the ice sheet.

"Did you see him leave?"

"No. Most of the house party did, however." She gave him a smile. It never hurt to be helpful. "He left at noontime four days ago, seen off in his carriage. It was quite cold, but didn't start snowing until afternoon."

He crossed his arms over his chest while he studied

her closely. "Where were you?"

"At a tenant's cottage. His child was ill."

"How is the child now?"

"Recovering, thank God."

"You had better luck with the child than you had with this man."

"I never had a chance with Mr. Mattingly. He'd been dead three or four days when we found him." She smiled sweetly at him, wondering why the oaf was trying to goad her.

"Are you sure? Could it have only been a day?"

"No. Two days ago, the ice where he was found was already strong enough to skate on."

"Then why wasn't he found before you saw him?"

"I wouldn't have noticed him, either, if I hadn't fallen. We were testing the ice to see if the entire pond was safe to skate on. I tried to skate directly across the middle when the surface cracked. I escaped, but once I fled to stronger ice, I tripped and found myself looking into his face."

"An unpleasant surprise."

She hugged her heavy apron closer to her. "Most unpleasant." It was an experience she never wanted to repeat, even with someone she disliked more than Mattingly. As she slipped off her examination garb and put her cloak back on, she said, "Why are you here looking for Mr. Mattingly?"

"I'm an investigator for the royal family. He was last reported to be here, and the crown wanted him to return to London."

Chapter Two

"His Majesty is looking for Mr. Mattingly?" Miss Franklin asked, staring at him.

Adam looked into her calm, dark brown eyes and wished he could tell her the truth. She seemed sensible and trustworthy, even if she didn't seem particularly awed by his position or his family ties. "Yes."

"And you can't tell me why."

"No."

She didn't seem ruffled or insulted by his reply. "Can you tell me why you were looking for him here when he left four days ago?"

"I found his coachman, his coach, and his horses waiting for him at an inn in Thudding Mill. The coachman said his employer returned here the evening of the day he left."

He watched her mull over his words. "No one mentioned seeing him. Of course, I had no reason to ask. You'll need to speak with everyone, above and below stairs."

"I intend to."

She nodded. "What time did the coach drop him off? And where?"

"What makes you think he didn't ride out here on horseback?" And then he added, his pride showing in his voice, "I did."

"You're not a dandy. You strike me as having been a soldier in Wellington's army, while Mr. Mattingly was most definitely a dandy. It was snowing that evening. He wouldn't care about the discomfort of his driver or his beasts, as long as he was dry and warm."

She seemed to have a higher opinion of him because of his stoicism than because he was sired by a duke. That made her different from most women he met. *Interesting.* "You didn't like Mattingly."

"He didn't seem to have a care beyond his own comforts. That's not the sort of person I like. Although if the crown is looking for him, he must have done something honorable in his lifetime."

If only she knew why he was being sought, her opinion of Mattingly would drop even further. But he wouldn't say anything about that. Not unless he thought it necessary. "The coachman said Mattingly had him stop on the drive before he could be seen from the house. He got out and had the coachman turn around there and go back to the town until the next day."

She blinked when she looked at him. "The next day? Mr. Mattingly had a plan in place to return there?"

"Apparently so. The coachman also said he came out the next day and asked at the servants' entrance for

Mr. Mattingly. He was sent away rudely, the staff denying he was here. As Mattingly had warned him they might say that, he followed his orders and went back to Thudding Mill to wait for a summons."

"You'll have to ask the servants about the coachman. I didn't hear anything about his return."

"No one commented on an unexpected carriage arriving the day after Mattingly left?"

"Not to me. With the poor weather, I've been busy with rheums and weak lungs. At least there were no other deaths here." She looked into his eyes, and he saw that dealing with death did affect her.

He glanced around the room, his breath making little clouds. "Do you have any more to examine here?"

She shook her head.

"I'll walk you back to the house."

She gave him a smile that made him rethink his assumptions that she was plain, mannish, and bossy. Her skin was creamy, not just pale. Her face was well-formed and robust, not just common. Her voice was calm and well-modulated. The voice of a lady.

Adam held her arm as they walked back to the house so she wouldn't slip, the maid following behind.

There was no danger of Miss Franklin sliding. She walked faster than he did, and it was his boot that slipped off the path into the snow, nearly upsetting them both.

He decided a man not as secure in his own worth as he was would find Miss Eve Franklin to be an insurmountable challenge.

She stopped him once and pointed toward the pond. "In the dark, with the ice covered by snow, I wonder if Mr. Mattingly headed straight for the lights of the house. He might not have realized the drive curves around the edge of the pond. In the dark in bad weather, it's easy to lose your way."

"That may explain how he ended up on the ice, but it tells us nothing about the manner of his death." Still, he'd keep in mind what she'd said.

They walked in the side door of the house and removed their cloaks as a footman came up to them. "Beggin' your pardon, but Sir Isaiah Truwell wished to speak to you when you returned."

"Tell him I'll be there right away." Adam handed off his cloak, hat, and gloves to a waiting servant and stepped toward the messenger.

"Um, he meant both of you," the footman said, looking uncomfortable as he glanced at Adam.

"Of course," Miss Franklin said, not appearing at all surprised at being summoned by the magistrate. She handed off her cloak with regal grace, unexpected in someone so practical. At least, unexpected by Adam.

He followed her and the footman to a small parlor where Sir Isaiah sat in front of a roaring fire, a tea tray and biscuits at his side. "Bring my young friends some tea," he said to the footman.

Adam quickly saw he could either freeze or share the sofa by the fire with Miss Franklin. Had Sir Isaiah planned the seating ahead of time? He nodded to her before sitting beside her. They both made an effort to leave the maximum amount of room between them on the small settee.

"As the magistrate in charge of this mysterious death, I would appreciate regular updates on your investigations. Miss Franklin, has the body warmed sufficiently to give up its secrets?"

"Not yet. I have learned the body was almost completely under the ice rather than frozen into it."

They waited in silence while the tea arrived and Miss Franklin poured. Adam watched her long graceful hands prepare his tea and accepted it gratefully. He'd had an icy ride and then a frigid time in the cold larder.

Her smile warmed him almost as much as the tea.

When they had their cups in hand, Sir Isaiah asked, "Have you drawn any conclusions based on Cousin Adolphus's records?"

"Cousin Adolphus?" Adam asked quietly.

"You haven't met Cousin Adolphus?" Sir Isaiah asked.

"No."

"You are in for a treat," Miss Franklin said with a tiny smile.

Adam could tell he was being set up. He wished he knew for what.

"I know several inches of snow have fallen since Mr. Mattingly left, and the weather had turned cold before he left and has not moderated," the woman said.

"Beyond that, nothing."

"And you, Lord Adam? What have you learned that has brought you here?" Sir Isaiah asked.

Adam told him what the coachman said.

"Good. The two of you need to question all the servants. Someone must know something about at least one of these two arrivals."

"The two of us?" Adam asked in a quiet voice. He didn't want his investigation to be hamstrung by a headstrong female. He'd promised his parents he'd be home for Christmas, and all women did was slow a man down.

"Yes. Working together, you'll learn a great deal more. Now, off with you." Sir Isaiah helped himself to another biscuit and turned toward the fire.

When they'd left the parlor, Miss Franklin asked, "What do you suggest as our first line of inquiry?"

"The servants' hall."

She glanced at him and shook her head. "Let them have their dinner in peace. We'll question them when their stomachs are full. Then they'll be more likely to tell us all."

He suspected she'd be running this part of the investigation. *Oh, well. Let her.* He'd found the coachman. It was Mattingly's killer he needed to find. "What do you suggest, then?"

"Visiting Cousin Adolphus."

"I thought that was where you received the meteorological data."

"I did." She smiled at him. "But I suspect he may have more to tell us."

He gestured for her to lead him. At this rate, he'd be lucky to get home by New Year's. He was glad she walked quickly for a woman. They reached an upstairs wing in time to hear a loud boom and see smoke emanating from beneath a door at the end of the hall.

Adam pushed the woman behind him. "Quick, alert the staff to a fire."

She stood there, shaking her head at him.

"Go!" He pushed her away.

"Oh, for pity's sake." She elbowed past him and walked down the hall to open the door. "Cousin Adolphus, was that a success or a failure?"

Adam heard coughing, and then, "Oh, a success, I believe. A modified success."

Cousin Adolphus must be the crazy member of the family. Most families had at least one. Adam walked down the hall and looked in at a laboratory set up in what had once been a fine bedroom. Now it was singed and sooty, filled with molting, stuffed small animals, charts, a telescope, scales, and a large metal box from which smoke was still drifting.

"Cousin Adolphus, this is Lord Adam Downing. He's investigating our corpse." Miss Franklin turned to him and smiled.

Adam had the sensation that Cousin Adolphus wasn't the only batty member of the family.

The two men greeted each other as if potentially

blowing up wings of country houses was an everyday occurrence, and then Adolphus asked about his journey. Adam, who'd been brought up to have good manners despite wanting to chuck them away in the face of a houseful of lunatics, asked about his current scientific enquiry.

The elderly man launched into a long technical explanation. Before Adam could stop the flow of information, Miss Franklin linked an arm through the old man's and said, "We're very glad you're all right."

"I'm always all right."

"We worry about you. Now," she said in a conspiring voice, "do you know any reason why Mr. Mattingly would have returned here the day he left?"

"No. How odd. Did he forget something valuable?"

"Not that we know of, but it makes a line of inquiry. When did you go out to make your scientific observations the evening he left?"

"I go out several times a night. Rigorous investigation is required for well-thought-out papers. What time did Mattingly come here?"

She turned to look at Adam. He'd tried to stand back, but now he had to come forward. "His coachman says he dropped him off once it was fully dark."

Cousin Adolphus rose and went over to consult one of his ledgers. "With the clouds and snow, last light might have been any time between three and four in the afternoon. He could have arrived here any time after three. I take observations at four and again at six."

"Did you see anyone outdoors during either of these observations?"

"No. At least I don't think so."

What kind of a scientist was this man if he couldn't be certain of something as basic as seeing anyone outdoors on a cold, snowy night? Adam kept his voice level with effort. "You don't think so?"

"Well, I'm rather short-sighted. I saw movement at a distance, but it was dark. This was during my four o'clock observations. It may have been a man. It may have been an animal."

"What size was this thing?"

"Larger than a hare. Beyond that, I'm not ready to speculate."

Not ready to speculate? A man who a short time ago tried to blow up the house? Adam turned on his heels and walked out.

Behind him, he heard Miss Franklin say, "Thank you, Cousin Adolphus. Where was this thing?"

"On the lane leading to the house."

She caught up to Adam and tugged on his arm when he was a distance down the hallway. "Where are you going?"

"Somewhere I might find sensible people."

She stared at him, eyebrows raised.

He'd had a nanny who'd looked at him that way when he was a badly behaved little boy. Well, he wasn't a little boy now. He looked at his arm where she gripped it, and she loosed her hand as if he'd burned her. Then he stalked off.

It took him a few minutes to realize he was lost, and even longer before he would acknowledge this to the woman silently following him. "Where is the servants' hall?"

"If you'll follow me." She led him back, down, and around until they found an open doorway to a well-lighted room with a long table and plenty of uncushioned chairs. Somewhere close by, he could hear pans clanking and a voice giving orders. No doubt the kitchen. Here, the table had been cleared and scrubbed, and several people were seated working on sewing or cleaning projects. A few more, with some moments of free time for themselves, were hanging ribbon for Christmas decorations.

They greeted Miss Franklin with a mixture of friendship and deference. They glowered at Adam. Miss Franklin folded her arms over her chest and watched him.

"I know when I'm beaten," he murmured to her.

"Oh?"

"A joint investigation into Mattingly's return and cause of death."

He looked at her closely then and realized, while her expression was solemn, her eyes twinkled. "All right." She turned to the occupants of the table. "We've been told by Mr. Mattingly's coachman that he returned here with the coach the day after Mr. Mattingly left. The coachman asked at the servants' entrance for someone to tell Mr. Mattingly that his coach had returned for him."

One of the maids said, "He was as boastful as his master was rude. He came to the door the next day, saying the butler had sent him down here to ask after Mr. Mattingly. We told him we'd seen the last of his master the day before."

Another added, "He accused his lordship of kidnapping that weasel. Can you imagine? Lord Farnleigh. Really."

They were obviously loyal to their employer. Getting the truth out of them might take a long time and a lot of effort. Adam opened his mouth to begin asking questions when Miss Franklin said, "Boastful or not, the coachman said he returned Mr. Mattingly here a few hours after we saw him leave. By then it was full dark. The coachman said he was following orders that evening and following them again the next day when he came out to get his master. All of you understand the need to follow nonsensical orders. Now, who got to know the coachman best while he was here?"

"That would be Vince and Wally in the stables." There was a general nodding of agreement.

"Do you know if they're in the stables now?"

Again, a lot of heads nodded.

"Shall we get our cloaks and brave the weather?" Miss Franklin asked him.

"Certainly. We'll meet in the front hall in five minutes." When she raised her eyebrows at him again, he said, "Is that acceptable?"

She smiled at him. "Now you're learning how to deal with sensible people, should you find them."

He couldn't resist smiling in return at her beautiful, cheerful face. "I suppose I deserve that. But don't expect me to deal with your cousin."

"Oh, no. He's Lord Farnleigh's cousin."

He suspected she was laughing at him now. "Five minutes," he growled and went up the nearby staircase.

To his surprise, she showed up on time. Most London ladies would never dream of doing that. Once outside, they walked together toward the stables, picking their way along icy walkways.

"I could tell in the servants' hall that you realize the coachman is the leading suspect in Mattingly's death," he said, his words forming clouds in the cold air.

She nodded. "We only have his word that he dropped Mattingly off alive and well and returned to town. Thank you for not judging him before we learn all we can."

"I don't want to hang an innocent man any more than you do." The idea of it made him angry, and he grumbled his words.

"Good, because I like you and I couldn't if you were careless with people's lives."

I like you rang like a bell through Adam's mind. Women generally found him too hard, too cold, too distant. Had this woman seen through his exterior? He took the last steps in silence and opened the small door on the side of the barn for her to enter first.

Vince and Wally were nowhere to be seen, but noises came from the storerooms which were attached to the far side of the stable area. Miss Franklin led the way through an area noisy with the nicker of restless horses and pungent with the smell of beasts and leather. They reached a smaller area where two men were repairing and sharpening axes, pickaxes, scythes, saws, and other farm implements. Both men set down their work when they saw Adam and Miss Franklin.

"Don't let us slow you down," she said. "We just need to ask you some questions about Mr. Mattingly's coachman. What did you think of him?" She lowered herself onto a stool and Adam leaned against a wall, hoping he'd be forgotten.

"Mouthy," Wally said, settling comfortably on a bench.

"But that could be because he was Mattingly's only servant. He had no one to talk to, no one to confide in," Vince said.

"And a braggart. Always going on about how many rich men's houses he'd seen in London. He even said he'd been to the palace and seen the Prince of Wales," Wally said.

"He wasn't very knowledgeable. Remember those questions he asked about fixing a leak in the carriage? We ended up showing him how, and it was a simple job. He was grateful for our help, and it weren't much." Vince studied Miss Franklin as if trying to understand why she was asking these questions. "He did know horses, though."

Wally nodded. "He did, that. Took care of those mounts like they were something special."

"He said that was because he shared a stable with them, and a lot of times they were his only company."

"Were the carriage and horses owned by Mattingly?" Miss Franklin asked, and Adam had to stop himself from reacting to her savviness.

"They were," Vince said. "But the coachman's service, and the horses and carriage, were won in a card game, and quite recently, too. Mark, that's the coachman's name, said he figured there was something funny about that card game, but it wasn't his place to say anything."

"Who were they won from?" Miss Franklin glanced at Adam, but he merely shrugged and let her continue. Just how much of the truth would she learn?

"Mark called his former employer 'His Highness,' but I have no idea if he was being truthful or sarcastic. He sounded to me like a careless man, to lose a valuable thing like a carriage and team of well-matched horses in a card game." Vince shook his head and picked up the pickax he'd been sharpening.

Wally just shrugged.

"Did you see the coachman or the coach back here the day after Mr. Mattingly left?"

"No, but we heard about it at dinner that night. No one could figure out what game Mr. Mattingly was playing."

"Did people think that Mark and the carriage returning here was some sort of trick?" Miss Franklin leaned forward on her stool. The lantern on the table cast a warm light on her dark hair, catching red and gold strands mixed in with the darker colors. She had gorgeous hair.

"Yes." Vince checked the sharpness of the pickaxe with his thumb.

"Any idea what this trick was?"

Wally shook his head. "The butler thinks it's something to bring disgrace on this house."

"No. Mattingly wanted something from someone," Vince said, "and sending his coach out was part of his plan to get this something."

The two stablemen argued a few more ideas, each more ludicrous than the last. Adam listened quietly, knowing it didn't matter what Mattingly had planned. He was dead and would never carry out his scheme.

More importantly, he now knew Miss Franklin was lovely by lamplight.

Evidently, she had heard enough. She thanked the two grooms and pulled her cloak more closely around her before she walked to the door. Then she stopped. "These look like they'd make great weapons. None of them are missing, are they?"

"None have gone missing since the ice melted last spring," Vince told her.

Wally made a sound of disgust. "Lord Farnleigh had

the footmen help gather the ice for the ice house last spring. Everything went wrong. Vince and I had to search for a tool they lost, restack the ice, and still carry out our usual tasks of feeding the livestock and cleaning out the barn. I hope his lordship doesn't try that again." He sounded as if this were a longstanding grievance.

Vince nodded agreement.

Adam was already bracing for the cold when Miss Franklin thanked the two for their help. Then he opened the door for her, and they both hurried toward the house.

Before they reached the relative warmth of the hallway, she stopped him. "Who owned the horses and carriage before Mattingly supposedly won them in a card game?"

"Oh, Mattingly won them in a card game."

She stared into his eyes. "You wouldn't be here if that was all there was to this. The card game was rigged?"

"I believe so. I was sent for proof. And to speak to Mattingly."

"Someone powerful is against cheating at cards?"

He found himself sucked into her gaze. She was too smart for her own good. "Yes."

"Why? I thought all aristocrats cheat."

He had to smile at her naiveté. "Oh, on their wives. On their debts. But not at cards."

She glared at him, and the smile slid off his face.

"Why would the Prince of Wales care if Mr.

Mattingly cheats at cards?"

Since she'd guessed that much, he might as well tell her more. "Because Mattingly fleeced a nephew of everything but the clothes he stood up in. A nephew Prinny is actually fond of."

Chapter Three

EVE LOOKED AT LORD ADAM through widened eyes. "I take it Mr. Mattingly very quickly relieved this member of the royal family of his worldly goods."

"He did. And now that you know, I beg you not to mention any of this to anyone."

"I won't."

When Lord Adam made a move to go into the house, Eve leaned against the door and stared up at him. "When am I going to get the full story? If I'm to help you, I need to know as much as possible."

"I can't believe how much you've learned in a very short time." He sounded sincere in his surprise.

"I've learned a great deal because I know the people here, and now I want to hear the rest." When he remained silent, she said, "I can be helpful in this investigation." Why did she always have to convince men that she had a brain and could be useful?

"It must be about time to dress for dinner. May we continue this discussion after dinner? Privately? Perhaps we can find an unused parlor?"

She shook her head; sorry she was unable to meet with him then. She wanted to hear the rest of what he knew about Mr. Mattingly and hoped he wasn't trying to dodge her questions.

More than that, she wanted to spend more time with this man. Most men of his station would have ignored any help she offered, but Lord Adam, like Sir Isaiah, was willing to at least hear what she had discovered. And he was certainly more handsome than Sir Isaiah. Or any other man here. "We'll be expected to take part in the entertainments."

"We could meet when people start going upstairs for the night?"

She smiled. "We'll talk then. And don't get any ideas about avoiding me."

"Miss Franklin, I would never want to avoid you." He looked into her eyes with such intensity she had to believe him.

She *wanted* to believe him. There were men who didn't avoid her company, who didn't turn away from a poor relation. However, none of them were eligible bachelors. Then there were those sorry few who sought out her company to curry favor with Lord Farnleigh, but she didn't want to be a stepping stone on some man's path to success. But this man, this second son of a duke, was different.

There was little she could say about dinner. The food was good. The conversation was bland, everyone trying to keep Ann from getting too excited about the topic everyone wanted to discuss. The drowned man.

Instead, they talked about Christmas celebrations, past and present. Lord Adam told how Christmas was celebrated at Castle Northbrook, and later shared a funny tale from his childhood involving the vicar, the sheep from the crèche, and two naughty boys who had to spend the entire day before Christmas cleaning out the church.

Cousin Adolphus invited Lord Adam to join him in making his weather observations immediately after the game course, but Lord Adam graciously declined, claiming he was very fond of the next course. Eve decided to come to his aid and mentioned that roasted nuts and sharp cheeses were some of her favorite foods, too.

The smile of gratitude he gave her warmed her more than the toasty fire. She must have blushed, because Ann pursed her lips together and ducked her head to hide her laughter.

Why did her sister have to read her every thought? Ann frequently knew what Eve felt before she was ready to admit such feelings to herself.

Shortly thereafter, the women adjourned to the large parlor while the men stayed behind with their port. Lady Chandess, a cousin of the marquess who normally ignored Eve, and that Eve gladly had nothing to do with, came up to her and asked in a loud voice, "What were you and Lord Adam up to, skulking about the house and grounds all day, avoiding the rest of us?"

Eve immediately remembered previous visits and why she'd avoided her. Lady Chandess yearned for nasty gossip like a rogue craved women and wine. "I've been asked to assist his lordship in his investigation."

"Ooh. What fun," Miss Woodward exclaimed. "I'd like to assist him." Then the man-chasing young woman giggled. Eve wondered if there was a brain behind the pretty face.

Eve barely disguised her distaste. "You find rotting corpses to be fun, Miss Woodward?"

"Eew. No. Of course not."

Lady Deborah Rogers, a pudgy, pasty-faced heiress sitting nearby, sniffled. Eve would try to remember the girl in her prayers if Lady Deborah didn't vanish from her mind the moment the bland woman was no longer in sight. Lady Deborah seemed to have that effect on everyone.

Eve walked away from her to where Ann was sitting. "Are you comfortable?"

She received a weak smile. "I've learned in the last few weeks that nothing is comfortable." Ann had barely tasted dinner yet looked swollen from head to toe.

Eve smiled back at her sister in encouragement. "It won't be much longer."

"Maybe it'll be a Christmas baby," one of the ladies said gleefully. That set off a round of horrid remembrances and misinformation that Eve ignored. She hoped the soon-to-be mother ignored it as well.

The tales stopped the instant the men rejoined them. Cards were decreed the entertainment of the night and tables were set up. Members of the house party joined in enthusiastically. Eve stayed on a sofa as long as possible and then slipped out of the room.

Moments later, Lord Adam joined her. "I professed myself weary after my travels today. Shall we find someplace private so I can tell you the full story," he grinned and added, "before I fall asleep in truth?"

Eve couldn't help grinning back at him conspiratorially. "Follow me." She led him to a seldom used parlor, old-fashioned and unheated. The room lacked oil lamps. All she could find for light were candles, and Lord Adam soon had them burning merrily. He was such a practical man she felt certain he could make do with anything. Just the kind of man she liked.

They sat down facing each other. Immediately, she wished she'd worn her cloak, but she was afraid going to fetch it would alert someone to their location. Then she would have to wait to hear the rest of the story until tomorrow.

"I won't name the nephew who lost his fortune to Mattingly," he began.

"I understand. I can picture the situation. This nephew of the Prince of Wales, this product of an unapproved liaison by another of George III's sons, goes to a den of iniquity and gets into a game with Mr. Mattingly. Things go from bad to worse, no doubt fueled by strong drink and young friends with whom he wants to make a good impression. He ends up losing all and making a midnight raid to give Mr. Mattingly all he has promised him."

"It's worse. The young man is very young. He gets into what he thinks is a friendly game with Mr. Mattingly and others at a party at an aristocrat's home. And it is friendly. However, as the night wears on, this new acquaintance, Mr. Mattingly, urges the nephew and a couple of equally young friends into going with him to a den of iniquity. Just to look around. Just so they can say they've been inside one."

"They travel in the coach driven by Mark the coachman?"

"The coach belonged to a relative, but the young fool told his new-found friend, Mr. Mattingly that it was his own."

"Oh, dear." The full extent of how badly this night was going to go for the young man was becoming clear, even to a young lady who'd never been to London. She rubbed her cold hands to try to warm them.

"Oh, dear, is right. With stupidity not seen since the prodigal son, he loses a year's allowance, valuable jewels, and the coach, coachman, and horses in a few hours. A single night."

Eve was staggered by his folly. "How did you get involved? By the owner of the carriage?"

"If only. As the sun rises, Mattingly and the young fool travel to the palace where the debt is partially settled before the idiot begins to sober up and complain.

Mattingly beats him to a pulp, takes anything he wants from the royal apartment, and leaves in the coach. He has the fool's signature on a paper transferring ownership of the coach and horses to him. He has vowels promising him all sorts of wealth signed by the little fool."

"Amazing." It was. She pulled her sleeves over as much of her hands as the fabric would reach to try to warm them. "How did you get involved?"

"The fool finally sobers up, his man cleans his injuries and straightens his cravat, and he goes to see his favorite aunt. He tells her all, or at least a good part of the story. She is also Prinny's favorite sister. She knows of my role with the royal family and so she summoned me."

He looked exhausted from his journey, exasperated by his job, and handsome in the way knights must have looked when they returned from the Crusades. Eve would have loved to have been in the group to welcome him home to his castle.

She shook her head. It wasn't like her to be fanciful. He was the son of a duke; she was the daughter of a physician. He aided the royal family in hushed affairs; she investigated unexplained deaths for a country magistrate who hated dead bodies.

There was one bright spot in this mess. "Well, one part of your investigation is made much easier by Mr. Mattingly's death. You can return the coach and horses, and the coachman, to their rightful owner without a fight."

"If he didn't leave a will or have heirs." He moved to sit on the sofa next to her. Picking up her hands, he blew on them to warm them. Then he wrapped them inside his larger hands.

"Thank you. That feels wonderful." How could she be so silly as to fall for a man because he warmed her fingers? Then his words made her eyes spring wide. "Did he? Have a will or heirs?"

"I hope not." He gazed into her eyes for a moment. "You're freezing, and I'm falling asleep. Let's call it a night. We'll meet at breakfast tomorrow and plan our strategy."

She nodded, and they stood with him still holding her hands. She'd have been pleased if he'd continued to hold her hands until spring. Then the door opened and Robert, Earl Stonehill, strode in. "Eve, what are you doing in here?"

Her cheeks heated as she pulled her hands away. "Discussing what needs to be done about Mr. Mattingly. We didn't want to speak where Ann might hear." Thank goodness her wits hadn't abandoned her, or Lord Adam might be more embarrassed than he currently was. At least she guessed the grim look on his face was embarrassment.

She turned and looked into Lord Adam's eyes with hope and admiration. "I'll see you in the morning. By then, we may find our way clear to the answer. I bid you goodnight." Then she turned to Robert. "Goodnight, brother. I pray you and Ann have a quiet night."

"That is to be hoped for. Goodnight, Eve," Robert said. Then he turned to glare at Lord Adam. "A word with you, if you don't mind."

"Not at all." Lord Adam glowered back at Robert.

Eve hurried toward the door, the cold air in the room freezing her limbs. How could they stand to stay in there? When she glanced back from the doorway, Lord Adam smiled at her. "Sleep well, my lady."

The next morning, after Eve washed and dressed, she scratched on Ann's door before she went down to breakfast. Ann's lady's maid opened it, and Eve walked into the overheated room. "How are you this morning?"

"Feeling the cold. I've been hot for months, and now, all of a sudden, my hands and feet are like ice. Feel them."

Eve did as her sister wanted. "They are indeed cold. I think the baby will be here before the New Year."

"I can't wait. I can't sit down properly, my feet are too swollen to fit into my shoes, and sleeping is impossible."

"That's what I like about you, Ann. You never complain."

Eve was relieved to see a smile on her sister's face. "I've given up not complaining until this child arrives."

"A wise choice."

"Wiser than yours," Ann said, trying to sit up in bed and swing her legs over the side.

After Eve and the lady's maid got her into position, Eve said, "What unwise choice have I made?"

"Spending time in an empty parlor with the Duke of Northbrook's second son. You'll get a reputation."

"Your husband is unhappy with me?"

"He doesn't want to see you disappointed or gossiped about. He fears you'll bring disgrace to the family."

How could she say anything about her role in the investigation without upsetting Ann? "Sir Isaiah asked me to help Lord Adam. Something else Robert does not approve of."

"No, he does not. It isn't very ladylike."

"Then it's a good thing he didn't know I used to help Papa on his rounds or he never would have married into our family." Eve dropped lightly onto the bed next to her sister. "I'd go mad doing nothing all day, waiting for some man to marry me. Sir Isaiah has been a godsend. I enjoy healing the sick and tending the dead. Please don't ask me to stop, Ann."

"Never. I may have need of your skills. Even Robert won't go so far as to tell you to stop healing."

Eve saw Ann's untouched breakfast tray and knew Robert wouldn't stop her healing work. Not now when his wife or their newborn babe might have need of her training. "But he'd like to tell me to stop aiding Sir Isaiah. I won't. It's necessary work."

Ann smiled and patted her hand. "Then we won't say anything to him."

Eve smiled in return. "Sir Isaiah can't stand to even look at the dead. Fortunately, the rest of his skills and temperament are such that he's a good magistrate."

She rose then and walked toward the door. "I'm going down to breakfast. And if I see Robert, I'll immediately start talking about the baby. That will keep me on his good side."

Ann laughed. "You do that."

Eve arrived in the breakfast room to find Robert, Lord Farnleigh, Lord Adam, and several of the relatives visiting the house for Christmas seated at the table. She chose tea and toasted bread and carried them to the place next to Lord Adam that he indicated as he rose and greeted her.

Only when her food was safely on the table did she curtsy to him before she sat down.

"That was the safest choice," he said, grinning at her.

"I don't practice curtsying enough to make it safe for me to carry hot liquids and attempt anything graceful." She smiled in return, only to look up and find Robert glaring at them.

"When will you be visiting Mr. Mattingly again?" Lord Adam asked quietly.

"After breakfast. Then I'll go to see Sir Isaiah. Afterward, I'll visit some of the tenants' cottages where there is sickness." She kept her voice neutral, aware that Robert was trying to make out her words. "I believe you'll be a father again before the New Year, Lord

Stonehill," she said, directing her voice toward her brother-in-law.

Robert immediately puffed up and accepted some murmured congratulations. "Are you certain?"

"So certain I'll send a message to the midwife in Thudding Mill before luncheon."

Robert and his father began making plans for the child if it was a boy.

"Now we'll be able to carry out investigations this morning without interference," Eve said to Lord Adam in a murmur.

"I'll meet you in the front hall, ready to go outside, at nine." Lord Adam nodded to her and then began to discuss the weather with the pudgy, pasty-faced young woman sitting across the table.

Despite Lord Adam's best efforts, he couldn't get more than a word or two out of the woman. If he used those same charms on Eve, they wouldn't stop talking until bedtime and never lack for a topic. What was wrong with that girl? With effort, Eve dragged her name from the back of her mind. Lady Deborah Rogers. The blandest, most forgettable debutante of all time.

Lord Adam was waiting for her in the front hall when Eve appeared, already dressed in her cloak and gloves and trailed by a maid. She led him to the side hall, and then they hurried through the freezing air to the cold larder.

"I think it will snow again," Lord Adam said.

"Don't say that. The midwife is planning to stay in

town until she is actually needed. I don't want the roads blocked with drifting snow at the worst time."

He turned his head to look directly into her eyes. Lowering his voice, he said, "You're afraid something will go wrong."

That was her fear. It had been since Ann had grown too large and weary. No one before had voiced her thoughts, and she wished Lord Adam hadn't now. "Let's see if Mr. Mattingly is ready to give up his secrets."

Once in the cold larder, the maid again stationed at the door, Lord Adam helped her lift the measured chunks of ice off the body and toss them outside. Then, dressed in Eve's spare butcher's apron and using his own gloves, Lord Adam helped her by undressing the corpse and then wrapping him in a sheet.

While he worked, she began to give him helpful directions for lifting a weight she knew she couldn't manage. Without looking up, he said, "I helped a surgeon on the battlefields in France. I learned how to hold patients down. And I know how to move bodies and prepare them for burial. This isn't the first time I've done this task."

"I can't imagine working where there is such a poor chance of success. You must be very strong willed to survive such a difficult environment." Her admiration showed in her voice as she meant it to.

His voice became distant. "I saw miracles there. A few of them. And isn't this the season for miracles?"

Something comforting about him made it possible

to trust him with her thoughts. "That's the Christ Child's promise to us. Of all the promises of happiness and freedom at this time of year, Christmas's greatest promise is miracles."

After a glance that spoke of understanding, he cleared his throat and said in a normal tone, "You found him face up under the ice?"

"Yes."

"Was there a reason for him to be lying on his back in the water?"

"None that I know of. He could have lost his balance and fallen backward. But even then, the body should have turned over. Drownings are always found face down in the water."

"How deep is the water there?"

"Just a few feet." Now that he was dressed in a sheet, Eve came over and stared at Mattingly. "Maybe there wasn't room for his body to turn over."

"Maybe. Let's examine his back." Lord Adam lifted one of the dead man's shoulders and checked the back of Mr. Mattingly's head. A deep gash in the lower part of his head cut through the hair and skin. She measured it to be four inches across and less than an inch wide.

"What could have caused a wound like that?" Eve asked. She'd seen plenty of accidents, particularly at harvest time, but nothing like this.

"I don't know. It looks too wide and heavy to be a knife or a sword. A scythe, perhaps?"

"That appears to be bruising along the wound." She

began to feel carefully along the length of the damage, using her fingers more than her sight. "It feels like not only the skin is cut but the muscle and bone beneath is broken."

"How much of this damage is because he was frozen?"

"He wasn't. The water below the ice is cold, but not frozen. Let's see if there is water in his lungs." At her direction, Lord Adam maneuvered the body so fluid would run out of the mouth.

Some froth came out, less than a cup in all.

Lord Adam looked from the body to Eve. "I'd suspect there isn't enough for him to have drowned. He was dead when he went into the water."

"Or died shortly after falling through the ice." As the two of them lay Mr. Mattingly on his back once again, Eve asked, "What has happened to the coach and coachman?"

"I told the coachman to take the coach and horses back to London to his previous employer, and sent a message to the fool's aunt telling her the coachman should be returning shortly. I suggested he be reemployed so he will be readily available should it become necessary."

Lord Adam marched up and down the cold larder for a moment, avoiding the meat hanging from the ceiling. "I wish we knew what type of weapon left that mark. Was anything found around the pond that would explain this?"

Eve shook her head. "Since he couldn't have done this to himself, we need to find out who was outside that afternoon and evening. Someone did this to him."

"Agreed. Shall we finish going over the body before reporting to Sir Isaiah?"

They continued their examination. Eve was grateful they didn't find any bullet or stab wounds to confuse things. Definitely no signs of starvation or disease. "Poison at this late date would be impossible to detect," she said aloud without meaning to.

Lord Adam gave a strangled laugh. "Which is unfortunate, because the only thing we're left with is that inexplicable wound in the back of his head."

"That's what we'll have to report to Sir Isaiah, and he's not going to like it any better than we do."

Lord Adam began to search the dead man's pockets. "Happy Christmas, what is this?"

Eve hurried over to see what he'd found in the jacket pocket. She gasped as it sparkled in the lamplight. "Have you ever seen such beautiful stones?"

"These jewels were reported stolen at the same time as the coach and horses. The young fool signed them over to Mattingly, but he had no right to pledge them for a gaming debt." Lord Adam held up a large ruby to the light.

"Ooh. That stone alone must be worth a fortune. What will happen to the nephew?"

"The jewels will be returned to their rightful owner. I doubt much will happen to the lad. Not that we and the rest of the world will see, anyhow."

Eve continued to stare at the jewels in his hands. She'd never seen anything like them before, and probably never would again.

Lord Adam put the stones in his pocket and finished searching the clothes. "The inquest will have to come back with a verdict of death involving person or persons unknown. Murder or misadventure, though, who can tell?"

Eve gave him a weak smile. "This isn't getting you home for Christmas any faster. I'm sorry." At least she could say that, even though she wasn't sorry.

"I don't mind. If it weren't for the corpse, I'd be enjoying my time here immensely." He took her hand. "Especially the time I'm spending with you."

Her cheeks heated. "I enjoy the time I get to spend with you as well, but I've been warned not to expect anything. You're the son of a duke; I'm the daughter of a physician."

"That's another wonderful thing about you. You say what's on your mind. You are a very honest person." He moved closer. "I'm the second son. No title except a courtesy one. No claim on anything. I live by my wits, and I have nothing to offer."

"You have a great deal to offer. You're clever, and insightful, and I'm very glad I've met you." She stared into his eyes, hoping he'd kiss her, despite the butcher's aprons and the carcasses waiting to be prepared for Christmas dinner.

He leaned in, and Eve felt her heartbeat speed. She closed her eyes, waiting for the magic to begin.

"Ah, there you are, Eve." Robert stood in the doorway, the bright snow behind him, blinking in the darkness inside the room. "I've been looking for you everywhere. Ann wants you."

Eve opened her eyes as she stepped back. She heard the longing in her voice when she whispered, "She's the reason I don't like not knowing who was behind this death or how it was done."

Eve walked into the nursery to find Ann curled up with Frances on a sofa. "Robert said you needed me."

"I just wondered where you were. I don't know why I'm feeling so fearful." She clung to Frances harder, and the little girl squirmed out of her hold.

"Here. Let me, milady, and then perhaps Miss Eve can get you to eat or drink a little," the nursery maid said. Ann slowly loosed her hold on her daughter. The woman took the child away to the next room where the other children attending the house party played.

"Would you like tea? Toast and jam?"

"I can't eat a thing. My stomach revolts at the thought. And then I worry."

"We've had an unexplained death and not knowing if some malevolent force was behind it is preying on your mind. Cheer up. You're not likely to be wandering around the pond in the dark and neither is anyone else in the family."

"Are you certain?"

Ann looked so frightened Eve had to laugh. "You've never been the timid one before. What has brought this on?"

Ann patted the seat next to her, and Eve sat. "About a week or two ago, I went looking for Robert. It was a warm, clear day for a change, and I wanted to ask him to go for a walk with me. The door to the small parlor was open, and I heard Robert's voice come from inside. 'That's the deuce of it. I'm afraid you might be right.'

"Then Mr. Mattingly's voice, saying 'If your wife doesn't produce an heir this time, if she and the babe both die, what options will you have?' I ran away. I couldn't stand to listen to my husband's plans for my death."

"Oh, Ann." Eve threw her arms around her sister. "Robert loves you. He adores Frances. He'll love the new little one. Nobody is dead except Mr. Mattingly, and if you think he could have had any premonitions, he would have saved himself."

Ann clutched her tighter, leaving finger marks on Eve's wrists. "Tell me, Eve. What do you think they were planning?"

"I don't know, but I intend to find out. This might explain why Mattingly was really here so close to Christmas." Eve knew Robert was a good man, but he was old-fashioned and sometimes a bit of a fool.

"You mustn't let Robert know I overheard him." Ann begged, her grip making Eve's wrists hurt.

"I won't. I plan to use Lord Adam for this conversation." Eve patted her sister's arm as she tried to extricate herself.

"Can you trust him?"

Eve considered for only a second. "I believe I can."

Chapter Four

ADAM MET WITH EVE AS SHE RETURNED to the main floor. "I've reported our findings to Sir Isaiah. He's mystified by what we've discovered, too."

She signaled him to follow her into a side passage, and he went with her willingly. "I've learned something, and I need you to ask Lord Stonehill about it without giving away where you heard it."

Adam nodded. Her position in her brother-in-law's house must be tenuous.

"Robert said to Mr. Mattingly, 'That's the deuce of it. I'm afraid you might be right.' The person who overheard this heard nothing before it to indicate the subject under discussion."

"And after it?" Something had to make this lovely, sensible woman worried over these innocuous words.

"Mr. Mattingly asked Robert about his options if Ann and the baby both died." She looked up at him, wringing her hands and biting her lower lip.

He stared at her lips and felt himself drawn toward them. *Hold steady, you fool. She needs your help.* "Ah, er, that hardly sounds like a reason for Mattingly to come all the way out here from London. In winter weather."

"What was Mattingly's background? Is he a relative of Lord Farnleigh that I haven't heard about?"

Sir Isaiah had shown him the family tree that morning. "If he was, he was born on the wrong side of the blanket." When he realized he'd spoken aloud, he added, "Pardon me. He doesn't show up in the family records."

"It's hardly something to apologize for unless you were responsible, and it's obvious you weren't. Mr. Mattingly was at least your age and possibly a few years older." She was staring at the wall and tapping her fingertips together, probably too busy thinking to worry about how her words could be taken.

Adam wanted to laugh. It was such a relief to hear an unvarnished opinion.

"But what was his family background? Were there any rumors?" she asked him.

"Oh, yes, plenty. Many started by Mattingly himself. A firm of solicitors paid for his schooling, including university. When I made inquiries, I was told they had given their word never to reveal who paid for his education or his army commission, which he cashed out after only a couple of years."

"So he never faced Napoleon?"

"No."

"But you did. Second sons go into the army, don't they?"

"Yes, I was in the army and fought against Napoleon." He forced the words out past paralyzed lips. He tried never to think of the war during the day. It reduced the number of bad dreams he faced at night.

He glanced down to discover she had taken his hand. "I'm glad you returned."

"So am I."

She smiled at his words. Somehow, her smile alone was enough to make the nightmares he'd carried home recede.

"Now, perhaps I should ask Lord Farnleigh directly if Mattingly was here because he was an unacknowledged relative."

"If the solicitors wouldn't tell you, why would they tell Mattingly?"

"Perhaps they had a letter they'd given Mattingly on an important birthday. A letter from his benefactor, whoever that might be."

"Then I suspect you have no choice but to talk to the marquess next." She patted his arm with her free hand. "And I'll send a message into the town to put the midwife on alert."

He gave her hand a squeeze and went in search of Lord Farnleigh. He found him in his study going over accounts.

"May I interrupt you, my lord?"

"Yes. I've had quite enough of figures for today." The gray haired man set his pince nez on the desktop and blinked his eyes into focus. "We'll be called into

188 • Kate Parker

luncheon soon. Will this take much time?"

"Hardly any, my lord. First of all, I need to leave these in your safe."

When he opened the soggy sack of jewels, Farnleigh's eyes widened. "Mattingly was carrying those when he died?"

"Yes."

"Incredible." Farnleigh quickly locked the jewels away.

Now came the part Adam regretted. Farnleigh was a decent man. "As part of my investigation, I need to know why Mr. Mattingly came here for a visit, and why you all but escorted him off the property a few days later. And why you found him carrying jewels to be incredible."

"You're right. This won't take long at all. The matter is none of your business. Good day." Lord Farnleigh picked up his pen, and Adam saw it shake in his hand.

Adam took a deep breath to calm his own nerves. His guess had to be right. "Whose son was he, my lord? Yours? Your older brother's?"

He crushed the pen in his hand. "Those fool solicitors have been talking again, have they? By gad, can't they keep their mouths shut?"

"Please, Farnleigh. I'd like to hear the whole story from you."

"He was Gerald's by a well-paid mistress. Too well paid to let such an accident happen. And then Gerald, the damned fool, broke his neck racing a horse. I was next to inherit the title, so my father asked me to see that this little problem was handled discretely. Over the years, Mattingly had received more than he deserved, but now he'd been through the money from selling his commission and the swine wanted an allowance."

"To keep his mouth shut."

"He said he was going to mount an appeal of the title to the crown. He threatened to bring proof that his parents were wed. That he should have the title."

Adam felt himself move forward slightly at this shocking news. "Does he have such proof?"

"No. It was clear the so-called proof would be manufactured. Apparently the Regent has a nephew he's fond of, and Mattingly threatened his life and reputation if Mattingly wasn't declared rightful holder of the title of Marquess of Farnleigh."

That explained his fleecing the young man. He'd proved to Prinny he could drag his nephew through all sorts of debauchery. Proved he could cause all sorts of damage if money wasn't given to him one way or another. "He offered to drop his suit in exchange for an allowance?"

"A very healthy allowance. I couldn't afford it. In the end, I had no choice but to tell him to leave and not come back. He could run to the Prince Regent and be damned." He slumped back into his chair.

A moment later, a discrete knock sounded on the door before the butler came in. "Luncheon is served, my lord."

"Thank you," Farnleigh said. "Shall we go through?"

Adam stood and glanced over his shoulder until the butler departed. "I'm sorry, Farnleigh. This must have been very distressing for you. Who killed Mattingly?"

The man's head jerked up. "I don't know. It wasn't me. It wouldn't have been any of my people. They didn't know what Mattingly was up to. Maybe his coachman knew why he was here and killed him in the course of a robbery, hoping to obtain those jewels Mattingly was carrying when he died."

"Do you know who Mattingly planned to meet when he returned here that night?"

"No. I'd given him no hope of a better answer, and I'm the only one here likely to give him the money he wanted."

Lord Farnleigh was already on his feet and walking around his desk. Adam knew time was running out. "What about your guests? Could any of them have offered him employment? Were any of the girls soft on him?"

"I don't think any of them could be so foolish, but please, question all of my relatives. I doubt anyone in this family has any sense. Shall we go?"

Adam bowed, knowing he'd get nothing further here. He walked with Farnleigh toward the dining room, planning to sit with Miss Franklin and arrange another meeting to discuss the investigation. Instead, he was waylaid by Miss Woodward, a young woman of rapid speech and ferocious giggles.

He tried to catch Miss Franklin's eye, but she was

too far down the table, speaking with two men he was certain he'd been introduced to. One was too young for the lady, the other too old.

On the other hand, Adam was the right age. Old enough to be settled and experienced, young enough to be vigorous and flexible in his attitude toward a woman who dealt with cadavers.

And while thinking this, he completely missed what Miss Woodward was saying. "I'm sorry. I wasn't being attentive."

"You could have taken lessons from Mr. Mattingly. He was always attentive."

Was that the reason he was killed? "Did you know him well, Miss Woodward?"

"I only met him here at this party, but I liked what little I saw of him."

"A pleasant voice and face?"

She giggled. "Oh, much more than that. He had a gift for conversation, quoted poetry with ease, had a flair for fashion, and knew the latest gossip at court."

"In short, what every young woman wants." The entire ton, when they met in London, did nothing else. Adam found them all boring.

She giggled again.

Was a romance budding that any sane parent would tear out at the root? Adam found it a compelling reason for murder. "Did you have hopes for furthering your friendship?"

She giggled, then pouted. Adam made a mental note

to warn his friends away from an entanglement with this lady. "I never had a chance. Lady Deborah Rogers, the Earl of Chandess's daughter, monopolized him from the start. She was ready to run off with him. It was mad."

"Really?" He'd never be considered a great conversationalist with responses like that.

Fortunately, it didn't take much to keep Miss Woodward talking. "I found her crying in the picture gallery the morning after he left and tried to comfort her by saying she'd be sure to see him in London in the spring. She cried all the harder. I finally got it out of her, and you'll never guess."

"What?"

"Miss Woodward, would you like to go sledding after luncheon?" a young man said from across the table.

"Oh, yes, I would." She began to talk to him, leaving Adam to steam. He gripped the silverware so hard the pattern left an impression on his palm. Picking up his wineglass, he gulped down the contents.

At least he knew Lady Deborah Rogers was aware of something about Mattingly at the time of his death. But life would be much easier if he could just get the Woodward chit to finish her story.

He kept trying to break into their conversation without luck. The chit on his other side sniffed and sighed to get his attention. He did try to pay attention to her drivel, but really, he'd much rather listen to why a girl was sobbing over Mattingly's absence than to a girl attempting to sound witty in schoolroom French. He still hated French because of the war.

When the next course was brought around, Adam said, "Miss Woodward, you've left me in suspense. Why was Lady Deborah crying?"

"I told you."

"You did?"

"Yes. She was going to run away with him, but he never showed up."

"The day he left here. He was supposed to return?" This was news to Adam.

"Yes. They'd spend the night here, and then confront her father in the morning so he'd have to bless the marriage."

"Dear heavens."

"Yes. Mad, isn't it?"

Leaving her father, Lord Chandess, as new principal suspect. He needed to talk to Miss Franklin. Would luncheon never finish?

When the meal finally ended, Adam nearly knocked his chair over to reach Miss Franklin before she disappeared. "Miss Franklin, Miss Franklin," he called as he reached her. "Sir Isaiah wants to speak to us. Urgently."

"Of course." She led the way to the parlor where they'd met the older man before. Heat still rose in the chimney, but the magistrate wasn't there. "Do you know where he is?"

"It doesn't matter. I heard at lunch that Mattingly planned to return here to spend the night in Lady Deborah Rogers's room, thereby compromising her. Then her father would be forced to let them marry."

"Oh, dear. I'm glad Ann hasn't heard about this."

He grabbed her by her upper arms, feeling the steel inside the narrow flesh. "This is no time to worry about Ann's hearing about anything. We need, or rather you need, to have a talk with Lady Deborah immediately."

"While you talk to her father."

They split up outside the room. Adam found Lord Chandess alone in a parlor looking morosely out at the snowy landscape. "Hoping someone will appear?"

"Too late for that, I'm afraid."

"Mattingly?"

"Yes."

"I've heard he had hopes where your daughter was concerned."

"He did. You can too if you want."

Adam's hands went up in surrender. "No. Sorry."

"Ah, well." He sounded like a man who'd been disappointed too many times to have any hope left.

"Is that why Mattingly came back the same day he left?"

"Yes. So foolish. I'd have said yes if they'd only asked me."

"For your permission for Lady Deborah to marry Mattingly?"

"Of course, man. She's had five seasons. Five! And

every year I've raised her dowry, and still no offers."

Adam began to open his mouth, but snapped it shut. He had no recollection of ever meeting Lady Deborah Rogers.

Chandess apparently didn't notice Adam's silence. "She has the personality of a brick wall, the intelligence of pond water, and the looks of a muddy carpet. I should know. I'm her father."

"So there was no reason for him to spend the night in Lady Deborah's room to gain your blessing?"

"None whatever. Although I do applaud her resourcefulness. But personally, I don't care who she marries, as long as she's off my hands."

Adam was becoming certain everyone in this house was quite mad.

"The second I'd have found out about Mr. Mattingly setting foot in my daughter's room, I'd be slapping him on the back and calling for the vicar, followed by drinks all around."

Lord Chandess strode off and Adam dropped onto the nearest sofa. He was still sitting there when Miss Franklin joined him a few minutes later. Stunned, he said, "Why would Mattingly travel through bad weather to carry out a charade if all he had to do was have a short conversation with Lady Deborah's father?"

Miss Franklin sat down next to him. "I've talked to Lady Deborah and some other guests. My guess is he didn't know anything about Lady Deborah. I don't know anything about her, and I spent ten minutes trying to get her to tell me anything useful."

She shook her head at the experience. "I had the impression he'd not spent much time among fashionable young ladies. He's not on anyone's invitation list, according to some of the mamas here. They wondered why he was invited. Few people know he wasn't invited."

"Miss Franklin. I haven't thought to ask you about Mattingly's arrival, and you seem to have paid more attention than anyone else I've spoken to."

She sat next to him and gripped one of his hands. "He showed up one day in his fine clothes and his fine carriage and asked to see Lord Farnleigh. He looked so much like one of the family that the butler didn't think anything of it. His lordship invited him to stay for a few days while they talked. Negotiated was the word the marquess used with Robert."

She dropped his hand.

His hand felt cold without her touch. "So you and your brother-in-law and his father knew Mattingly was here under somewhat false pretenses. Did anyone else?"

"No. They decided to keep it between themselves and I overheard them. I've not repeated any of this until now." She tilted her head back to gaze at the ceiling. "You won't tell anyone, will you? I don't want people to know I listen. No one pays me any attention, and so I learn things."

"My dear Miss Franklin, I wouldn't dream of telling anyone. But I would love to see you dressed in jewels and finery. You'd outshine every woman here." She already did, wearing a gray gown of plain wool, with a locket as her only jewelry.

"If I did that, I'd embarrass Ann and Robert and be sent away from here. As long as I am demure and useful, I can stay with my family instead of being cast out."

"Who would be fool enough to send you away?"

"Robert."

"Why?" She was exquisite. He had been right. Everyone here was insane.

"I don't know. Robert says they have enough useless people hanging around here as it is. Without a husband, and with no money, I have to rely on the kindness of Ann's husband."

She snapped her mouth shut as scratching was heard on the door and then Cousin Adolphus stuck his head in the opening. "My data is very clear. We're about to have a large storm. Probably snow."

Adam was about to say, "It's December and it's freezing outside. What else do you expect?" Good manners kept the words from forming on his lips.

Then he noticed how the news had turned Miss Franklin's creamy complexion pale. "Oh, dear. I must send a note to the midwife immediately."

"Surely the babe isn't coming yet," Cousin Adolphus said.

"We must be ready for when it is." She hurried from the room.

Adam wandered off to search for Sir Isaiah and

when he found him, discovered the magistrate was as confused by what Adam had learned as he was. Then they spent part of the afternoon discussing odd cases, court gossip, and good literature. He was surprised when they rose to find it dark outside and snow falling at a heavy rate.

There was nothing else he could do on this investigation, and so he wrote a letter to his client, telling her only that Mattingly had met his death under suspicious circumstances and he would need to investigate further to separate the innocent from the guilty.

When he arrived at the dinner table, it was to discover that neither Ann nor Eve were there and Robert was drinking more than usual. No one mentioned the reason, but everyone seemed to be holding their breath.

"So close to Christmas," Miss Woodward said to him over the game course. "It must be a blessed baby."

Across the table from them, a dowager said, "Quiet. It's bad luck. Besides, it's a second child and it's only the twenty-third."

Miss Woodward giggled. It was such a fiendish sound that Adam expected horns to appear in her ringlets. They were all crazy here.

The dowager glared at her. Miss Woodward loosed peels of giggles.

Adam downed the contents of his wine glass. He'd follow Robert after dinner to see if he could have a word with Miss Franklin. Try to learn if the midwife had arrived and whether he could do anything to help.

Besides pace the floor with Robert.

When dinner finally ended, he followed Robert, but the man disappeared into the study with his father.

Undaunted, Adam went upstairs and followed a serving maid with a steaming bowl of water. He saw which door she entered and waited in the hall for someone to come out.

He heard voices, cries, grunts, and wailing. After what felt like an eternity, another maid came out with dirty linens. "Is the midwife here?" he asked.

She shook her head no.

Another maid came past carrying clean linens. "Excuse me..." Adam said. She started to hurry past when he grabbed her arm. "Who's in charge in there?"

"Miss Eve."

He felt marginally better about Lady Stonehill's chances with her sister running the affair. "Ask her to come out to speak to me when she can."

The maid nodded and slipped inside.

Miss Franklin came out an hour later; sweaty, her hair disarrayed like an old mop, and her dress stained. She looked at him through old eyes and said, "I can't work on the Mattingly investigation right now. Ann is trying to deliver."

"I gathered as much. Can I do anything? Go for the midwife?"

"Two people have already tried, but thank you for

200 • Kate Parker

offering. It was a fool's errand. No one has made in or out of here for hours, and Ann has been in labor since late afternoon." She gripped his hands for a moment. "You didn't need to spend the evening waiting for me in the hallway. You're a guest here. It's almost Christmas. Go enjoy yourself."

She started to turn away when he said, "Not without you."

What he didn't expect was for Eve Franklin to fall into his arms and sob uncontrollably.

Chapter Five

FEAR OF LOSING ANN ECLIPSED every other thought. Before this, Eve would never have acted so embarrassingly, so emotionally, so childishly, in front of anyone, much less Lord Adam Downing. Tonight, she didn't care.

She sobbed out the mourning she was sure would come, for her sister and the baby both. She cried until she was out of tears and beginning to hiccup.

And then she felt the strength and the compassion in Lord Adam surround her. It was in his murmured words, in his embrace, in his feather-soft kisses on her forehead.

Eve straightened up and mopped her face with the handkerchief he kindly handed her. "I'm sorry."

"Don't be. You needed to release your fear so you can return to the battle."

She looked at his encouraging expression. "Thank you."

"Can I do anything for you?"

"Not unless you're a midwife."

"I'm afraid not."

"I've only helped with simple births. This baby won't come, Ann is swelling up, and she's growing weak. I don't know what to do."

"What have you tried?"

"I've had her up and walking until she's cursed me. I've had her lay first on one side and then on the other. She won't eat. I can barely get her to drink watered wine. And then we go through it all again."

He put his arms around her and she felt her fatigue fade away. "Then you'll have to be strong for both of you. Unless some of the other women in the family can help."

"Ann won't have any of them near her, and I can't blame her. They prattle on until I want to scream, and I'm not in labor."

She felt his chuckle rumble in his chest. "At least have someone bring you dinner."

"They have already."

He kissed her forehead, and she wanted to linger.

Except she couldn't. As she pulled away, she said, "Please, come up and check on me in the morning if there's no word. I may have need of your shoulder to cry on again."

"I will."

It was the longest night of Eve's life. Frances had taken longer than this to be born, but the midwife had been in charge. When one of the maids opened the curtains and let light—cold, gray, snowy light—into the room, Eve sighed in relief. It was Christmas Eve day. Surely the heir of the heir would arrive today.

Another maid came in and said, "Lady Chandess is outside, saying she'll stay by Ann's side while you get breakfast."

"Ann, is that all right?"

"I don't care. Just get out of here." Then she flopped on her other side and shut her eyes.

Eve nodded to the maid and Lady Chandess came in. "How is she doing?" she asked in a whisper that could have been heard in London.

"I'm trying to rest. Shut up," came from the bed.

"Won't be long now," Lady Chandess said knowingly and took the chair Eve had been sitting in.

After washing and changing clothes, Eve went down to breakfast. She took tea and toast and sat uninvited next to Lord Adam. "Where's Robert?"

"Passed out after drinking half the night. He's scared," Lord Adam murmured.

She looked into his lake blue eyes and said, "We all are."

"Can you get some rest?"

"Lady Chandess is with her now."

"I guess the answer is no," he said, making her smile.

Hope made her ask, "What is the weather like?"

"They keep shoveling the paths to the outbuildings, but then the snow covers them again. No one's going anywhere for awhile."

She felt like he had hit her in the chest.

"Eve. Miss Franklin." She found she was clutching his hand and let go. To her joy, he held her hand in such a way that she could grab his and squeeze again. She knew of no other man who treated a woman of no standing with such compassion.

She blinked back her tears. "Oh, dear heavens, it's all up to me."

The day went on like the night, and still no baby. Robert entered the room in the afternoon looking hung over, and soon he and Ann were both crying. Eve ended up suggesting he leave, although they all knew it might be the last time the couple saw each other in this life.

A tray was sent up at dinnertime along with the good wishes of Lord Farnleigh. Eve found she was growing too tired to eat, and she wasn't the one having the baby. Ann cursed Robert, the marquess, Eve, the maids, and the tray, since the smell of food was making her nauseous. The tray was sent down. Eve wished she could be so easily removed.

By late evening, Ann visibly weakened. Eve could tell the baby was close, but Ann's pushing had become feeble.

Then a maid said, "Lord Adam is outside for you."

Eve squeezed her sister's hand and rushed from the room into his arms. When he saw her damp eyes, he stopped whatever he was going to say and held her.

"Where is Robert?"

"Passed out drunk."

"Damn the man. Damn him for the weakling that he is." Then she gave in to the hopeless tears she couldn't spill in front of Ann.

Lord Adam held her, rocking slowly side to side and whispering shushing noises in her ear.

When she got her tears under control, she said, "The babe is finally close to coming, and Ann is too weak to push him out. I'm losing her. I'm losing both of them. And I can't. I can't lose my little sister."

"Is there any way to push for her?"

"If we could get her in a different position. Maybe. Sitting on the edge of the bed so the baby could fall out of her..." She looked at him. No. She couldn't ask. Men didn't get involved in what was women's work.

Frail little women. Ha!

"I helped army doctors. I'm not afraid of blood and guts." He was looking into her eyes, and it felt like he was encouraging her to ask him.

"That's nothing compared to a woman in labor."

He smiled as she meant him to, but then he turned serious. "I know what it's like to help someone dear to you."

"Wait here. I may need you soon." She strode back into the bedchamber and looked into her sister's face. Already her lips were cracked and she'd soaked through her nightgown and the bedding. What little water they could get into her wasn't helping.

"Ann. Ann dearest."

Her sister tried to focus on her face, but Eve could

see the effort even that simple task took.

"I want to try something different. I want to sit you up on the edge of the bed and let the baby fall out."

Ann smiled at her words. "Can't. Too weak. Tell Robert..."

"Tell Robert yourself when you show him his son. Wait here."

Oh, good heavens. What a stupid thing to say. Did she believe Ann would rise up and run around the room? Eve opened the door. "Lord Adam."

He walked in, taking in at a glance the chaos in the overheated room.

"Strip off your coat, your boots, your cravat, your waistcoat. I'm going to slide Ann down the bed so she's at the bottom. I want you to climb up behind her, slide your legs on either side of her, and hold her up in a sitting position. Do you think you can do it without fainting on me?"

"Miss Franklin, have a little faith in me."

"Call me Eve. We're going to get to know each other very well tonight."

"Call me Adam."

"Yes, my lord."

"Don't..." Then he must have seen her weary smile. He started to undress.

Eve and two maids moved Ann down the bed so her legs were hanging toward the floor. At her direction, Adam climbed in behind Ann. He'd stripped down to his shirt with his sleeves rolled up above his elbows, his trousers, and his socks. He levered himself into position and supported Ann's back against his chest. The maids piled pillows behind him on the bed, but Eve suspected they wouldn't be needed.

Ann blushed and jumped slightly when Adam first spoke to her, but quickly calmed. He spoke softly to her, encouraging her to push whenever Eve felt another contraction starting in her stomach muscles.

Eve checked the way she'd been taught. During the contractions, the baby's head was close to crowning. From the outside, all appeared ready. The baby simply wasn't making his way out.

Much more of this, and both Ann and the baby would die, the babe still inside her. Eve had felt the promise of this being a joyful Christmas. She could now feel her hope shriveling within her.

The next contraction started. "Push, Ann."

"I can't." The words were said so softly Eve wasn't sure Ann had spoken.

"Mary, take one foot. Sally, take the other. Both of you, push her legs up toward her body. Adam, hold her in place."

The first time, nothing appeared to have happened. The second contraction was weaker, but they worked together and the head crowned. Too large to slip out easily.

Eve picked up the knife to cut the umbilical cord. When the contraction ended, she slipped it in and cut her sister's flesh, widening the hole for the baby.

Ann came alive with curses that would have embarrassed a sailor. Adam chuckled. "That's the idea, my lady. Curse that baby out."

Another weak contraction started. "This is it." With Mary, Sally, and Adam all pushing toward the middle, the head appeared. "Keep pushing." The rest of the body followed.

The baby was slimy, bloody, and limp.

"Adam, put Ann back in a reclining position. Mary, give her a drink of watered wine. Sally, help me with the baby."

It took two slaps to the upside down backside, but thick matter slid out of the baby onto the floor. A weak cry followed.

Ann must have asked if it was a boy, because Eve heard Adam say, "Only a male could be so much trouble, my lady. You have a fine son."

While Eve tended to the chores required after a birth, Sally quickly cleaned the baby. The child, annoyed by cold or handling, whimpered, kicked, and then cried loudly.

Eve gave a sigh of relief as she wrapped him in a soft blanket and gave him to Ann. The mother was too weak to hold him, so Eve helped her hold the infant while he began to nurse.

"Sally, Mary, take all this away and bring warmed fresh water and towels. Her ladyship will feel better once we get her washed and into a clean nightgown and fresh sheets."

The servants, helped by an army outside the door, quickly completed the tasks while Adam, seated facing away from the activity, fought to pull on his tall boots without the aid of his valet. Then Mary took over aiding Ann while Eve went to thank Adam for helping to save her sister's life.

"Hungry little beggar, isn't he?" Adam said, half-dressed, unkempt, and ravishing.

Eve nearly jumped into his arms, and they hugged each other in relief and triumph. "We did it, Adam. Isn't this much better than investigating Mr. Mattingly?"

"Less likely to cause nightmares."

Tears poured down her cheeks. "We brought a new life into the world."

"Better than sending them out," he muttered into her ear.

They stepped apart, still holding hands. Then Eve had to drop her grip to move away to check on her sister. She saw Adam turn away, pulling on his waistcoat. She yanked on the bell rope. When a footman answered the call, Sally told him to get Lord Farnleigh and the new father.

The words had no more than left the servant's lips when a commanding voice said, "What is the meaning of this?"

Eve turned to face the marquess, his son Robert swaying right behind him. Adam, who'd begun to button his waistcoat, continued to dress. There was no help for it. She curtsied to Robert and said, "You have a son."

Robert hurried to the bed, sounding much more sober. "Oh, Ann."

Mary dropped the laundry she was holding and pushed a chair under the unsteady earl. He sat there grinning, one hand on his wife's shoulder.

Eve watched the new parents smile at each other and their son, the rest of the room forgotten.

Lord Farnleigh rounded on Adam. "Explain yourself, Downing."

"I have battlefield medical experience. I offered a strong back and Miss Franklin accepted my help." He rolled his sleeves down, hiding his muscled, sinewy forearms, and picked up his coat.

"You wouldn't have a grandson, or a daughter-in-law, without his help. You should thank him, your lordship," Eve said.

His glower slowly smoothed. "The babe is truly whole and well?"

"Yes." She glanced over at the trio and smiled. "They both must have great care given to them after their ordeal, but they'll make it. There's no reason why the little boy shouldn't grow up to be tall and strong."

"I didn't realize you were a midwife in addition to your other talents, Miss Franklin."

Eve stared at the marquess. "I'm not. I have assisted at births before, and I have experience healing. Without a midwife, we had to do our best. And now we all need to thank God for our little Christmas miracle."

The marquess watched his son and grandson for a

moment before he said, "My thanks to both of you as well."

Eve slept through what was left of the night and breakfast Christmas morning. Exhausted, she awoke tired and sore but happy. Once she was dressed and had checked on Ann and the baby, she discovered the marquess was leading the entire family and staff in prayers for Christmas, victory over Napoleon, and the new arrival.

She slipped into the back of the ballroom and found herself next to Sir Isaiah. Not until they began to sing a carol did the older man whisper to her, "After luncheon, Lord Adam is going to lead a party out onto the ice to check the bottom of the pond below where Mr. Mattingly was found."

She asked, "What good will that do?" but he only shrugged his shoulders.

After more prayers and carols, the group disbursed. By the time they reassembled for Christmas dinner, served at midday by family tradition, nearly everyone had viewed the newborn heir. They commented on his large size, lusty lungs, strong grip, and big feet. Catching Adam's eye across the table, Eve saw he was as relieved as she was that no one commented on his irregular presence at the birth.

With luck, no one would ever know.

The meal seemed to go on forever. Finally, everyone rose from the table, and Eve met Adam in the hall. "Get your cloak and join us outside," he murmured, standing too close for propriety.

A couple of dowagers cleared their throats.

"Sir Isaiah told me. I'll meet you at the pond," she replied, staying close to Adam. Let the old tabbies fuss. She'd never meet another man like him.

When she reached the pond, Vince and Wally were there with ropes and buckets laced with holes. They also carried saws capable of cutting through thick ice, pick axes, and other farm implements, as well as the brooms used to sweep the ice free of snow.

"Where is everyone?" she asked.

"His lordship and the magistrate won't be out until we have the ice opened up and have found something," Vince told her.

"Smart," Wally added, blowing on his hands hidden in his thin gloves.

Eve burrowed further inside her cloak, shivering as the air bit the exposed skin on her face. "You might as well start and open a hole in the ice. The activity will keep you warm."

Vince nodded and began to chip a hole in the ice with a pick. The temperature had been cold long enough that the frozen water didn't crack with each blow.

Eve was glad to see they weren't in danger of falling through. She'd nearly gone in a few days before and she didn't want to be so close to the icy waters again.

Vince had chipped through the ice and Wally had started sawing away a slab when she heard male voices behind her. She turned to find Adam coming toward her with the marquess. They seemed to be arguing, but they were keeping their voices lowered.

She bobbed them a curtsy and then turned back to the hole, which was growing by the minute.

"This ice is easier to break through, since we opened it up here just a couple days ago," Vince told her as he helped Wally move a block cut from the surface to be hauled to the icehouse.

"When you're ready, I'd like you to send down a hook to the bottom and see if it hits anything," Adam said.

"You have an idea," Eve said. "You're expecting to find something specific."

Adam nodded solemnly to her. "I'd seen something like this before. I finally remembered where I'd seen that type of wound. In the French countryside. In a fight with some farmers."

"It's some sort of farm implement?"

He nodded.

After a few minutes, Vince said, "We're hitting against something sticking far up from the bottom. A tree branch, maybe."

"Where?" Lord Farnleigh asked.

The stableman lowered the hook and then dragged it forward. In a moment, it caught on something and wouldn't move no matter how much he pulled.

"How deep is it here, Vince?" Adam asked.

"Three feet, maybe four. The whole pond's not that

deep."

"Let me have a length of rope," Adam said. Wally handed him a coil. Adam walked to the far side of the hole and tossed one end of the rope to Vince.

Vince looked over expectantly. "You want to drag the bottom and find out how far up this branch sticks out?"

"Yes."

The two men nodded to each other and began to work. It was quickly obvious whatever this thing was, it came close to the surface and was stuck in the mud in the bottom. "Let's get a second rope across and trap whatever this is from the other side."

Wally sprang into action, and Eve rushed over to stand by Adam and catch the second rope as the stableman threw one end.

It didn't work. The second rope, pulled from the opposite direction, slid smoothly up from the bottom along an arc. Eve looked at Adam and shook her head.

She felt as if she had failed him after all he'd done for her and Ann the night before. That wasn't right. She owed him for his help, and she wanted his good opinion of her. Frustrated, she clung to the rope, wishing she could think of something, anything, to assist.

"At least we know there is something solid less than a foot below the bottom of the ice. Something that may have caused the injury we saw to the back of Mattingly's skull." Adam stared at the hole in the ice, his gloved fists against his waist. "We're going to have to reach in and try to pull it out."

"Why?" the marquess demanded.

"It's evidence in an unexplained death."

"I'll do it, my lord," Vince said as he began to take off his jacket and gloves.

"Thank you," Adam replied. "I'll reward you for this, whether or not we succeed. Don't take unnecessary risks. Wally, get a rope around his waist and hang on, just in case."

Wally did as he was told, and Vince was soon laying on the edge of the ice, reaching into the frigid water. He muttered curses and then, "I feel something metal. I can't pull it out."

To Eve's surprise, Adam shed his coat and gloves, too. Before he lay down to reach in where Vince struggled with the weighty object, she tied the rope she held around Adam's waist and gripped the other end. She wouldn't let him freeze or drown. She'd take care of him.

A man's voice next to her said, "Yes, your lordship." Eve turned to find a footman beside her grabbing the rope at Lord Farnleigh's signal. As much as the marquess's lack of faith in her hurt, she was glad of the footman's help.

Together, Adam and Vince raised the object enough to break through the surface where they all saw what they'd searched for.

Chapter Six

"IT'S A PICKAXE," THE MARQUESS SAID.

Wally and Eve looped a rope under the edge showing above the water and in a minute, the four managed to get the implement onto the ice. Adam and Vince quickly put on their coats and rubbed their cold hands. Eve could hear their teeth chattering.

"Let's get you both into the kitchen to look after your fingers. I don't want you to get frostbite," Eve said. "Wally, bring the pickaxe along to the kitchen as well. It's evidence. Sir Isaiah will want to see it."

The marquess left without a word.

They made a fast moving parade back to the house. When they reached the kitchen, Eve sent one of the maids after Sir Isaiah and shed her outerwear as she called for two bowls of warm water for Vince and Adam.

"When did you figure it out?" she asked as she examined Adam's skin in the heated water.

"Early this morning. I'm fine. Hand me a towel and look after Vince. He's the one whose arm was in the pond the longest."

"So someone was out there to strike down Mr. Mattingly, and then threw the murder weapon into the pond after him?" Eve gently patted his arm dry, taking tender care of his still cold arm.

"In that case, the pickaxe would have weighed down the body." Adam looked her in the eye as he rolled his sleeve down. Eve noticed the fabric was still wet in spots and no doubt was uncomfortable against his skin.

"What are you thinking?" She admired his clever mind. She would miss him in investigations she undertook for Sir Isaiah in the future. No, she'd miss him all the time.

"We need to talk to Sir Isaiah." He rose from his seat and headed out of the kitchen.

"Sally, keep giving Vince hot tea and make sure the water in that bowl stays warm, not hot." Eve rushed after Adam, wanting to hear their conversation.

When she arrived in the parlor, Sir Isaiah was planted in front of a roaring fire. Lord Farnleigh sat a small distance away and Adam took a seat on the sofa between them. She sat next to Adam and incurred a wrathful stare from the marquess.

"Miss Franklin is here at my invitation," Adam said, staring back at Lord Farnleigh as if daring him to say a word.

"Quite right," Sir Isaiah said into the lengthening silence.

"Go on," Farnleigh finally said, brushing the matter of her presence away with one hand.

Eve breathed a sigh of relief. She could stay.

Adam leaned back and crossed one booted foot over the other knee. "I think Mattingly's death was an accident. He'd made plans to spend the night under your roof with Lady Deborah Rogers in order to force a marriage. Ironically, Lord Chandess wouldn't have objected to their being married if they'd asked, and no one else cared. Lord Farnleigh was ready to fight Mattingly's claim on the title, because he knew he and his legitimate heirs would win. Therefore, no one present had any reason to do Mattingly harm."

"How could it be an accident?" Sir Isaiah asked. "You said yourself that there was a straight wound across the back of Mattingly's head."

"From a weapon just below the surface of the ice. When he felt the ice give way beneath his feet, he fell backward and landed on his back, shattering the ice along the entire length of his body." Adam then nodded to Eve.

She continued his thoughts as if they thought as one. "His head went into the water and struck the pickaxe sticking up from the bottom of the pond. Unconscious or dead, his body fell as far as it could while the ice formed over him again. When his body refloated, it didn't have room to roll over and so rose straight up, leaving him face up under the newly formed ice."

"What was he doing on the pond?"

Eve answered, "It was dark out and the grounds

snow covered. Mr. Mattingly was on foot. He took the direct route to the house, forgetting that the lane here doesn't go straight, but around the pond."

"That's all good and well, but how did the pickaxe come to be in the pond?" Sir Isaiah said.

"I think I can answer that." The marquess looked only at the magistrate as he said, "Last spring, when we took the ice off the pond to use in the icehouse, I was informed a pickaxe had fallen into the pond and become affixed on the bottom. I gave orders that it should be retrieved. Apparently, my orders were ignored." His expression darkened.

"With your permission, my lord, I'll investigate what you've told us. If I can find anyone who can verify the pickaxe wasn't salvaged, I think Sir Isaiah will be able to close the ledger on this unfortunate incident." Adam rose and bowed to both men before turning his attention to Eve. "If you'll assist me?"

"Gladly, my lord." Her heart leaped as she rose and hurried from the room as if she were escaping. She could feel Lord Farnleigh's glower aimed at her back.

"Any idea how to learn what happened?" Adam asked when they were in the hall.

She smiled at him, glad to be useful once more. "I have an idea."

They went back to the kitchen, where Vince and Wally were retelling their tale to the household. "Vince, Wally, I have a feeling that the search for the missing pickaxe last spring would have fallen to the two of you,"

Eve said.

"Yes, but we weren't around when it went missing," Wally said, exasperation evident in his tone. "Footmen, who didn't know how to do the job right, were assigned the task of cutting the ice into blocks and carrying it into the icehouse."

"They didn't do a good job?"

"Oblong blocks, round blocks, all sorts of sized blocks thrown every which way in the ice house. Tools scattered all over the banks of the pond. They even—" Wally warmed up to the subject.

"Hey," one of the footmen said, "we've never done that work before. I bet you weren't any good at it your first time. And wet! We—"

Vince cut him off. "And then we learned one of the pickaxes was lost somewhere in the pond."

"Some fool of a footman broke through the ice with it and the force of his blow buried it in the bottom," Wally said.

"Hey, you don't know who did that," the footman replied.

"Who else would be so foolish?" Wally asked.

"We searched twice, but closer to the meadow rather than toward the lane." Vince looked at Eve and shook his head in sorrow. "Do you think if we'd searched longer, that fellow might still be alive?"

"No," Adam said, drawing all eyes to him in the cozy kitchen. "There are too many 'ifs' in this tale. If he'd asked the Earl of Chandess outright for the hand of his daughter. If Mattingly had gone back to London like he said he would. If he'd not tricked another man out of his horses and carriage. And, yes, if the pickaxe had been found."

A change in any one of them, Eve knew, would mean Mattingly would still be alive. And she would never have met Adam. Mattingly's death was a terrible thing, but...No, his death was a terrible thing. Period.

"Think they'll call it an accident?" Vince asked.

"Yes."

"Where will they bury him?"

"In the church graveyard. It might be too good a place for him, but Stonehill thinks it would be a good thing to do, and Lord Farnleigh agrees." Adam told them.

Adam turned toward Miss Franklin, toward Eve, but behind him he heard, "And there'll be no trouble for Wally or me for not finding that pickaxe?"

"No," Eve assured him. "We're just glad to know how it ended up there."

Adam took Eve's arm to escort her upstairs. The walk suddenly seemed too short. "I've enjoyed working with you, Eve. Uh, Miss Franklin."

She grinned. "After working together to bring a child into the world, you should call me Eve."

He found himself grinning back. "That was good work."

"That babe is as close to a miracle as I ever want to

deliver."

He took her hand. "Didn't you say something about the promise of miracles being the greatest gift at Christmas?"

"That's more poetic than anything I would say." Her blush warmed him more than the overheated kitchen.

He spoke quickly before they were interrupted by one or another of the houseguests. "I'd like to see you again."

She looked wide-eyed and hopeful. "Will you be coming back to Farnleigh Park soon? I hardly get the chance to travel."

"I'd like you to come to Castle Northbrook in the spring. To celebrate Easter and new life in the gardens and the animal pens. Perhaps you can bring Cousin Adolphus as a chaperone. We have a wonderful observatory that he might enjoy."

"I'm sure he would, but are you certain your family will want more houseguests? I'm sure you'll already have a houseful arriving."

"Oh, they're going to want to meet you." He couldn't stop smiling. "I've met your family. It would only be fair for you to meet mine before you decide you want to spend a lifetime with me. A lifetime, I'd better make clear now, that will be spent in London."

"Would I be able to work as a healer in London?"

"There's probably more need for your skill there than there is here."

They'd stopped on the hall, and now Eve was

staring into his eyes. "I thought members of your class married other lords and ladies."

"I'm a second son. I can marry whom I want, since I have no responsibilities to form a dynastic marriage. You will only be Lady Adam Downing."

"That's very grand for a physician's daughter."

He had to smile at that. "Not as grand as Countess of Stonehill."

"Ann married Robert without the title. When they married, one of his older brothers was still alive and there was no talk of his inheriting the title. Please be certain I would listen to any proposal that you might give, with or without any title at all. And I look forward to meeting your family at Eastertide."

He kissed her then, and it felt as if they had practiced this to perfection. So perfect he forgot to stop until he ran out of air and broke away, gasping. "Eve, I want to give you a promise for Christmas. The promise that we will marry in the spring if you like my family. I know they will love you as I do."

She laughed, a sound he had grown to love. "Adam, if I love them as I love you, we will all get along splendidly. And a wedding for the two of us will be a grand affair if my sister has anything to say about it."

About Kate

Kate Parker grew up reading her mother's collection of mystery books by Christie, Sayers, and others. Now she can't write a story without someone being murdered, and everyday situations are studied for their lethal potential.

The main characters in *Christmas Promise,* Adam and Eve, are named for her great-great-great-great-grandparents who married in 1815. Unfortunately, neither were related to dukes or found themselves to be the in-laws of earls. They had twelve children and celebrated their 60th wedding anniversary, however, so perhaps theirs was the greater wealth.

This year, the first two volumes of the Deadly series, *Deadly Scandal* and *Deadly Wedding*, have been published. These feature society reporter Olivia Denis of the *London Daily Premier*, who, when her diplomat husband is murdered, trades in her ordinary housewife existence for that of a career woman who carries out special missions on the side for pre-World War II England. A third volume, *Deadly Fashion*, is in the works.

In the coming year, the fifth volume in the Victorian Bookshop Mystery series will be published. Fans of Georgia Fenchurch, a bookshop owner in Victorian London, and the Duke of Blackford will finally be invited to their wedding. The Archivist Society will be investigating the identity of a man who rescued a young woman and then disappeared, leaving Georgia distracted from her wedding preparations. After their long courtship, will Georgia make it to the church on time?

Follow Kate and her deadly examination of history at
www.KateParkerbooks.com
and www.Facebook.com/Author.Kate.Parker/

The Christmas Rose

by

Hannah Meredith

Chapter One

December 1819

"BLOODY HELL!" SIMON BIRCHE, Earl of Trenton, slapped the folded newspaper on the table in disgust. It took him a second to realize the curse that lived in his head had burst from his mouth. He quickly looked around to see who had noticed his loss of control.

His wife Emma continued to frown at the paper she was marking with a chewed pencil. She seemed oblivious to his outburst. The footman standing stiffly next to the sideboard hadn't removed his gaze from the far wall, but he was paid to ignore his employer's lapses.

This left only Simon to be irritated by his own behavior. He knew better. He'd been trained to govern his emotions. But exhaustion had frayed his normal restraint. Useless exhaustion, if he believed the article he'd just read in *The Times*—which at this point, he did.

"Emma, I'll take dinner at the club tonight," he said.

His wife looked up quickly, seemingly startled she'd

been addressed. When had breakfast become a silent affair? Simon vaguely remembered lively discussions and laughter, but that had been before he assumed the title and had taken his place in the House of Lords. For the past four years, he'd been absorbed with the duties of the estate and the responsibility of living up to his father's parliamentary reputation. Somehow, during that time, casual conversation at meals had leached away.

"You told me you could leave Parliament early tonight, so I accepted an invitation to the Pratmor's musicale in both our names." Emma's brow wrinkled. "Is there no way we could attend? Since so many people have already left town for the holidays, the guest list is limited and our absence will be noted."

He shook his head. "I need to spend the day canvassing for votes, and then I plan to leave the session early in the hope that I might find some untapped support at White's tonight. Men lose some of their rigidity after a good dinner and a few drinks. A great deal of 'work' gets done at White's. I still believe it's possible to find some sort of a compromise that will stop Lord Liverpool from forcing acceptance of these ill-conceived Six Acts."

Simon knew the chances of this happening were slim. But he had to try. Ever since the government's disastrous reaction to the huge mass meeting in Manchester last August, which had led to what was now being called the Peterloo Massacre, the Prime Minister and his cronies had been running scared. They imagined armed insurrection behind even the most benign of gatherings. Instead of addressing the root causes of the unrest—the inequities in male suffrage in the north, poor economic conditions exacerbated by the Corn Laws, and crippling unemployment—Lord Liverpool's government had responded with laws meant to repress the slightest dissent.

Simon was not alone in his opposition to these measures, but those who thought the Six Laws repugnant were in the minority, and many of those vocally in opposition were radicals whose ideas Simon found equally disturbing. His efforts to put together a coalition of centrists had not met with much success, leaving him both exhausted and discouraged. The last thing he wanted to do was attend an evening that featured someone's inept daughter plunking on the piano or screeching like an injured cat.

"Maybe you could go with your sister and her husband to the Pratmor's. I know Hadley is still in town, since I see him at the parliamentary sessions." Simon didn't mention that he would just as soon *not* see the Marquess of Hadley, who was one of Liverpool's most ardent supporters.

His wife glared at him. Glared? Emma didn't glare, but that was assuredly the look on her face. "Lucy has already taken the children up to Oakley. Hadley promised to join her within the next ten days. I assume we will be going to my parents' home within the same

232 • Hannah Meredith

timeframe. They're expecting us for the Christmas holidays."

Simon's enthusiasm for wasting a fortnight at his in-laws' drafty barn of a house in Cambridgeshire was limited. Emma's father would spend most of the time making it clear that Hadley was the favored son-in-law and pushing Simon to change his political views. The last thing he needed to add to his Christmas cheer was more political pressure.

He was also sure Hadley and Lucy's four demon offspring would escape the nursery as usual and create mayhem. During the Christmas visit to Emma's parents two years ago, the Hadley children had locked William, then three, in a chest, and it had taken a frantic hour to find their elder son. All in all, the Christmas season at Oakley was as much fun as having a tooth extracted.

But he had promised they would spend the holiday this year with Emma's parents, and so they would go. "Perhaps you could follow Lucy's lead and take the boys to Oakley next week. I'll follow as soon as Parliament finishes with these votes."

His wife's expressive face subtly shifted from irritation to disappointment. "How long will this take? Liverpool can't expect to keep both Lords and Commons in session through the Christmas season. I thought we would all go up together. As a... family."

He would swear he saw her lip tremble as she uttered the last words, but couldn't understand what had caused her to be upset. "Emma, I wish I had the freedom I enjoyed before my father died and I inherited the title—but that time has passed. I now have responsibilities, and I take them seriously. I don't know any other way to go on with my life. Since your uncle, rather than your father, inherited the title, you didn't see the toll that duty to one's estates and to the governance of the country can take. I'm sorry I can't stop what I'm doing and jaunt across the country at will."

"I wasn't asking you to stop anything. I simply wanted you to travel with the boys and me."

"And so I will. We'll just have to delay our departure a few days. And until we do leave, I know you'll stay busy with, eh, your charity."

"The Soldiers' Relief Committee."

Simon was glad he'd used a generic term since he'd thought Emma's favorite charity had something to do with orphans. He could have sworn he'd seen her stitching doll clothes. But he agreed that ex-soldiers were in need of help. So many brave men had returned from fighting Napoleon only to discover there was little work available for them. "Helping those who fought to preserve England is a worthy cause," he said, realizing he sounded pompous even though he meant the sentiment.

"I wish more textile manufacturers agreed with you. Two who promised to sell us blankets at a reasonable cost have increased their prices and one has reneged on his commitment completely. They all cite unrest in the

Midlands as their excuse."

Simon nearly smiled at Emma's providing him with the perfect exit line. "And it is to try to find a solution to the unrest in the Midlands that I have to get to the House of Lords." He placed his napkin on the table and stood. "Why don't you see if you can attend the musicale with one of the ladies in your soldiers' relief group? I'd hate to think you would miss something that you would enjoy."

He stopped by her place and leaned down to brush a kiss on her cheek. The faint scent of a spring garden that wafted from her soft hair stirred him. His sudden and inappropriate arousal surprised him, but it had been a while since he'd visited Emma's bed. When had that last been? He was chagrinned that he couldn't exactly remember. A fortnight perhaps? With parliamentary meetings lasting far into the night since the Peterloo Massacre, his attentions to his wife had been infrequent. He suddenly found this lapse disturbing.

He'd been working so hard on matters of the country's security, interspersed with the need to confer with his land stewards about getting the fall crops in, that he'd fallen into his own bed in a stupor for an embarrassing long period of time. But that was a failure of duty he would be able to address shortly. Will was five and Ben was nearly two. It was time they began working diligently on having another baby. A slight smile tugged at his lips. This was a responsibility he didn't begrudge.

Satisfied that he would soon put his domestic house in order, Simon's thoughts had turned to matters of state before he even stepped into the carriage.

Emma sat back with a contented sigh as she watched Diana, Lady Stanley, make neat stacks from the papers the other ladies had left strewn around the top of the dining room table in Diana's gracious home. The board meeting for the Soldiers' Relief Committee had been more successful than she could have anticipated.

"I can't believe you managed to get Lady Fairbourne to underwrite the additional costs of the blankets," Emma said. "Good Heavens, is the loosening of her purse strings a sign of the coming apocalypse?"

Diana's face crinkled into a mischievous smile. "Instead of the apocalypse, I think you might observe Lady Fairbourne's son dropping some of his rakish behavior and actually begin pursuing a wife in the months to come. I whispered some information into her ear that will allow her to bring him to heel—something she's been wanting to do for years."

"Oh, some choice gossip!" Emma sat up straighter in her chair. "No one ever tells me anything, so confess all."

Diana shook her head. "No one tells you any gossip because they know you will never circulate it, and what good is gossip if it simply stops with a single person told and doesn't make the rounds? Unfortunately, Emma, you have no talent for skewering your fellow man. In this case, however, the information I gave Lady Fairbourne only had the power to prompt her generosity if no one else is privy to it. I made her that promise, and I'm sticking to it, since the result is that our Boxing Day gifts to indigent soldiers and their families will be greatly improved."

"A worthy reason," Emma conceded, "but it's still frustrating that I never know anything scandalous. I'm sure notorious behavior is going on all around me, and I'm stuck being as oblivious as some naive young girl in her first season."

Diana laughed. "Well, you're my friend, and by some people's measure, that's scandalous all by itself."

Emma couldn't disagree with Diana's statement, since it was true. As a young, attractive widow of a much older man, Diana drew society's attention—and since she was frequently surrounded by adoring men, it was easy for the more malicious to arrive at the wrong conclusions. "Some people don't know what they're talking about," Emma countered.

Diana reached across the table and patted her hand. "Emma, you are a true friend. And since I'm your friend as well, I need to caution you not to loudly proclaim my innocence to every rumor or innuendo you hear. It could lead to embarrassment since I will admit to bending society's rules on occasion."

"What—"

"No, don't ask. I like your naivety. Being around you, as you are, makes me feel good. Just know that not all of us were as fortunate in our marriages as you are."

"I'm sorry if yours wasn't everything you'd hoped..."

"Don't be." Diana gave her a grin with an artificial edge that tugged at Emma's heart. "I pleased my parents and in the end, got what I wanted—wealth and independence. Even if I'm not someone mothers can hold up as an example to their daughters like you are, I'm still satisfied."

"I'm hardly an example." The idea was embarrassing.

"But you are. With so many girls reading those silly Minerva Press novels and, consequently, harboring unrealistic expectations of romantic love, you and Lord Trenton are the perfect illustration of an amicable partnership."

Emma wasn't sure she much liked her marriage being described as an *amicable partnership*. It sounded like it should characterize a couple in their seventies who tottered around holding on to each other to keep from falling. Surely, she and Simon weren't like that? They did get along well enough, so she guessed they were amicable, and like a pair of good carriage horses they pulled in the same direction, so in this respect, they were partners. Nonetheless, there was something about the description that stung.

"I suspect we both grew up reading those same Minerva books," she said.

"But we didn't believe real life was like that." Diana was adamant. "We knew compromises had to be made—and we made them. You and Lord Trenton have made a marriage that turned out as it should. Incredibly, you've been married for six years and you've supplied the necessary heir and a spare, and neither of you has strayed. I'd say that was worthy of emulation."

Emma wasn't sure if she was incredibly naive or if Diana was simply cynical. "Good Heavens, Diana. Being faithful to one's wedding vows is hardly something to celebrate. It's perfectly ordinary."

Her friend raised one skeptical eyebrow.

"All right," Emma conceded. "I'll admit that some men aren't faithful. Even I'm not that uninformed. But married ladies? No, I can't image that. How would they go about finding a... partner?"

Diana laughed. "For a woman, finding a partner is simple. Just go to any of the *ton* entertainments and flirt a bit. Propositions are thick on the ground at such places."

"Maybe for someone like you. You're not married. You're beautiful and—"

"And men think I'm available for an affair." She shrugged. "I might be, of course, if I could find the right man, but so far that hasn't happened. But if you even hinted that you were looking for some extramarital entertainment, you'd have more offers than you could handle."

Emma opened her mouth to disagree, but Diana held up a hand for silence. "Because *you* are beautiful," she said with certainty.

The idea seemed so foreign, Emma sat stunned. Her sister Lucy was the beautiful one in the family. That had been the consensus the whole time Emma was growing up. When she debuted, more than one gentleman was heard to lament that the younger Hightower daughter was brown haired, tall, and thin whereas her older sister had led them to believe that all the ladies in the family would be blonde and curvaceous. No, Emma had never been beautiful.

But when Simon had first started courting her, he'd acted as if she were. That was part of his magic. He made her feel beautiful and witty and cherished. All in all, heady feelings for an eighteen-year-old girl.

Now that she'd matured, she appreciated him for his more enduring attributes—his constancy, steadiness, and consideration. She was confident that Simon had always remained faithful, and that he would continue to be.

But somewhere deep inside lived the young girl who wished he still made her feel beautiful.

Emma shook her head. "No, I own a mirror and know what I look like. And I'm satisfied with myself. I have a pleasant face. Since my mother no longer controls what I wear, I dress well. I'm considered a more than adequate conversationalist, and my dinner partners are never bored. But I don't strike any prurient interest in men."

"Oh, how wrong you are. To prove my point, why don't we try an experiment? You asked me if I wanted to

240 • Hannah Meredith

attend the Pratmor's musicale—"

"And you said you weren't interested in an evening of caterwauling."

"Well, I've changed my mind. I'll go with you if you are willing to follow my lead and act as if you're interested in the men who are there. And I don't mean in their ideas. I mean interested in them, as men. I promise you'll have a definite following and at least one veiled indecent proposal."

Emma laughed. "Now you're being ridiculous. A following, no less, *and* an indecent proposal? That has never happened and it never will. You're describing men's reaction to you, not me."

"So you're afraid to even try the experiment?"

Diana certainly knew how to goad her. Emma liked to think of herself as fearless and her friend knew this to be the case. "I have no desire to have an affair," Emma said sharply.

"I know that! I'm not suggesting you actually do anything scandalous. You merely have to look as if you might entertain a gentleman's offer, and I'm sure you will get one. As a matter of fact, you probably already have and just missed the suggestion."

"Well, if I'm bound to miss this so called 'veiled proposal,' then there will be no way I can ascertain if your silly contention is right." Emma knew she should just tell her friend that she wasn't interested in doing any of this, but against her better judgment, she found herself intrigued.

"I'll be there to interpret. I've become very good at this since I've been widowed. It's important to recognize a proposition so it can be quickly deflected. This way there are no misunderstandings or hard feelings. I'll keep you safe, and it will be an adventure."

An adventure? That should not have sounded appealing, but it did. It might be fun to be the center of attention, just for one night.

"I'll do it," Emma said before she could change her mind. "But it will only prove I'm no good at attracting men."

"I'm quite sure it will prove the opposite, especially if you act like you know what you're doing. We still have time before you need to go home to dress for the evening. Let's ring for tea and I'll give you some pointers."

She shouldn't. This wasn't like her at all. But she was tired of being the competent matron whose marriage was described as a stupid *amicable partnership*. What could be the harm for a bit of playacting at a musicale? "Ring for tea," she said.

Simon found a vacant corner of the Members' Room at White's and collapsed into a comfortable chair. His efforts to find support for a compromise on the Six Acts had met with utter failure. Mostly, those he approached told him how disappointed his late father would have been in him—hardly a cheering message—and others had suggested he should perhaps seek membership in a more liberal club.

This last idea was not without merit, since White's seemed to house a collection of the most pigheaded men in London. The Earls of Trenton had been members of White's for over a hundred years, however. Simon believed his father would have understood his not following a Tory government if he thought them dangerously wrong. But his father would never have countenanced his abandoning White's.

He ordered a brandy and stretched out his long legs, hoping that position would ease the tightness across his back. He felt emotionally and mentally trampled, the result of frustration more than late nights, although this night had now crept into the small hours of the morning. Fortunately, this meant that most of the remaining members were gathered in the gaming areas and he could lick his wounds in private.

"Are you suffering an attack of the blue devils or did you drop more than you can afford at the faro table?"

So much for privacy, but the voice of an old friend was not unwelcome. "It's the blue devils, a condition partially induced by conversing with your esteemed father. Have a seat, Westmont."

David Grey, Earl of Westmont, slid into the chair opposite Simon and threw an order for a brandy over his shoulder to a nearby waiter. Then he held up his hand to stop the server's departure. "Did you want another, Simon? I know how trying my dear pater can be."

"Yes," Simon said with a nod. He had been abstemious with wine at dinner, wanting to keep all his wits about him. Now that seemed like a futile gesture.

"I'm assuming you asked my father to change his mind on parliamentary matters," Westmont said. "I could have told you that once he has formed an opinion, he cannot be swayed by logic. Lord knows I've been trying to do so for years. All to no avail."

Simon nodded. "This ability to ignore logic seems to be rampant within the House of Lords. I wish your father and his generation no ill, but I'd rather work with people who are not mired in the eighteenth century."

"I can agree with that, except I think my father is living in the fifteenth century. Since I'm his heir, he thinks he has complete control of my life. He is currently displeased with me because I haven't 'taken hold,' which in his lexicon means I haven't yet married and moved to one of the estates and begun producing the next generation."

Simon hated to give the Marquess of Fairbourne credit for being right about anything, but he agreed with the older man when it came to his opinions of what his only son should be doing with his life. He and Westmont were of an age, but his friend had, indeed, not "taken hold." Westmont spent most of his days, and definitely all of his nights, in pursuit of pleasure. Once one entered his thirties, there should be more to life than that.

However, past experience had shown Simon that trying to convince Westmont to change his ways was as futile as trying to get Fairbourne to reconsider his vote. Stubbornness was obviously a family trait.

The waiter arrived with their drinks, briefly forestalling any private conversation. When he left, Simon asked, "Other than haranguing you, what can your father do? And since it hasn't changed you yet, I'd think he would have concluded that yelling is ineffectual."

"Oh, he's figured out what he can do—and he's done it." Westmont's voice had risen, and he quickly looked around to see if anyone had noticed. The men in the nearby seating areas seemed oblivious, but he did continue in more modulated tones. "I've been getting the income from the estates that are assigned to the Westmont title since I reached my majority. But two weeks ago, my father called me in and informed me that he and a contingent of lawyers have determined those properties are still Fairbourne properties. The upshot is that those monies will now go into my father's accounts and I will be given an allowance.

"My God. I'm thirty-three years old and I'm supposed to live on an *allowance*?" Westmont took a large slug of his brandy as if the liquor would wash away what he evidently considered a dirty word.

"It's not all that peculiar," Simon said, trying to sound a reasonable note. "I was given an allowance until I married and took over the direct control of my own estates. But my father was mindful that a young man needed a generous amount to cut enough of a swath to be seen as an acceptable *parti* for the type of lady I should be pursuing. I'm sure your father will take that into consideration."

Westmont sat up straighter, his face a mask of incredulity. "You've just been dealing with him, and you think my father is a reasonable man? He's discovered he holds the leash and he's shortened it until I'm choking. To keep the money flowing, I even went to a musicale tonight."

"Pratmor's?"

"As if there could be two on one night? But I notice that you wisely were absent, although I did fight my way through the adoring crowd to give your lovely wife my regards."

"Oh, good. She found someone to attend with. When I left this morning, her plans were uncertain." Simon thought he sounded pleased to hear Emma was there. Westmont's comment that she was surrounded by men was irritating, however. Other men should most definitely *not* be buzzing around his wife.

"Lady Trenton was there with Lady Stanley. They held court during the intermission and at the supper afterwards. That was as it should be, of course, since they were the two delicious morsels at an otherwise tasteless feast."

"I would prefer if you didn't refer to my wife as a delicious morsel." The surge of anger that had shot through him at Westmont's suggestive comment shocked Simon. He'd never thought of himself as particularly possessive. Of course, the idea of Emma "holding court" also seemed profoundly wrong. He remembered his surprisingly physical reaction to the fresh, springtime scent of his wife's hair this morning. Had any of the men surrounding Emma this evening noticed and been similarly enticed?

He should have stayed at home or even gone to the stupid musicale. Instead, he had wasted his time in a quixotic attempt to make his fellow peers see reason. "To hell with them all." He gathered his legs under him and prepared to rise.

Westmont's hand on his arm stayed him. "I didn't mean any disrespect." His friend's face flushed with embarrassment. "You know I think highly of Lady Trenton, and I hope my choice of words didn't lead you to think otherwise."

Simons settled back into his chair. "No, my foul language wasn't directed at you. I've just come to the end of my tether with the stupidity of those who think they govern when they are only protecting their own importance. I suspect I will try again tomorrow, thus proving my own stubborn stupidity, but I'm now ready to call it a night."

"Before you go, I have a favor to ask of you. In honesty, I came here looking for you specifically to do so."

Simon was intrigued. He and Westmont had been friends since they both attended Eton, and he couldn't remember a single time Westmont had asked for anything. "If it's in my power to help you, you know I will."

Instead of immediately speaking, Westmont watched his hand as he moved his glass in a slow circle on the side table. "I need you to buy something for me."

His eyes then came up to meet Simon's. "I'll give you my vowels, and I'll repay in less than a week. Oh, Hell, this is demeaning. I told you my father has decided I'm to live by begging him for funds. Well, I don't have money for a large outlay, and he won't give it to me unless I have a legitimate need. I'm sure he'll give me the money to cover a debt of honor, however, so I'll tell him we gambled, and I lost, and I need to redeem my IOU."

"Just how much will you be losing, and what am I supposed to buy?" Simon was normally not inclined to do something underhanded, but the idea of tweaking the nose of the pompous Marquess of Fairbourne was definitely appealing. Fairbourne had been one of those who suggested Simon's behavior would have distressed his father, and that particular criticism had cut.

"I want you to meet me at Marshall's tomorrow and purchase a necklace I've already chosen." Westmont reached into his coat pocket, pulled out a folded sheet of notepaper, and handed it to Simon. "Here's my IOU to cover it."

The first genuine smile of the evening crossed Simon's face. "You seem quite confident that I would agree." He flipped open the note to discover a number that gave him pause. "My God, David. Are you buying the crown jewels? No one will think that I would have been playing this deep."

"My father has no idea of your gambling habits or of my level of play, so I don't think he will doubt this. And the necklace is a nice matched set of rubies."

"This necklace is for your *chère-amie*? Miss eh..."

"Makepeace. Belinda Makepeace. And before you begin to castigate me on the cost, it is a parting gift, only she will not immediately realize it. The rent on her house is paid up only for the next two months, and I won't have the money to extend the lease. So she will be leaving me. In fairness, I need to give her time to find another protector, but I shouldn't have to say anything for another month."

"And the price of this necklace is worth another month?" Simon had never had a mistress and had not realized keeping one could be so costly. He had heard of Belinda Makepeace, however; she was one of the most sought after of the demimonde. He'd not realized Westmont was her current protector.

"God yes, she's worth it."

"Do you harbor some affection for the girl?" Simon had heard of this happening, and had always thought it very sad.

His friend looked perplexed. "Affection? Probably not. But I burn for her. She's wildly inventive and the things she can do with her mouth..." Westmont's normally ruddy face darkened. Simon was surprised to realize the man was blushing. "I'm sure you know what I mean. You stole the march on all of us and married Emma Hightower before anyone realized what a gem she was. But I suspect I'm going to be stuck with one of the whey-faced warblers from tonight's musicale. At least that's my mother's idea. So I need something inspiring to remember when I'm doing my duty and producing an heir."

Simon refolded the note and placed it in his own coat packet. "I'll do it, but I need to tell you that I think you're a fool."

Westmont gave him a chagrinned smile. "And I don't need to tell you that there are some things that men are willing to be fools about."

They made arrangements to meet at the jewelers, and then each went his own way into the near-dawn of a cold, damp night. Two disturbing thoughts kept swirling through Simon's head while he was riding home in his carriage. The first was his reaction to Westmont's referring to Emma as a tasty morsel. He judged it to be more possessiveness than jealousy. Emma would never do anything untoward. But he did want every man to know that she was his.

Westmont had been correct. He had stolen the march on others when he asked for Emma's hand early in her first season. He remembered her as he had initially seen her. A slender reed of a girl with lush, coffee-colored hair and expressive, amber eyes. She'd been one of the ladies on his father's list of potential spouses. She was from a good family and had an adequate dowry, although not one that would tempt the impecunious. She was attractive but hadn't the flashy looks that so often accompanied those proclaimed to be one of that season's incomparables. Her open countenance and shy smile appealed to him.

In Emma Hightower, he saw a woman who would please him as well as please his father. So he'd begun a courtship that quickly saw them betrothed before the rest of the herd of expectant swains had realized she was there. He'd been proud to marry her and thought they would live a happy life—which for six years, they had.

But the timber of Westmont's voice when he said, "I burn for her," haunted Simon. He suspected he had never burned for anyone. And he now wondered if a part of life had slipped by him without his noticing.

Oh, he didn't wish to have a mistress. If nothing else, Westmont proved they were an expense that Simon felt was not worth having. Perhaps what disturbed him was his friend's assumption that Simon felt this way about his wife.

He had come to his marriage bed only slightly more knowledgeable than his virginal bride. He'd been trained to think that lusting after a woman showed a lack of moral fiber and so had resisted most of the temptations that lay before a wealthy, titled, young man. Most, but not all. He hadn't wanted to seem odd while at university. Nonetheless, his experience had been limited.

The sensation of being left behind stayed with him until he'd arrived home and prepared for bed. He went so far as to quietly open the connecting door to Emma's bedchamber, but the room was dark and Emma's breathing even. He could hardly rouse her and ask if she burned for him. She would think he had lost his senses.

So he returned to his own bed and finally slept as the first fingers of a dull day sneaked around the edges of his drapes.

Chapter Two

EMMA WAS DOWN ON THE NURSERY FLOOR where she simultaneously rolled a ball to Ben and made suggestions on the deployment of Will's troops. She wanted to interact with both boys, but if Ben got too close to Will's soldiers, he would immediately put one in his mouth. To avoid this, she'd seated him at a distance with his legs splayed to create a funnel to help him capture the ball. The problem was in getting Ben to return it with any accuracy. He was getting better, but the exact direction the ball would take was still questionable.

Since he faced the room's entrance, Ben was the first to see his father and alerted the others by shrilly calling. "Papa, Papa," as he ungainly clambered to his feet.

Emma looked over her shoulder to where Simon lounged in the doorway with one shoulder braced against the frame and a soft smile on his face. Diana had been right. By appearing to be more accessible, she'd been surrounded by men last night. But none of them had looked as inviting as Simon now did, standing in the nursery door.

As Ben approached his father, he held his hands above his head and imperiously demanded, "Up!" Simon reached down and swung their younger son onto his shoulders. Ben giggled and clenched his father's hair.

Will, ever on his dignity since they had explained to him a few months ago that he was Viscount Merrill and could expect everyone but close family to call him that, stood, bowed, and said, "Good morning, Father." Then he reverted to five-year-old Will and dashed to meet Simon as he walked into the room while his shoulder-rider bounced and laughed.

"Are you winning the battle?" Simon asked as he ruffled the curly hair of his older son.

"Yes, sir. The French are getting a trouncing."

"As they should be. Show me how you have your troops positioned."

Will proudly led the way to where Emma still sat. Balancing his burden until he was seated, Simon gracefully lowered himself to the floor. Then he leaned forward and tumbled Ben into a delighted heap on the nursery rug.

"I missed you at breakfast," Emma said, "but Vickers said you'd gotten home very late and were still abed. I hope your evening was successful."

"Very unsuccessful, and this contributed to my decision to miss the morning session at the House of Lords. I suspect there will be nothing but speeches by those who want their words preserved for posterity." He shook his head. "The fact that time will prove their shortsightedness hasn't occurred to them, since they are primarily enamored by the sound of their own voices."

"So these acts you feel are regressive will probably pass?" She read the answer in the slight slump to his shoulders. Emma felt her spirits similarly dip. Simon had worked so hard to change this outcome.

"I think there is little doubt. But I'll play it out until the end and have the satisfaction of knowing that I tried to do the right thing. For this morning, however, I'll have the pleasure of enjoying the boys, something I've been missing."

She could have told him that Ben and Will had missed his visits as well, but she didn't want to add guilt to his despondency. He'd invested a lot of his energy, as well as his time, in trying to defeat the Six Acts. Simon now seemed to think their passage was inevitable, and that had to be hard to accept.

But even the inevitability of defeat couldn't dim the essential man. He sat in a spill of pale winter light that slanted through the broad nursery windows and seemed to glow. Sandy haired, with a face made for smiling and a lanky fencer's body, he would have been arresting even without his expressive moss-green eyes. With them, he was devastating.

She had found him attractive from the first, and six years of marriage had not changed her opinion. Not for the first time, she wondered what he had seen in her. Was he satisfied with their *amicable partnership*? A shiver of doubt sneaked down her spine.

"While Ben and I try to help the French put up a decent fight and keep General Lord Merrill on his toes, tell me how the musicale went last night," Simon said.

Emma acquiesced to his suggestion and recounted her evening, bringing a smile to his face when she described some of those asked to sing. "What some of the performers lacked in talent, they made up for with enthusiasm," she concluded. "It was an enjoyable evening."

"I saw Westmont at the club later and he said much the same thing." As he spoke, Simon reached over and removed a toy soldier from the now-sleeping Ben's grasp. Will seemed oblivious that no one was actively opposing him and continued to give orders and attack.

"Yes, he greeted me there. I'll admit I was surprised to see him, and when I told him so, he said something cryptic about being there to placate his mother."

Simon grinned. "I think Lady Fairbourne has determined her eldest son is to marry and may have even chosen some potential brides. Westmont mentioned something about one of the singers being a possible candidate for marriage."

"Then one of his mother's requirements can't be the ability to stay on key." Emma doubted any prospective spouse had ever been eliminated for having a poor singing voice, but she did wonder if Westmont's sudden interest in marrying had anything to do with the information Diana had passed on to Lady Fairbourne.

Simons chuckled at her quip. The sound made her chest feel warm. Odd how none of last night's attentive gentleman had made her feel this way.

"How would Westmont's expectations differ from those of his mother?" she asked in honest curiosity.

"I doubt Westmont has specific requirements for a wife. With a mistress, he is probably more exacting. I hope my saying this doesn't offend you. I only mention it because he is currently keeping one of the demimonde who is in high demand."

He paused and toyed with the soldier he still held in his hand. "I think he will eventually marry a young lady of whom his parents would approve. You know—a girl from a good family who can eventually fulfil the duties of the Marchioness of Fairbourne. Someone who has a pleasing personality but no strong opinions that might threaten the present Lady Fairbourne's position. Attractive without necessarily being a beauty, since gorgeous women are often demanding. I think he will end up with someone who meets those rather standard expectations."

The flush of warmth Emma had felt watching Simons care for his younger son instantly disappeared. She realized *she* fulfilled the standard expectations. As had most of the girls she debuted with. Were they all interchangeable pieces from which one was chosen by a specific man simply because she seemed like the best fit—the one who could be the female half of a cursed *amicable partnership*?

She wondered if Simon had even chosen her or if he'd simply obeyed his father's dictates. She'd been so ridiculously proud when he'd shown her his marked favor. Handsome, charming Viscount Merrill, heir to the Earl of Trenton, was considered a major catch, and he had singled her out. Oh, she understood that one married for a host of logical reasons, but her eighteen-year-old heart wanted the attraction to be a love match. And even now, after years of marriage, she had still convinced herself that perhaps it was. Simon just had so many important things on his mind that he sometimes seemed to forget her.

She was a fool. She had thought she was special, and it was lowering to discover she was not. She'd been so pleased that her husband had deemed to spend a portion of the morning with her and his children. As if they should be thrilled with the crumbs of his attention.

Although she hadn't moved, Simon must have felt her withdrawal since he took her hand and said, "I need to leave for an appointment, but I'll be home in good time for dinner for a change. And I thought afterwards I'd... eh... like to visit your room." He gave her a hopeful, boyish look she now suspected was false. He'd been to her room so seldom recently, she was surprised he didn't need a map. She kept her mouth closed on that thought.

"I look forward to dinner, then," she said, since

there was no other reply possible. But she mentally added broodmare to the list of standard expectations.

Although Simon was a little early, he found Westmont pacing in front of Marshall's. The jewelry sparkling in the window normally attracted gawkers, but the blustery day had kept them away, leaving Westmont as the only person hovering near the door.

"You should have gone inside where it's warm," Simon said.

Westmont shrugged. "No, I'll wait out here. Keep myself at arms' length of the purchase, if you will. I doubt the parents would check on who bought the necklace I hope they never know about, but I'm being very careful. If they continue to restrict my funds, I'll be a pauper."

Simon thought his friend was overreacting, but subterfuge wasn't normally part of Simon's makeup, so he wasn't sure what degree of stealth was needed. "All right. Then tell me what I'm supposed to buy."

"Third case to the left. It's a ruby necklace set in gold and is the only one in that case. The price will also match the amount on the vowels I've given you."

Simon nodded and left his friend on the pavement. The transaction took surprisingly little time, although the owner, obviously delighted to have the Earl of Trenton as a customer, attempted to entice him to buy other baubles. There was a pair of delicate emerald earrings Simon thought would look lovely against

Emma's dark hair, but the style was so different from the rubies he didn't think the owner would believe they had both been purchased for the same woman.

When he exited, he saw Westmont looking in the window of the next store down. They met between the two shops. "I had your folly put in a suitable box but not wrapped." Simon held out the purchase. "I assume that's what you wanted."

"Perfect." Westmont happily took possession of the package with a broad grin.

"Well, you must let me know how your *chère-amie* likes it." Simon looked around for his coach.

"Now we need to go to White's and play some cards so there is a record of our game." Westmont continued grinning.

"Now wait a moment!" Simon was incredulous. "I agreed to buy the bloody necklace, but I didn't anticipate an entire mummer's play. This is hardly espionage for king and country."

"Come on, Trenton. It will only take an hour, and then I'll be completely covered. If anyone asks, we'll have witnesses to your winning the money I'll need to pay off my IOU."

Simon and his father had not always had the smoothest relationship. His father had been very exacting. But he could not imagine how Westmont interacted with his parents. Of course, if his father had been as idiotic and pigheaded as Lord Fairbourne, Simon might have had to descend to subterfuge. The decision seemed to be made when his coach arrived and Westmont stood at the door, expecting a ride.

In short order, he and Westmont were ensconced in White's blessedly warm cardroom. "What are we playing?" he asked.

Westmont looked up from where he was admiring his mistress's gift. "Piquet. I know you are the superior player, so it is a game you'd obviously win. That's why it's only going to take an hour for me to lose the price of this necklace."

Simon began shuffling the cards. "I appreciate your getting this over quickly. I promised Emma I would be home for dinner for a change. I fear I've been ignoring her and the boys with all this parliamentary mess, and she has subtly let me know she is becoming irritated."

"Subtly? How does one's wife indicate irritation subtly? I thought once a woman had the ring in your nose, she could jerk you whichever way she wanted."

"David, your concept of marriage is decidedly skewed. First of all, there is no ring in my nose. The only ring involved is the one on Emma's finger. And after years of marriage, a wise husband can tell irritation from his wife's behavior. You know... how she holds herself, the expression on her face, things like that."

Or in his case, a wife who distanced herself, but Simon couldn't bring himself to explain that. It was embarrassing to admit that he really didn't know what was going on in Emma's head. If there were such a person as a "wise husband," he doubted he qualified—

especially since just using those words made him sound like a bit of a prig.

Westmont looked dubious. "My only in-depth experience with married people comes from observing my parent's behavior, and there is certainly nothing subtle about either of them. Everyone in the entire house can tell when my mother is angry, since this attitude is punctuated by shouting and the slamming of doors. My father simply becomes absent, which does tend to calm the situation.

"Needless to say, watching them for my entire life has not made me want to leap into marital bliss. I'm going to have to declare for some chit shortly, however, whether I want to or not. I can only hope I'm as lucky as you are and find an attractive, willing wife. But even then, it seems like a lot of work for limited reward."

"Well, considering the massive outlay of coin that has necessitated this charade, I hope you are getting a lot of reward from your mistress, since you're definitely paying for it." Simon pushed the deck toward Westmont. "Cut."

Westmont drew a ten of hearts and Simon a queen of spades. "I'll take first deal," Simon said, knowing this would put him in an advantageous position when they reached the sixth and final game of the match.

"Of course you will," Westmont said dryly. "And for what it's worth, I'm well rewarded, usually more than twice a night. As I said earlier, Belinda is very talented."

Simon's hand froze mid-air before he flipped a card

onto the pile that would be Westmont's basic hand. "Define talented." Westmont had mentioned something like this before and it made little sense. Simon could understand talent in relation to things like drawing or singing or dancing, but sexual congress was simply what it was. Once again, he had the vague feeling that he was missing pieces of life.

"Using words to define something like this is difficult." Westmont grinned as he picked up and fanned his twelve cards. "It's more something one has to experience. But I'll try." He sat quietly for a moment, seeming to study his cards. "Belinda is limber and willing to attempt numerous exotic positions. She knows how and where to touch a man to heighten pleasure. She can make you last half the night and when you do reach the peak, it's shattering. I don't know what else to say. I'm sure you know what I mean."

Unfortunately, Simon really didn't. "You mean there is no affection?"

"Affection has nothing to do with it. This is recreation. Fun. If I wanted affection, I'd buy a dog."

"A dog would be a lot less expensive," Simon muttered.

Westmont laughed. "I heard that. And as an old married man, you should have said something about finding affection in marriage. I feel like you're letting your side down. Now, it is possible that I'll be delightfully surprised when I do get leg shackled, but, to be honest, I suspect the whole process within the bounds of matrimony will be... boring."

"Boring? Ye gads, where would you get that idea? Of course, it's true that you should treat your wife like a lady and be respectful and considerate, but no one wants to be bored."

"Your last statement is definitely true. There are quite a few wives who are looking for a little extracurricular entertainment—and they almost universally complain of being bored with their husbands." Westmont looked at him seriously. "Did you ever consider there is such a thing as too much respect? Wherever did you come up with these ideas?"

Simon felt he was on the defensive and wasn't quite sure why. "If you must know, my father sat me down before I married and pointed out that I was marrying a virginal lady and shouldn't expect her to act like a tart. He said I should always ask if it were a convenient time to visit and that I should control my urges and not do so too often, since constant breeding is bad for a lady's health. He told me there were some activities I should not expect or ask for—I can tell you that part of his lecture was damned uncomfortable—and that I should be considerate enough to leave shortly after, eh, it was completed."

"Oh, my Lord." Westmont looked down, shaking his head. Then he reached across the table and retrieved the score pad and pencil.

"What are you doing?"

"I'm scoring this bloody game. You'll be glad to

264 • Hannah Meredith

know you won all six hands in the *parti* and that at five pounds a point, I will owe you the amount shown on my vowels. I've decided we could more productively use our time talking rather than in pretending to play cards."

Westmont suddenly looked as serious as Simon had ever seen him. "Simon, there are things you need to know. The first being that your father gave you very bad advice."

Simon's first impulse was to be offended. But he was also intrigued. "I'll go get us a fresh drink while you finish the tally," he said.

Emma surveyed her reflection in the dressing table mirror as her maid slipped the final pin into her hair and stepped back. "It looks lovely, Dorcas," she said, turning her head from side to side. "While it is a bit elaborate for a family dinner, I think Lord Trenton will like it."

A knowing smile accompanied Dorcas' curtsey and she departed the room—leaving Emma beset with the insecurities and irritation that had bothered her all day. She wore a blue velvet gown Simon had once complimented. Her hair was set in a loser style that she thought made her look younger. All in all, she was as attractive as she could make herself.

But she couldn't understand her motivation for this concern. Whatever she did, she would never be more than someone who met the dashed *standard expectations*. How she wished she had never heard of them. She was attractive without being beautiful. She thought she had a pleasing personality, and she tried not to voice any strong opinions—although if Simon thought she didn't have any, he was a fool.

And, of course, she had been trained from birth to fulfill the duties of a peer's wife. Her parents' expectation had been that she would marry well. And she had. But she was beginning to wonder if she, and perhaps Simon, had fulfilled everyone else's requirements but had never asked themselves if this was what they wanted.

Had Simon had a list and carefully checked off each desired attribute? He had asked for her hand early in the season. Perhaps she was the first lady to reach the required number of checks, and he didn't want to be bothered with looking further. Heavens, what a depressing thought. But that would explain why his interest in her seemed to have waned after Ben's birth. She'd supplied the necessary heir and a spare, so there was no pressing need to produce other children.

Broodmare. Right, she didn't want to leave out that prerequisite. Was his interest in visiting her this evening because he wanted to try to catch up with her brother-in-law Hadley's number of offspring? She knew Simon and Hadley were politically at odds. Maybe this competitive impulse carried over into procreation. Well, if this were the case, Simon was bound for disappointment since the Hadleys already had four children and Emma was fairly certain Lucy was once again increasing.

She might take Diana's suggestion and bolster her self-worth by looking for some gentleman with whom she could have a discreet affair except... she cared for her husband. It had been rather fun to flirt at the musicale, but she couldn't imagine following up on it with any man she'd talked to. Simon was the only person who attracted her in *that* way.

Perhaps she was still holding on to her youthful hope of a love match. More likely, the physical intimacy she'd enjoyed with Simon had formed a bond that she was unwilling to break. More than flesh was joined in the act, and she could not take it casually.

She took one last look in the pier glass to make sure her appearance was all it could be and left her room. She felt ridiculously nervous, but she was going to get some straight answers from Simon tonight. She desperately needed to know his reasons for marrying her. Would he have been as satisfied with anyone who fulfilled the basic requirements or had there been something about her specifically that called to him?

If it did, indeed, turn out that she was interchangeable, she had the right to know. Simon's answer might hurt for the moment, but it would give some direction to her life. One had to know which direction was true north to chart a course.

By the time she reached the dining room, she'd mentally prepared herself. Whatever happened, she would know where she stood.

One of the footmen opened the door at her approach and she sailed in, battle flags flying—and stopped. The dining room glowed with candlelight as if they were entertaining, but only two places had been set, Simon in his usual place at the head of the table and a place for her to his immediate right. He quickly came forward and took her hand.

"You look lovely tonight, Emma," he said. "You've always been striking in rich colors."

Simon held out her chair. As she slipped into it, she noticed a potted plant to the left of her charger. Delight filled her when she recognized the flower. "Oh, a Christmas rose."

To Emma, the Christmas rose had always been a hopeful sign, since it bloomed in the dead of winter, sometimes even pushing its delicate blossoms through the snow. For this reason, it was much beloved in the cottage gardens near her father's estate and, consequently, spoke to her of her youth and a more innocent time. It wasn't a true rose, of course, but rather an evergreen member of the buttercup family with delicate, pale, rose-like flowers rising above dark, leathery leaves.

"I saw it in a florist's window and had to get it for you," Simon said. "You always comment on those that grow around Oakley, and I thought that since we were not yet there, I'd bring a bit of your family home to you."

Emma reached out and gently touched the soft

petals. They were a pale pink in the center that shaded to ivory at the tips and did look amazingly like an old-fashioned rose. "Thank you, Simon. This is a lovely gift." And then, as if noticing the hovering servants for the first time, nodded and said, "You may serve."

She had steeled herself to speak bluntly with Simon and realized to do so during the meal was impossible. She had no intention of airing her grievances in front of the staff. Grievances that now seemed so much less pressing. Ridiculously, her resolve had been weakened by the Christmas rose. Simon didn't usually give presents for no reason, and she was touched by the idea that he'd impulsively chosen something just to please her.

They spoke of innocuous things as the courses came and went—the boys; improvements that needed to be made at Friar's Hill, their estate in Essex; whether they would host a ball for Emma's cousin in the coming season. It had been so long since just the two of them had dined together, Emma had forgotten how congenial Simon could be. He had been so often absent, or they had been entertaining. But this meal was so enjoyable that the desert course seemed to come too soon.

"I'm assuming you will not sit here in solitary splendor and have some port," she said at the dinner's end.

Simon chuckled. "No, I'll sit with you while you have tea in the yellow parlor and have a brandy there instead."

As she stood, she picked up the small pot containing the Christmas rose. "I want to look at it," she said in answer to Simon's quizzical look.

"If I'd known a flower would have met with such enthusiasm, I would have been packing the house with them for years." He settled her shawl over her shoulders and escorted her into the hall.

"Why haven't you?"

"Why haven't I what?"

"Packed the house with flowers."

Simon hesitated and then guided her into the yellow parlor. A cheerful fire burned in the grate, making the room pleasantly warm. "It's hard for me to admit, but I probably suffered from the male misconception that flowers are only part of courtship. It was recently pointed out to me that I should have been bringing you flowers all along. This made me realize that I may have been putting emphasis on the wrong things."

He seated her on the sofa and backed away as a footman placed the tea tray on the table in front of her. As soon as the man exited, Simon closed the door and headed to the table that held decanters of liquors.

"I'll take a brandy instead of tea." Emma thought she sounded authoritative.

Simon raised one expressive eyebrow, but poured two glasses of the amber liquid. He handed one to her. "Dutch courage? I can tell you have been waiting to talk to me about something, and I assume it is not a comfortable topic or you would have broached it over dinner."

"Not Dutch courage. I simply felt like a brandy."

He smiled. "You've had it so often before?"

"On occasion." She didn't admit it was only one occasion, when she had sneaked into her father's study as a girl. She hadn't much liked the taste. After taking a sip, she discovered she still didn't, but she managed to not wince or make a face, so she hoped Simon wouldn't notice her reaction.

"Then it is I who evidently needs the courage." Simon sat down next to her, rolling the glass in his hands. "I've done some soul searching in the past few days, probably brought on by my failure to sway a significant number of peers to my way of thinking about the Six Acts. But whatever the motivation, assessing how I was living my life was overdue."

"How odd," she said, "since I too have been wondering how I ended up with the life I have."

A strange look that might have been alarm washed over Simon's face. "Well, I've come to realize my priorities were in the wrong places. My father always stressed parliamentary duty, and so, I thought I should be as conscientious as he had been. My responsibility to the earldom and all those associated with it had been drummed into my head from an early age; consequently, I needed to give that a lot of effort. I was the sole branch on the family tree, and it was essential I attend to these things. The upshot is that four years after his death, I am still trying to impress my father, a man who was more absent from my life than he was present."

He paused, but Emma simply nodded encouragement. She could have written a treatise on filial obligations. She well knew the frustration of never quite achieving parental expectations. What she had not known was that these same doubts plagued Simon. How disturbing that she'd missed this aspect of her husband.

Simon moved his glass towards his mouth again, but did not drink. "I now realize these duties are important, but they're not the *most* important. That position belongs to attention to family—and is the one thing my father did poorly. Maybe it was because my mother died when I was very young, but my father didn't know what to do with me as a boy, and this didn't change as I matured. He continued to give me the lowest priority in his life. I was horrified to discover I was doing the same thing to you and the boys. So, I wanted to tell you that I'm sorry, and with your help, I'll try to change." He raised the glass and took a long swallow.

Emma sat amazed. All her arguments were cast to the wind. All her guns spiked. A feeling of great tenderness welled up in her for the boy who had tried to make his father love him by treating the man's every utterance as if it were gospel. But one question still needed to be asked. "Did you marry me to satisfy your father or yourself? When you mentioned it this morning, I realized I met all of the standard expectations for a wife, and I wondered if I were just a convenient choice."

Simon placed his glass on the table with such force the sound made her jump. But the hands he brought to the sides of her face were gentle as he turned her to look directly into his eyes. "Emma, I married you because I wanted to live with you for the rest of my life. I didn't care who approved, or who didn't. From the moment I saw you, I knew what I wanted and I pursued you more diligently than I've ever pursued anything else. But then, when you *were* mine, I foolishly stopped the pursuit. I let the rest of life weigh me down and gave you the scant time that was left. I hope you will find it in your heart to forgive me."

And then he kissed her. Not the brush of lips she had become accustomed to, but a passionate, open-mouthed kiss that stirred her to her toes. She met him with equal abandon, her tongue dueling with his, her hands gripping his shoulders and then his neck. She'd forgotten what a kiss could be. It lasted minutes, hours, she wasn't sure, but when he pulled away, they were both breathless.

"Come to bed, beautiful Emma," he whispered, pulling her to her feet.

"Yes," she said, holding his hand as he led her from the room. At the door, she glanced back at the Christmas rose and knew the promise was true. There was hope when flowers bloomed in the middle of winter.

Chapter Three

EMMA SAT IN THE YELLOW PARLOR admiring the flower Simon had given her and feeling at peace with all the world. Last night had been a revelation. Simon had taken her to his room, saying he thought they needed a change of scene, and had convinced her that there was no need to ring for Dorcas since he could easily perform the duties of a lady's maid.

He'd proved to be rather inept at the task, but what followed was a mixture of embarrassment, titillation, and laughter. She'd never thought physical intimacy could be combined with such silliness. The result was a great deal of fun, which was a word she thought never to use in connection with marital relations. Simon had surprised her with some of his suggestions, but they all seemed to work. She felt a smile crease her face. Yes, some had worked rather spectacularly.

In the process, all her insecurities were swept away. She felt beautiful and cherished and somehow more in control of her own future. Emma had no idea what had brought about the change in Simon's attitude, but she liked it very much. Today, he'd even accompanied her for an hour of play with the boys before he'd had to leave for the House of Lords. He wanted to be there to record his "no" vote whenever the question was called.

She was feeling drowsy and contemplating a nap when Lady Stanley was announced. Good Heavens. Had she forgotten a meeting? Emma didn't think the previous evening had scrambled her wits to that extent. She was delighted to see her friend, but hoped there hadn't been some sort of disaster with getting the baskets for the soldiers put together.

No problem was evident when Diana came breezing into the room, her face split by a grin. "Sorry for the intrusion, but I just had to come by and tell you that Lady Fairbourne has outdone herself. She purchased some lovely warm scarves and hats in addition to the promised blankets. I know all the recipients will be delighted."

"Goodness, Lady Fairbourne has always held her purse strings tightly closed. Whatever was the impetus for this miracle?" Emma was truly delighted. The addition of hats and scarves would make the boxes seem more like gifts than just necessities.

"I believe the information I gave her has borne fruit." Diana looked very pleased with herself.

"Then please sit down and tell me all. Don't pretend this still needs to be kept a secret. I know you're dying to divulge every last detail." Emma grinned back at her friend. "I'll ring for tea."

"Oh, all right."

Emma nearly laughed aloud at Diana's unconvincing show of reluctance. She ordered refreshments, and they talked of innocuous things until the tea tray arrived and they were again alone.

After pouring their cups and offering her guest a choice of sweets, Emma could stand the suspense no longer. "So... what was the information that allowed such wonderful improvements to our Boxing Day offerings?"

Diana looked around as if expecting an eavesdropper to appear from under a table. Then she leaned forward. "Lord and Lady Fairbourne have been frantic to get their only son, Lord Westmont, to the altar. He's now over thirty, and they fear he will never fix on a suitable *parti*. Lady Fairbourne is convinced David's reluctance—"

"David?"

"Yes, David. I've known Westmont since we were children. And don't give me those raised eyebrows."

Emma consciously relaxed her forehead. "Well, continue."

"Before I was interrupted, my point was that Lady Fairbourne is convinced her son isn't looking for a wife because he's too attached to his mistress. But neither she nor her husband could ferret out the woman's name. If they asked Westmont's friends or acquaintances, they've been met with a conspiracy of silence."

"And you were evidently not part of this conspiracy."

"Not at all. I discovered the name by accident. But once I knew it, I decided to use my knowledge to the advantage of The Soldiers' Relief Committee."

Emma smothered a laugh. "For shame, Diana. You let Lady Fairbourne bribe you for the name."

Her friend gleefully nodded. "Yes, for a good cause."

"But I don't see how having the name will help the Fairbournes."

"Emma, even if Westmont has developed a tendre for his ladybird, I doubt the feeling is mutual. Oh, I'm not saying these women don't sometimes feel affection, but for them, this is a business, and they expect to be paid. Because he didn't know which woman Westmont was keeping, his father cut off his funds, assuming this would force Westmont's mistress to look for another protector."

Diana took a couple of dainty bites from one of the tarts. Emma recognized a stalling tactic to increase anticipation when she saw one. "Oh, cease your nibbling and get on with your tale."

Diana's demeanor could only be described as smug. "Well, the relationship between father and son has never been good, and Lady Fairbourne was concerned it would worsen if Westmont blamed his father for his mistress's loss. So, once she knew the woman's identity, Lady Fairbourne eliminated this possibility by buying the woman off. As far as Westmont knows, his ladybird will leave on her own, and she will be the only person he can, therefore, blame."

Emma knew she should be pleased that Diana had discovered a way to increase donations to destitute soldiers and their families—and she was, really. But she still felt a nagging sadness for the woman who was being paid to leave Westmont. It was entirely possible that his mistress did love him. Westmont was, after all, an appealing man. But such a woman won't have the luxury of loving where she willed. Lacking the protection of marriage, her situation was precarious. She had to be concerned with money.

"I can't imagine what it would be like to be a mistress," Emma said. "You have to feel sorry for women who are relegated to such a position. They have to do whatever some man wants for any type of security."

Diana barked out a loud, unladylike laugh. "Emma, you are such a goose. You have described most wives as well as mistresses. We all have to follow some man's dictates in exchange for security. The only difference is that a mistress may leave whenever she wants. Wives are stuck with whomever they, or more likely their parents, pulled out of the hat."

Emma opened her mouth to protest, but Diana hurried on. "I've told you before that you lead an exemplary life. You can't judge others' marriages by your own. Most wives are quietly smothering in their regimented lives."

Emma suspected Diana was describing her own life before she'd been widowed. With a jolt, she realized she might have said the same about her own, at least until last night, when Simon had apologized for ignoring her and made her feel like a bride again. She *was* a fortunate woman. She unconsciously touched the container holding the Christmas Rose. She was tempted to tell Diana what a discovery the last twenty-four hours had been, but that seemed indelicate.

Instead, she hugged her secret knowledge to herself and changed the subject. "I know it isn't Christmas yet, but I've put together some ideas for food to fill Easter baskets. I believe we can't start planning too soon. Would you like to see my ideas?"

Diana brightened. "Yes, I'd love to see what you've come up with. And we really should be making plans." Diana's feigned enthusiasm probably reflected her friend's relief at the return to a safer topic.

Emma got up and rummaged through the papers on her desk. After a few minutes of fruitless searching, she remembered she'd asked Whitman, Simon's secretary, to get her the prices for the foodstuffs she wanted to include in the baskets. He must have inadvertently left the list on Simon's desk.

"Give me a moment to retrieve the information from the office," she said and hurried down the hall.

As she'd anticipated, her list lay on top of a neat pile on her husband's desk. Whitman had carefully written prices next to her notations. As she snatched up her list, she dislodged the paper beneath it, and some sort of receipt fluttered to the floor. Emma bent to pick it up, more absorbed in the prices listed for the items she wanted—Heavens, hams had gotten dear—than in the fallen paper.

She glanced at it as she returned the paper to the stack and walked away—only to return to the desk for a second look when the name and the price on the receipt registered. Marshall's. It was an upscale jewelry store, although not one the family normally used. And the price... was astronomical.

A necklace. Rubies set in gold? Well, that made no sense. There was a magnificent ruby suite that was part of the jewelry passed down through the Trenton family, and Simon knew she seldom wore those pieces. She was simply not fond of that type of stone. So why would Simon spend such a ridiculous amount to buy a ruby necklace?

The answer came with a pain so sharp she had to grip the edge of the desk to remain standing. *The necklace wasn't intended for her.*

Against all her firmly held beliefs, Simon must have a mistress.

Any empathy she'd felt for these grasping harpies who prayed on other women's husbands immediately evaporated. How could Simon do this to her? Yes, they had grown apart recently, but they'd both been busy with their own concerns. Or at least, she thought it had been governmental or charitable endeavors that had taken up so much of their time.

Perhaps Simon had been involved in trysts with his mistress when he said he was in Parliament until the wee hours. Emma had a vivid mental image of some big-busted seductress wrapping her limbs around Simon's lanky form. Beautiful. Of course this woman would be more beautiful than she was. Someone without the hint of fine lines Emma had noticed radiating from the corners of her eyes. Someone without the pale abdominal marks that came from carrying her husband's progeny. Someone who knew what she was doing in bed and…

The teacakes she'd recently consumed threatened to make a reappearance. Last night's magic suddenly became tawdry. She'd wondered where Simon had gotten his new ideas—and now she knew.

Distress turned to anger. How could he do this to her? The list of supplies for the food baskets fell unheeded to the floor, but she clutched the damning receipt and left.

She must have looked as badly as she felt, for when she entered the yellow parlor, Diana jumped to her feet and asked, "Emma, whatever is the matter?"

"Simon has a mistress." the words blurted out before she had fully gotten into the room.

"*Your* husband? No, you must be mistaken. That's not possible. I've put this idea in your head with my foolish talk."

"It is most definitely possible. He left the evidence

of his illicit tryst out in plain sight. And don't suggest I buy her off. Simon has bought her a necklace that is worth more than what I have for pin money for the entire year."

And then, like the idiot she was, she burst into tears.

She felt Diana's arms come around her and guide her to her chair. Her friend handed her a handkerchief and ineffectually patted her shoulder. "Don't take on so. This has to be a momentary aberration. Just ignore it, and I promise things will go back to normal very soon."

Emma scrubbed at her eyes and blew her nose without concern for the propriety of her actions. Since she undoubtedly looked a mess, she might as well act uncouth. "I can't ignore this." She hated the way her words came out all breathy and choppy. "Simon spent a huge amount to satisfy his paramour, and he bought me a bloody flower. And I was so stupidly pleased with it. I thought it was a symbol of love enduring in adverse conditions. Love? Now there is a foolish thought, a childish wish I should have long ago outgrown. He never loved me or even expected to. I'm simply someone who met the standard expectations."

Diana continued to thump her shoulder as if she could think of no other method of comfort. "You're distraught. You need to calm down and then you'll see more clearly how you should respond."

Emma doubted she would ever calm down, but she was already coming up with her response.

❖ ❖ ❖

Simon slipped out a side door, feeling like he was a poor scholar escaping his tutor. It was obvious the question would not be called tonight, and he had better things to do than sit around the House of Lords. He unconsciously smiled. Yes, he had *much* better things to do.

Although he hadn't told Emma he would be home in time for dinner, he hoped it would be a happy surprise. The kitchen always had an abundance of food, so his arrival should only require setting an extra plate. Or perhaps he could enter through the kitchen and arrange something more intimate—like dinner in his bedroom. It could be a picnic, dining *al fresco* except this would be... he searched his mind for the Italian word for bed... dining *al letto*. Oh, that had a nice ring to it.

By the time his coach was brought around, he was actually chuckling at the mental images that presented themselves when he expanded the idea of dining *al letto*. His father had certainly never mentioned such a possibility when he took Simon aside before his wedding. But judging from last night, Simon was beginning to think his father had gotten more than a few things wrong. He was sure his father had never mentioned anything about laughing in the bedchamber. He had made the very act of intimacy sound like dreary duty.

Yes, his father would have been appalled if he'd witnessed Simon and Emma's recent behavior. It had been wonderful fun. But he did need to check with

Westmont about one of the positions they'd tried. Neither he nor Emma could figure out exactly how to bend to get things to, well, fit. The attempt, however, had been quite enjoyable.

Of course, his father would also be appalled with his leaving the House of Lords before the session had ended. But he now doubted that his father had prioritized aspects of his life correctly. His father had been absent so often, Simon felt he had never really known the man. How sad. This wasn't how he wanted his children to remember him. While he would not shirk his duties, he didn't want them to be the measure of his life.

When the coach arrived at his townhouse, he leaped out before the steps were set. He felt amazingly young and energetic as he strode through the front door just as it was being opened. He put his finger to his lip to indicate quiet and then softly asked the butler, "Where is Lady Trenton?"

"I believe she's in her chambers," the man said.

Good. Emma was not yet down for dinner. Simon grinned. His *al letto* plan could work. "Would you ask the cook to pack a picnic basket with whatever is handy for such a meal. And include a couple of bottles of the better Claret. Then send it to my bedchamber."

If the butler looked briefly nonplussed, Simon didn't notice. As soon as he had made his request, Simon was taking the stairs two at a time. He stopped in front of Emma's door to tug down his waistcoat and finger-comb his hair. Should he knock or just walk in? Dorcas was probably helping his wife dress for dinner, and Emma might be in dishabille. On that lovely thought, he grinned and opened the door.

Dorcas was indeed helping Emma, but his wife was fully clothed and engrossed in choosing gowns to go into a truck Dorcas was packing. Emma looked up, surprised by his entry.

"What do you want?" Her voice was as cold as the winter wind.

This was not the reception Simon had anticipated. "I was going to ask you to join me for a picnic in, eh, my rooms." The look on her face dissuaded him from mentioning anything about dining *al letto*. "What are you doing?"

"Packing to take the boys to my parents." And she returned to the task as if he weren't there.

"I thought you wanted us to all go up together."

"Circumstances are such that I've changed my mind."

"What circumstances?" Simon could tell Emma was angry, but he had no idea of the cause.

"Dorcas, please leave us." Emma said.

They both stood frozen as the maid departed. The minute the door clicked shut, Simon turned back toward Emma and was just in time to dodge the shoe she flung at him.

"Emma, what in blazes is going on?"

She picked up the shoe's mate, but didn't throw it at

him. Instead, she charged across the room, her arm raised to pummel him. While one part of him remained baffled, another part, located below his waist, registered that Emma looked magnificent in her fury.

She took a wide swing at him that he easily avoided. "Did you think I wouldn't discover you had a mistress? Here I've been dutifully waiting at home for you to finish your 'parliamentary business', putting off going to my parents for the Christmas holidays, and all this time, you've been visiting your ladybird."

"I do not have a mistress!" Simon was baffled by her behavior. Where had this peculiar idea come from?

"Then I'd like you to explain your purchase of an expensive ruby necklace."

Simon relaxed. So *that* was the problem. "Emma, I bought that necklace for someone else."

It was then she threw the second shoe. She was so much closer he didn't have time to take evasive action, and the shoe connected solidly with his shoulder. The damned thing hurt.

"I know you bought rubies for *someone else*, since it's not a secret that I don't like them. Consequently, you can just spend your Christmas with this wonderful *someone else*. You obviously don't need either me or the boys."

As she turned to begin shoveling clothes into the trunk, Simon saw the tears in her eyes. How in the Hell had he gotten into such a coil when he was blameless? He held out his hands in a placating manner. "You must

286 • Hannah Meredith

listen to me. There is no mistress. There never has been a mistress. I purchased the necklace for a friend so he could give it to his m... eh, friend. He is paying me back for the purchase price." He smiled reassuringly.

"There are entirely too many *friends* in your explanation—and I don't believe a word you're saying." Emma wouldn't look at him. She just continued going through the motions of packing.

Simon approached her as he would a skittish horse. When he was close enough, he softly wrapped his hands around both her upper arms. "Sweetheart, you need to listen to me. Your conclusions are completely wrong."

"Don't call me sweetheart and don't touch me. I feel like you're using my emotions against me." She spoke quietly, but tears streaked down her face. Her desolate expression stabbed Simon like a knife in the gut.

"What can I do to make you understand?" Simon was at a loss. He was noted for being truthful and had no idea why his wife would suddenly choose to question his honesty.

"For right now, could you just leave? Having you around hurts me."

Simon let his hands drop. He'd been upset by his inability to convince his peers that the Six Acts would be a disaster, but that emotion didn't compare to the feeling of defeat Emma's doubt engendered. He would have to drag Westmont here to explain what had happened. Sadly, Emma would continue to question whatever he told her—but would probably recognize the truth when someone else showed it to her.

Yesterday he'd thought he and Emma were moving toward a better understanding. Today, that hope was gone. He desperately wanted it back, however, and he'd make it happen.

"I'll do as you ask," he said quietly and left the room.

As soon as the door closed behind him, his subdued attitude fell away. He needed to find Westmont and get him back here quickly. He would do everything he could to stop Emma and the boys from leaving London without him.

He passed a footman bringing up the picnic basket. Refusing to be saddened by opportunities lost, Simon told him to take it to Lady Trenton's room. He was sure Emma hadn't eaten and she would be hungry.

Urgency burning through him, he paced the front hall until the coach arrived. He hoped Westmont would be at White's. Unless he was with his mistress and receiving his just rewards for his magnificent gift, White's was the logical place to start. If Westmont wasn't there, at least someone might be able to give Simon his direction.

When he reached the club, Simon told his coachman to stay close in case they had to leave again and dashed inside. The doorman was perplexed when Simon refused to relinquish his coat. "Is the Earl of Westmont here?" Simon asked the frustrated man.

"I'm sorry milord. The earl is not here this evening."

This was the first of a dozen times that Simon was

to hear that same, hateful sentence. Westmont had gone to ground and no one knew where he was. Of course, that didn't keep those he asked from offering suggestions of where to look, and Simon had no option but to follow the slightest lead.

Simon visited more gambling hells than he thought existed, and since most of these establishments wouldn't confirm who was in attendance, Simon had to prowl through a series of progressively seedier gambling dens and stare through the smoke at every likely figure.

Finally, shortly before dawn, one drunken sot was able to give him the address of Westmont's love nest. Or at least Simon hoped it was the address. Westmont had been very closed mouthed about where he'd sequestered his mistress.

Hurrying outside, Simon roused his sleeping coachman. The man had begun to leave the carriage where it had stopped. A wise decision considering how many locations they had visited on this ridiculous search. The coachman, wrapped in a great coat and multiple scarves against the cold, grunted in what Simon took to be assent. The man was due some days off and a nice bonus to compensate for this exhausting night.

In fairly short order, they arrived at a well-kept property in a solid middle class neighborhood. Simon's first blurry thought was that this location was costing Westmont a pretty penny. His second was to note that no lights were visible from inside the house. With a hint of sun glimmering on the horizon, Simon thought the servants should be stirring, but everyone inside must still be in bed.

Well, it was time for them to be up and about anyway. He banged the knocker vigorously. And waited. When a candle's gleam showed in the sidelights, he knocked again. The door cracked open to reveal an older woman with her cap askew and wrapped in a bed robe. Presumably the newly awakened housekeeper.

"Is Lord Westmont here?" Simon asked for what seemed the hundredth time. His tired voice sounded hoarse.

"Yes, but he's abed." The woman started to close the door.

Politeness, propriety, all of those supposed virtues fled. Simon stuck his foot in the crack and gave the door a push. The woman opened her mouth, probably to cry murder and mayhem.

"I'm sorry," Simon quickly said in an effort to keep her from screaming the house down, "but this is an emergency. I must see Lord Westmont."

"Has something happened to Miss Makepeace?" the housekeeper was suddenly all concern. As far as Simon knew, Belinda Makepeace was currently sharing Westmont's bed and nothing had happen to her. Simon could not guarantee the same could be said for Westmont once he got his hands on him.

"No, this is about another matter, but it is most

urgent."

The older woman scuttled toward the stairs and Simon stayed right with her. She looked at him askance, but if she thought he would remain in the entry hall, she was mistaken. Evidently resigned to his forward behavior, she continued up the stairs and knocked softly on the second door.

"I'll do this," Simon said, banging his fist on the door panels.

There was a sound. Probably a groan, but Simon took it as permission to enter. A narrow shaft of pale light filtered in around the edges of the drapes and illuminated the single figure on the bed. Dressed in his pantaloons and shirt, Westmont lay diagonally across the rumpled covers.

"Westmont, you ass, get up. I need you." Simon's shout as he charged across the room elicited only another groan. A gasp from the doorway behind him reminded him of the housekeeper's presence. When he yelled for her to go, she quickly disappeared.

Unfortunately, Westmont didn't respond in the same manner. Instead, he responded not at all. Simon grasped him by the shoulder and gave him a solid shake. Westmont batted at Simon's hand and grunted. Was a grunt an improvement over a groan? Simon had no idea, but the miasma of alcohol that surrounded Westmont left no doubt that the man was well and truly foxed.

In desperation, Simon grabbed the pitcher from the washstand and poured its contents on his friend. That brought Westmont to a wavering, sitting position. He wiped the water off his face and squinted his eyes in an attempt to focus on Simon.

"What are you doing here?" Westmont asked, then his face crumpled. "She's gone."

Simon glanced at the light coming through the curtains. "No, she's not gone yet. It will take some time to assemble the traveling coach and a baggage coach not to mention the time needed to load everything and get the boys settled and—"

"What in the hell are you talking about. Belinda doesn't have coaches. If she's left town, she probably took the stage. But that makes no difference; she's still left *me*."

Simon didn't care in the least what had happened to blasted Belinda. "I'm talking about *my wife*, not your ladybird. Lady Trenton is going to leave me if I don't get you to my house to explain about that damned necklace before she departs."

Westmont made a hiccupping sound that may have been a sob. "Oh, God, the necklace. I didn't even have a chance to give Belinda the necklace."

"Good. Since she's already departed, you can return the bloody necklace and get your—well, my—money back. But right now you can get your carcass up, get dressed, and come talk to my wife."

Westmont began moving off the bed with the speed of a slug. Simon grabbed his shirtfront and had him standing upright on the floor in one move.

"I'm getting there," Westmont said, brushing at Simon's grasping hand. "What does your wife need to know from me, anyway?"

"She needs to hear from you that the necklace is yours. That I bought it as a favor and you're going to pay me back."

"Your wife is worried about money?" Westmont looked so happily incredulous that Simon had trouble controlling the urge to shake him until his head snapped off.

"No, you bloody idiot. My wife thinks *I* bought the damned necklace to give to *my* nonexistent mistress—and she's taking my children and going home to her parents. And you are the only one who can stop her."

"Oh, I say. Then we should get moving." Westmont matched action to comment and lurched across the room to begin stuffing his arms into his wrinkled waistcoat.

Finally! Simon gathered u the strewn clothing and acted as Westmont's valet. The process went more rapidly than Simon would have anticipated, although the result still left Westmont looking like a disheveled drunk. Simon had the terrible feeling that they looked like a matched pair, even though Simon had avoided alcohol all night.

Westmont was still trying to tie his cravat when Simon hustled him into the carriage. Their progress was slow, however, since at this early morning hour, the streets were frequently blocked by delivery drays.

When they finally arrived at the Trenton townhouse, Simon unceremoniously herded Westmont inside.

"Is Lady Trenton still in her rooms," Simon asked as they breezed by the butler on their way to the stairs.

"No, milord. Lady Trenton had everyone up and working before dawn so she and the young masters could be off as soon as it was light enough to see the road. She needed the early start since she plans to overnight at the Penhurst's estate." The butler managed to sound officious and put-upon at the same time.

His pronouncement stopped Simon cold with his foot on the second step. He swiveled around and collapsed onto the stair. Bloody, bloody hell. Emma was gone. His first impulse was to call for a horse and go pounding after her, but the discovery that she had left him brought the full weight of this horrible night down on top of him. He sat exhausted, unable to move.

He had to get some sleep before galloping off or he would end up falling into a ditch. He did some mental calculations. If he slept for even three hours, he could function, and if he rode hard, he could be at Penhurst's just shortly after sunset. He would simply have to drag Westmont with him and explain to Emma there.

It wasn't ideal, but it was doable. He raised his head from where it was resting in his hands and began giving orders to put his plan into effect.

Chapter Four

ONLY AFTER THE BOYS AND NANNY had finally dozed off could Emma release the tears that had been gathering all morning. She'd kept them at bay by strength of will, frantic movement, and the necessity to present a calm face to her children. But now, she was bereft of all three supports—the boys were asleep, she could do nothing but sit in the coach, and her will had crumbled. She pushed her hand against her mouth to help choke back the sobs. She didn't want to awaken her children or employee and allow them to see her pitiful state.

Dear Lord, what had she done? She had been so hurt when she found that damning receipt. The betrayal was doubly sharp because she'd thought she and Simon had just found a new delight in their marriage. She felt as if her husband truly saw her and she mattered. To discover it was all a lie was devastating.

Hurt had quickly turned to anger. No, fury was the better word, for she was indeed furious. At Simon for his inconstancy and neglect. At herself for allowing youthful fantasies to intrude into the real world—a world where she was simply a woman who met the *standard expectations* to form an *amicable partnership*.

How she hated both of those terms. She didn't want either to define her or form the parameters of her life. She wanted to be someone special, not some interchangeable piece. No, she was being disingenuous. She wanted to be someone special *to Simon*. The rest of the world could go hang.

And so, in her anger, she had rejected her husband, disrupted the household, and dragged her sleepy children out into a freezing dawn to flee to her parents' home. Could she have acted any more foolishly? If there was one place in all of England she was guaranteed *not* to feel special, it was at Oakley. There the important person had always been Lucy. Golden Lucy. Lucy who married a stanchly Tory marquess.

Growing up at Oakley, there had seemed to be little attention available for her, for Emma, the second daughter who had never developed into the society beauty so essential to her mother. Even after she'd somehow managed to marry an earl, the accomplishment was ignored since her husband had suspicious, liberal tendencies.

So why was she hastening to Oakley? Oh, she was foolish in the extreme.

Her greatest fear, however, was that she'd been wrong about Simon and the entire situation. His look of utter incomprehension remained vividly in her mind.

His stumbling explanation seemed to indicate guilt, but what if it simply showed shock?

Oh, dear Lord, what if she had been wrong?

Weeping would repair nothing, but it was all she seemed to be able to do. Sobs kept welling up from the depths of her soul. Logically she could tell herself that part of the problem was the season. Christmas was always an emotional time, a holiday when families would gather to celebrate the birth of Christ. And family is what Emma wanted most. Not the one of her youth, but a family made up of her, Simon, and the boys—a family filled with caring and support and laughter.

When she had first married, she believed she'd found what she most desired. She thought she could build this perfect family with Simon. When Will was born, she was sure she had. She remembered Simon holding his newborn son and looking at her as if she had wrought a miracle that had not been replicated in all of history.

Then Simon's father had unexpectedly died, and the loving family she thought they were building began to erode away. And now, by her leaving, she'd kicked over any remains and utterly destroyed her hope.

She needed to stop this useless blubbering and see if something could be rebuilt. Even if Simon were lying—and at this point, she couldn't honestly say that he was—she could win him back. She had won him once, and she could do it again. Even if she had been just a convenient choice, she had still been *his* choice.

The stupid experiment Diana had talked her into trying at Pratmor's musicale proved she was not without her own attraction. She'd simply had to pay attention to the gentlemen to have them pay attention to her. Perhaps part of the distance that had grown up between her and Simon was her doing. She was forced to admit that she didn't always make an effort to attract her own husband.

But she obviously continued to see some hope for the future. She had been unable to leave the Christmas rose behind, and it now sat in a box in the corner of the coach floor, carefully placed at a distance from the foot warmer to keep it from becoming overly warm. The fact that the flower was there acted as a talisman to ensure that her dreams could be resurrected.

By the time Ben's restlessness had awakened Nanny and Will, Emma's eyes were dry and her mind was at ease.

"I'm sorry I dragged you on a useless journey," Emma said to Nanny. "I've decided I should have waited for Lord Trenton to accompany us, so at the next change of horses, I'm going to ask the coachman to take us back to London."

The older woman gave no indication this news came as a surprise. She simply nodded and tried to keep Ben from kicking his brother. Ben had discovered this game early in the trip and seemed to delight in making Will either complain or retaliate.

"Oh, give the wiggle worm to me," Emma said

holding out her arms. "Perhaps then you and Will can enjoy looking at some of the books we've brought." When Nanny relinquished her charge and rummaged in the wicker basket that contained some of the boy's toys, Will, who had been looking bored, suddenly perked up. This ill-advised trip had been hard on all of them.

Emma settled Ben on her lap. "Shall we look for white horses?" she asked, pointing to the window. "I'm sure I saw some just a while ago."

Ben's nose went to the window like a hound on a scent. He loved white horses. It was quickly becoming apparent that his first pony would only meet approval if it were that color.

The day was cold and dreary with mist and occasional spits of sleet. The coachmen and the footmen on both carriages would be frozen to the bone. The weight of Emma's regret pressed down harder. But she was rectifying her impulsive action as quickly as she could.

Emma pointed out cows and the tall steeple of a church in a village they passed, but Ben soon became disinterested when no white horses appeared. "Down," he said, pushing against her.

"Mind the foot warmer," she said, lowering him to the floor. She didn't want him tripping over it, but the padded metal box had cooled enough that there was no worry of his being burnt. They would need to refill the warmer with hot coals at the next coaching inn if the trip back to London was to be the least bit comfortable.

And she hoped the inn had some small sweets. Cook had sent along chocolate biscuits, but the boys had already gobbled down the entire batch. Emma began making a mental list of anything else they would need to purchase as Ben happily trundled from bench to bench.

And then there was screaming. The loud, I'm-in-pain cry that is immediately recognizable to any parent. Emma's heart leaped into her throat and she looked down at Ben, who sat on the carriage floor, pawing at his mouth, and wailing.

She immediately swooped down and picked him up. "Shush, love. Mama has you. What's amiss?"

Ben continued to cry pitifully, constantly rubbing at his mouth. Emma caught his hands and pulled them away from his face. Nanny, who was partially standing and leaning over to see the problem, reached down and removed a piece of petal and a chewed piece of leaf from Ben's face. Nanny held up the foliage. "What is this, milady?"

Recognition jolted through Emma. "Ben's eaten some of my Christmas rose."

"Oh, no, milady. Christmas rose? It's poisonous. His mouth must feel afire. We need to flush it with water and get him to a doctor."

Poisoned! Dear Heavens. Poisoned by her flower. Emma was having trouble getting her breath. Calm. She must be calm and clear thinking for Ben's sake. "Water's in the food hamper," she said to Nanny in a rusty voice. Then she banged with all her might on the front partition.

The coach slowed. Before it had fully stopped, a footman thrust his head in through the door. "Is there a problem, Milady?"

How could there not be? Ben continued to scream as if tortured by devils. "Tell the coachman to get us to the next village at all speed. We need a doctor. Master Benjamin has been poisoned."

The information must have been yelled to the coachman since the coach suddenly rocked into motion and they seemed to be flying. Ruts in the road nearly bounced Emma from her seat, but she clutched the screaming Ben, held her position, and prayed.

She realized she was much more than foolish. She had left her husband and poisoned her child. Her behavior had led to disaster.

The morning had begun cold and overcast. Westmont, who still hovered somewhere between drunkenness and its later effects, kept up a constant litany of complaints about the necessity to ride horseback in such inclement weather. Within a few hours, however, he was silent. Simon assumed the man was as miserable as he himself was, and it took too much effort to keep voicing his discomfort.

The leaden skies had changed to a chilling mist that was interspersed with a fine, stinging sleet. The damp had finally seeped through Simon's greatcoat and every part of his body was cold. His hands in their sodden gloves were beginning to lose feeling and while he had two wool scarves wrapped tightly around his head, he was not sure his ears were still attached.

The one bright spot was that they were making good time. They'd pushed the horses hard, however, and would have to get some others at the coaching inn in Terrell. Simon hoped they had something worth riding available. He was miserable enough without being pounded to pieces by the gait of a heavy-footed carthorse. He glanced back to make sure the silent Westmont still followed and was relieved to see his friend's hunched form as they pressed doggedly on. Perhaps when they stopped for fresh horses, they could afford twenty minutes in front of a fire to reanimate their extremities. He could see the high steeple of the church in Terrell, so it couldn't be much further.

They had just rounded a copse of bare trees when a rider appeared from the opposite direction. He was coming at a full gallop and Simon thought enviously that the man must be nearing his destination to press his horse so. The rider was almost upon them when Simon recognized his own livery.

He brought his horse to a jarring stop and began waving his hands in the air. "Trenton, Trenton, ho!" he yelled in his most carrying voice, hoping the man could hear him over the noise of his horse's hooves. Behind him, a surprised Westmont uttered an expletive as he barely avoided riding into him.

The oncoming man sawed at the reins and overshot

Simon by only a short distance. He immediately swung his horse back to where Simon's horse stood. "Oh, Lord Trenton. Thank Heavens it's you. How did you know?"

"Know what?" Simon's voice was tight. Why would one of his footmen be rushing back the way they had come? He vividly saw a carriage accident. The mangled coach overturned in a ditch. Emma and the boys lying injured on the road. His agitation passed through his suddenly tightened knees to his horse, which sidestepped and tossed his head.

"Her ladyship sent me to ride like the wind to London and bring you back. Master Benjamin has been poisoned, and they're waiting for a doctor at a small inn in Merkton, on the other side of Terrell a couple of miles."

Before the man finished speaking, Simon was already in motion. He shouted his thanks to the footman and kicked his tired horse into a gallop. He heard hoof beats pounding after him. Westmont and probably the footman. Simon wished he had a doctor following him as well.

Ben poisoned! His tired brain now conjured the image of his youngest son writhing in agony. How could this have happened? But as soon as the thought crossed his mind, he knew how. Ben put everything within reach into his mouth. Rat poison was a likely suspect. It could be found in most any stable, and the coach would have stopped to change horses—good Lord. Rat poison! As a boy he'd seen a terrier pup die from eating it. Once conjured, the image of the whimpering animal would not leave his mind.

Simon was breathing as hard as his laboring mount by the time he arrived in the small village of Merkton. His family's location was immediately obvious. The Trenton traveling coach sat to one side of the courtyard of a small but respectable looking inn. In a move that would have made an equestrian at Astley's proud, Simon dismounted while his horse was still trotting. The momentum caused him to stumble and fall to his knees, but he clambered to his feet and sprinted through the inn door.

The small entry hall was empty, but the doorway leading to the common room was filled with servants and perhaps a few guests, all gawking at what must be an ongoing spectacle.

"Lady Trenton?" he asked. "Where is she?" When there was no response he tried, "Where's the sick child from the carriage?"

Immediately one of the servers leaped forward. "If you would follow me, sir. The party and the doctor are in the private lounge."

Simon more pushed than followed the portly woman, his need to get to Ben was so great, but he did feel some relief that a doctor was in attendance. He was able to take a full breath by the time he pushed open the appropriate door.

The room was cold in spite of a newly kindled fire. Ben lay on a settee pushed close to the hearth; a small man, presumably the doctor, leaned over him. Emma knelt next to Ben, but leaped to her feet when Simon entered. With a startled cry, she dashed across the room, threw herself into Simon's arms, and buried her tear-stained face in his wet greatcoat.

"Is he...? Is Ben...?" His voice didn't want to work.

"The boy will be fine," the doctor said, straightening to reveal a small, almost child-sized stature. "I've given him some laudanum to mask the burning in his mouth, which will dissipate naturally by tomorrow." He advanced toward where Simon held Emma and extended his hand. "I take it you are the father. I'm Dr. Ashe."

"Yes, I'm Trenton. I can't tell you how pleased I am to see there was a physician available." Since Emma stayed attached to his chest, Simon had to lean to one side to shake the man's hand.

Emma must have realized Simon's awkward position. She stepped back and took his hand. "Come see how Ben is doing."

Only the head of his younger son peeked out from what seemed to be a mound of quilts. Ben gave him a sleepy, drunken smile. Disturbingly, his expression reminded Simon of Westmont's when Simon had roused him from his bed. Westmont? Good heavens, after dragging him across a frozen countryside, he seemed to have lost the man—and it made no difference at all. His wife still clung to his hand and his son was hopefully safe.

"Ben will make a full recovery?" he asked the doctor.

"Oh, yes. Serious poisoning after ingesting *Helleborus niger* is rare."

"Helle...?"

The doctor gave him an impish grin that completed the impression that the man was an elf. "The Latin name for your Christmas rose." He laughed. "I'm trying to awe you with my university education in the event you thought you had only found a barber-surgeon in this out of the way place. I want you to rest assured I know what I'm doing and that your son will be fine. He probably swallowed very little of the plant since it is said to cause the mouth to burn and tingle. I've never tried it myself, of course, but your boy was smarter than pets and livestock, which have a tendency to continue to chomp away despite the discomfort."

During Dr. Ashe's discourse, Emma had come to lean on Simon's side, her arm around his waist. She felt good there. Simon pulled her closer, and that felt even better. "Thank you, Doctor." Now that the crisis was over, Simon wanted the doctor gone. He hoped Emma's closeness meant he had been forgiven for his nonexistent transgressions, but he felt a pressing need to put the rest of his world into order.

Dr. Ashe, obviously hearing dismissal in Simon's words, quickly replaced everything in his bag and opened the door. At which point the diminutive man said, "Westmont," at the same time as Westmont,

306 • Hannah Meredith

standing just beyond the doorframe, exclaimed,
"Marcus." Much backslapping and loud greetings
followed, all of which Simon ignored in favor of
dropping a kiss on Emma's forehead.

"You're wet and freezing," she murmured but,
thankfully, didn't pull away. Simon realized he was both
cold and wet, but he wasn't willing to relinquish his
hold on her to do anything about the condition.

"Eh, Simon." Westmont's voice intruded into the
intimate moment. "I'm assuming that we will all be
staying here for the night and have made arrangements.
If I'm in error, let me know now, as the rooms are being
readied."

"Thank you, Westmont. We will be staying." Simon
was appreciative that his friend had the presence of
mind to take care of this. He couldn't imagine pressing
on to anywhere, and suspected Emma felt the same
way.

His wife surprised him by calling, "And arrange for
a hot bath for his lordship."

Yes! A hot bath. He must be on his way to being
forgiven.

❖ ❖ ❖

Emma leaned back in a comfortable, upholstered
chair and felt the muscles in her shoulders and neck
relax for the first time in what seemed like weeks. The
rooms at The Gray Dove had turned out to be surprising
spacious. While the decor was decidedly of the
homespun variety, everything was clean and the room

smelled of cedar and beeswax. The landlord had lit generous fires in all the chambers they were using, so the temperature soon became comfortable. Dorcas reported that even the servants' rooms were nice. Emma was relieved their unplanned stop had turned out to be a fortunate one.

She also realized that much of her tension had dissipated with her anger. Even as the bathing tub was brought in and a phalanx of servants marched in and out with hot water, Simon insisted on having Westmont in to explain to her about the ruby necklace. The poor man had looked as miserable and wet as Simon, but he dutifully said his piece.

Watching him stumble through his tale like a poorly prepared scholar placed at the front of the class, Emma felt sorry for Westmont, who was so obviously embarrassed about speaking of a mistress to a lady-wife and then having to admit he had to ask for financial help to get said mistress a parting gift.

Westmont had actually blushed when he recounted that the woman had left without receiving the necklace or even hearing his explanation that he could no longer support her. Westmont evidently took his lover's departure as a personal rejection rather than one born of financial necessity.

Emma had to bite her tongue to keep from confessing what she knew about his mistress's departure. She doubted discovering the woman had been bought off by his mother would make him any happier.

Perhaps now he would find an acceptable lady to marry, but Emma didn't think many ladies of her acquaintance could tame Westmont's wandering ways. His behavior made her appreciate Simon even more. Perhaps Simon only felt duty and responsibility, but he had always been fair and kind to her, something she needed to remember in their coming discussion.

And the needed discussion *was* coming. There was no avoiding it. Westmont's recitation had removed her suspicions about Simon, but she had yet to explain her own overreaction. She'd steeled herself to talk about this as soon as Westmont left, but by then, the bath was ready and Simon said he could think of no other way to get completely warm. So her hour of reckoning had been postponed.

The heat of the water had drained what was left of Simon's stamina, however, and the minute he was wrapped in a quilt and seated in front of the fire, he dozed off. Another reprieve.

The delay should have increased her tension, but Simon looked so much like his sons as he bonelessly slept in the chair, she felt a welling of tenderness. When they finally talked, she would have to be forthright and acknowledge her foolishness in doubting Simon. She should have remembered his persistent honesty and not let herself be influenced by other's opinions. She suspected her behavior was prompted by listening to gossip and coming to believe that infidelity was common.

This attitude was as poisonous for her as the Christmas rose had been for Ben. She could only hope her recovery would be as easily accomplished. Much of this depended on Simon. Hopefully, their relationship could be mended.

The comfortable silence of the room was interrupted by a loud knock. Hoping the sound hadn't awaken her husband, Emma came quickly to her feet and hurried to the door. One of the footmen who had accompanied her party stood in the hall carrying Simon's clothes and boots. The man and some of the inn staff had made an effort to dry and clean these belongings. Until they were available, Simon was relegated to wrapping in bed linens. While Simon had packed a saddlebag with a clean shirt and unmentionables, they had become as soaked as the clothing he wore.

"Is Lord Trenton ready to dress?" The footman gave her a hopeful look. His status would be enhanced if he were seen even as a temporary valet.

"No, he's still asl—"

"Let him in," Simon said. "I'm awake."

Emma stood back so the man could enter. She then called over her shoulder, "I'll go check on Ben and Will," and slipped out the door.

The boys and Nanny were housed in the adjoining room. Emma tapped lightly on the door and walked in. She didn't want to disturb Ben if he were still asleep, but both boys were awake, at least marginally, snuggled into Nanny's ample lap as she sat by the fire.

"Is all well?" Emma asked quietly, noticing both boys opened their eyes at her voice, gave her weak smiles, and then seemed to doze off.

"Aye, milady. Ben didn't eat as heartily as is his wont, but that is to be expected. Will ate enough for the two of them. I think we will make an early night of it and Ben will be as right as rain in the morning." Nanny's face took on an odd expression that might have been guilt. "And I'd like to apologize for the worry I caused you. I was so concerned for our Ben that I panicked. I should have known he hadn't time to eat enough of that plant to do him real harm."

Emma patted the older woman on the shoulder. "At least you knew the Christmas rose could harm him. I had no idea the plant was poisonous. All I saw was pretty flowers. You have simply confirmed why I feel the boys are safe when they are in your care."

Nanny beamed up at her. "I'd do anything for them," she said. "I love these boys. It's that simple."

Emma's breath caught in her throat as she realized—it *was* simple. *Love* was simple. She had been trying to make it into something complicated. Something she could quantify. As if she could look at her life, point at a specific time or event and say, "This is when I loved, and this is when I was loved in return." But that wasn't how it worked.

She had loved her sons since they were born. No,

probably before that. She had loved them as each had grown under her heart. She couldn't point to an exact time because this love simply was.

With Simon, she had been waiting for some blinding lightning flash to occur that would change their *amicable partnership* into a love match. She saw now that her dissatisfaction had been building over the years when this didn't seem to happen. But on her part, it had. Like the roots of the Christmas rose that continue to spread unseen beneath the winter soil, her love for Simon had quietly grown. She would not have been so upset over his imagined transgression had this not been the case.

And did Simon's wild ride through freezing weather indicate that his love for her had also been quietly growing? She hoped it did. But even if her love was not reciprocated, it existed and would hopefully continue to grow until one day it burst into bloom when it was least expected.

She smiled down at Nanny, the catalyst of her insight. "Call if I'm needed. Otherwise I will see you in the morning."

And then she left the room, warmed by a good fire and the glow of love, to go to her own chamber, where she hoped to discover the same thing.

Chapter Five

EMMA HAD BEEN GONE for a long time. Simon was beginning to worry that Ben had suffered a relapse. Then the door finally opened, and Emma returned.

"Are the boys well?"

Emma stopped just inside the door. "Yes, Ben seems on his way to a full recovery."

Then they just looked at each other across the room. Simon cast about for another conversation starter. That last exchange had been mundane in the extreme and was not what he'd planned at all. Of course, he had also not planned to fall asleep in front of the fire like some gouty septuagenarian.

"I, eh, ordered dinner to be served in our room," he said. "I hope that's all right. We've both had a physically and emotionally exhausting day, and I thought we should follow the boys' lead and make an early night of it." That still wasn't what he wanted to discuss, but Emma nodded and moved in his direction, so that was some progress.

"What of Westmont?" she asked as she seated

herself in the chair she had earlier occupied and he sat back in his.

Westmont? Why were they talking about Westmont? But Simon thought it best to follow Emma's conversational lead. "He's well taken care of. He stopped by while I was dressing. Oddly enough, he and Dr. Ashe attended school together and so have planned to meet for dinner. He wanted us to know that the good doctor is the younger son of the Earl of Marle and a highly regarded physician with an Edinburgh education."

"I don't think I've ever met the Earl of Marle," Emma said.

"Well, I haven't either. Marle doesn't deign to leave Northumbria to attend the House of Lords. Instead, he controls a vast number of pocket boroughs and gets the Commons to do his bidding. Consequently, the so-called Gnome of the North is a power to be reckoned with."

Emma smiled. "The Gnome of the North? That really isn't what they call the man, is it? Of course, after seeing Dr. Ashe..."

"Yes, it would explain the doctor's lack of height." Simon smiled back at her. He had no idea why they were talking about such inane subjects, but they were talking—and smiling. Smiling was good.

Then Emma's smile blinked out and she leaned forward in her chair. "I need to apologize for my precipitous actions. I didn't give you an opportunity to explain the situation and instead jumped to erroneous conclusions. I now realize that there were contributory factors that had nothing to do with you that resulted in my rash behavior, but these are poor excuses for suspicions with no basis in fact. I hope you can forgive me."

The smile also faded from Simon's face and he shook his head. "No, I'm the one who should ask your forgiveness. The long ride here allowed me to see that I've been wrong about a lot of things. But I'm determined to change my priorities. I got caught up in the idea of being a crusader for justice. I wanted people to see that I was my father's son. That I could be a power in the government. And so I lost sight of what really matters."

Her eyes were suddenly luminous with unshed tears. "I love you, Simon." she said.

He knew he should answer her in kind. That's what someone like Westmont would easily do, whether he meant it or not. But Simon had to be sure before he could speak those words. And how could he be sure if he was in love, anyway? He could only tell her what was in his heart.

"I care for you, Emma. Your happiness is important to me, but I feel like we've recently let each other down. I can't pretend I wasn't hurt when you believed I could have ignored my wedding vows—for I meant every word of them when I said them, and I still do. But I also see that my lackadaisical attitude may have given you reason to wonder if this were the case."

"Making unfounded assumptions was my mistake,

not yours," Emma said.

While her statement was true, it was not all the truth. "Neither of us is solely responsible for the ridiculous mess we've recently made of our relationship," Simon said. "It was a combined effort, and, therefore, it will take the same combined effort to get us back to where we should be—where I want us to be."

"You didn't cause my ridiculous suspicions. That was my fault."

Simon didn't want her to feel guilty—especially when his behavior was contributory. "I'm equally at fault since I've never given you all the romance I suspect a woman wants and deserves. It took Westmont, of all people, to make this clear."

He broke eye contact and scrubbed his hand through his hair. Lord, this was embarrassing, but it needed to be said. "I realize now that I was lacking in the physical aspect of our marriage. I initially came to your bed without much experience." He gave a rueful laugh and again sought her eyes. "And I suspect I didn't get much better over time. I foolishly thought of something that should be a joy as a duty. But I'm willing to work on making this part of our lives better if you're willing to put up with occasional missteps."

Emma started to stand, but Simon was faster, taking the two steps that were needed to bring him to her chair. He captured both of her hands and knelt in front of her. He noticed her color was high.

"I hope you didn't tell Westmont about what we do when you come to me," she said. "I'd be too embarrassed to ever look at the man again if this were the case."

"No, he was appalled with me for some of my attitudes." He suddenly grinned. "But I now know things about him that could be equally embarrassing, so I suspect we will neither mention any of this ever again."

She tightened her fingers around his. "From all I've heard, Westmont is a rake, and I'd not want you following his lead."

"I don't think there is any danger of that. Westmont has mastered the physical act, but he doesn't understand about the emotions necessary for a real relationship, and in this area, I think my understanding is better than his."

She started to speak. Simon put a finger on her lips to stop their movement. "No. Let me finish my thought. I know I cherish you. I know I need you to help me become the best man I can be, since I'd be a lesser person without you. I want what is best for you, even if it is to my detriment.

"Is this love? I don't know. But I am sure that I will do all in my power to make you happy and that we will continue to grow as a couple."

He pulled her toward him and gently kissed her.

And there was a loud rap on the door. "Dinner, milord," echoed in the room.

Bloody Hell. The innkeeper's timing was perfectly

horrid—although in another fifteen minutes, it might have been worse. Simon rolled to his feet and stood behind Emma's chair, which effectively hid the part of his anatomy that was most disappointed by the interruption. "Come," he called.

The same servers who had brought his bathwater now trooped in with a small table and two chairs. Another brought in more logs and added them to the fire. A young maid hurried around setting the table with china and glassware. The room seemed invaded by a veritable horde of servants. These were followed by the innkeeper himself, who set a large tray of food on the table. "I hope the meal is to your liking," he said.

Emma rose from her chair and went to inspect the culinary offering. "It looks and smells wonderful," she said. "Thank you so much."

She then offered other compliments as she gracefully shooed everyone out the door. When only the two of them remained, she slid the bolt home and turned to grin at Simon.

"Thank you for getting everyone out of the room," he said. "You knew I was in an obviously, eh, interested state, didn't you?"

She laughed and looked pointedly below his waist. His arousal, which had been subsiding, again stirred to life. "I'm rather well acquainted with how kisses affect you. So it wasn't difficult to assume you were hiding behind my chair for a reason."

The minx. He quickly crossed the room and pulled

her into his arms. "Not just any kisses," he said. "Only *your* kisses."

He proceeded to demonstrate just how affecting kisses could be. By the time he released her, hairpins had fallen to the floor and Emma's hair tumbled around her shoulders. Her hands had also been busy and his shirt was untucked. They were both breathing erratically.

He started maneuvering her toward the bed, but stopped. Damned if the odor of the food wasn't making him feel quite hollow. "Are you hungry?"

"Well..."

Simon laughed when it was obvious Emma was equally torn. "Are you familiar with the old Italian custom of dining *al letto*?"

When Emma shook her head, he said, "Then let me show you."

This plan meant he would probably have to pay for new bed linens, but some things were worth the cost.

Emma stretched and wiggled her toes. She felt a slight need to use the chamber pot, but it wasn't persistent enough to make her leave her warm cocoon. She smiled, feeling absurdly happy. She could get used to dining *al letto*. It was a bit messy, of course. The pillow she rested on sported two large stains that might have been either gravy or wine. Sauce laden food wasn't a good choice for this type of activity.

Plainer fare would have been better—although the

food actually didn't make that much difference. What mattered was the closeness, the companionship, the laughter. She and Simon had never been silly together, and it was an unimagined delight.

Even this, the physical part of their relationship, had previously been serious. Dutiful. But how could an act filled with such joy ever be only a duty? Thank Heavens this had changed. Everything now seemed so wonderfully different. Simon may not think he knew what love was, but he could certainly make her feel that she was loved.

"Do you want to go on to Oakley?" Simon asked, his breath tickling her ear. She started with surprise. She hadn't realized he was awake. They were wrapped together like spoons in a drawer; the heat of his body was comforting as it radiated along her back and down her legs.

She rolled over to face him. Her hands stroked the sides of his face. She enjoyed the scrape of his night beard along her palms. "No, I want us all to go back to London. I want you to be there for the vote on the Six Acts."

"A useless effort, since my side will go down to defeat."

She leaned forward and kissed his nose. "A *temporary* defeat. When everyone comes to his senses, you will be on record as having been right all along. I want this for you."

Simon had worked too hard to not be present for

the actual vote on the measure. She loved his conscientiousness, his realization that with the privileges of his title came the responsibility to pass laws that benefited all of the country, not just a few aristocrats.

"We can leave for your parents' home immediately after the vote, then." Simon returned the quick kiss on her nose. Why hadn't she realized frivolous little things like a peck on the nose could be so, well, nice?

"Actually, I don't care if we go to Oakley or not. I'd just as soon we have our own Christmas celebration in our own house." There. She'd said it. She had finally voiced the unfilial sentiments that had been swirling through her mind.

Simon chuckled. "Well, I'll certainly never advocate we spend the holidays with your family. It's always so…"

"Tense," she supplied. "Going to Oakley has always been an obligation, not a joy." And being at Oakley always reminded Emma that she was second. The second daughter with the marginal looks and the less desirable spouse. As the coach went through Oakley's gateposts, she seemed to curl into herself like a leaf when the weather turned cold. And she didn't like that reaction. Especially since she felt she was blooming in her own small family.

"It's nice to know that I'm not the only one who feels like I've been called to the headmaster's office whenever we visit," Simon said, moving his mouth down to nuzzle her neck. "Do you want to go to Friar's

Hill or stay in London?"

"Friar's Hill," she said, but the name came out as a groan. Simon's wicked mouth had slid down to her breasts. Her hands caressed the hard contours of her husband's body, which felt simultaneously familiar and new. She decided she would worry about an upcoming journey as soon as she and Simon had finished this one.

Christmas morning, 1819

The room was chilly, but when Emma pulled back the heavy drapes to look out, the air that circulated from the window was positively frigid. After three days of snowy nights and melting mornings, the snow had decided to stay.

A white world met her gaze. The roofs of outbuildings looked as if they were covered in meringue. She smiled, hoping there was enough snow on the ground to use the sleigh to go into the village for church. The bells on the horses' harnesses always seemed a part of the holiday.

But she was thankful yesterday had been warmer when they gathered the greens for the house. The boys had been energetic helpers and if snow had been added to the fun, Emma feared they would never have come inside. She and the staff had managed to make the house look very festive—and this made her wish they had invited some friends to share Christmastide with them.

Their late decision to come to Friar's Hill had made

this impossible, although she had asked Lady Stanley to join them. To Emma's surprise, Diana had already planned to spend the holidays with the Lord and Lady Fairbourne—and presumably, their son. Had Diana anticipated spending the holidays with Westmont when she helped eliminate his mistress? Emma suspected she and Diana would have some interesting conversations when they were both again in Town.

"What are you doing up so early?" Simon's voice right behind her made Emma jump.

"Looking at the snow and obviously woolgathering, since I didn't hear you get up." Simon slipped his arms around her and she leaned back onto his chest, only to quickly straighten and turn around when she realized the man behind her was naked. "Simon! You're going to freeze off parts of your body I'm very fond of. You need to put on a warm dressing gown."

He laughed. "I would, except you seem to be wearing it."

Oh Heavens, she was. She hadn't wanted to awaken him, and his banyan was lying over the chair, so she'd slipped it on. If she was going to continue to sleep in Simon's bed—and she hoped she was—she needed to do some wardrobe rearrangement. "I seem to have appropriated your heavy wool socks as well," she said.

"I guess the clothes thief will have to come back to bed with me, then, and warm me up." He pulled her in the direction of the bed and she went without resistance.

He helped her out of his robe and pulled off the overlarge socks. She immediately slid over so he could join her under the covers, but instead he walked to the fireplace, kindled a paper spill from the remaining coals, and lit a candle.

Emma pushed herself to a sitting position. "Are you getting up?"

"No. But I thought since we're both awake and it is Christmas morning, I'd give you this." He handed her a jewelry box as he placed the candle on the table next to the bed.

"If this is a ruby necklace, I'll not be amused," she said with mock severity.

"No, it's nothing so expensive, but it is something I think, well, hope, you'll like better."

She lifted the covers to invite him into the bed, but he shook his head and said, "Open it first."

Bemused, she slipped off the ribbon and opened the box. Inside, attached to a gold chain, was an enameled pendent in the shape of a Christmas rose. "Oh, Simon, it's lovely."

He leaned over as if he too wanted to see what was in the box. "I know you like that type of flower, but after the poisoning problem, I thought this might be safer than the real thing." He removed the necklace and put it in her hand. "It's engraved on the back."

The reason for the candle now became clear. She tilted the gold back of the pendent toward the flame. *I love you, Simon* winked in the flickering light.

"It's perfect." She felt her throat tighten and tears threaten, so she could say no more.

"I've had trouble saying those words," he said, "although they have long been true. I wanted you to have something that would remind you that I loved you, even if I forget to tell you. I... Are you crying?"

"I'm touched, you silly man. Of course, I'm crying. As I said, this gift is perfect. Now get in bed before you turn into an icicle."

Simon snuffed out the candle and joined her in bed. He was thoroughly chilled from walking around the frigid room—but he didn't stay that way for long.

About Hannah

Hannah Meredith's father wanted her to be a doctor, so she dutifully trekked off to a university with this in mind. When she popped out the other side, however, she had a Master's Degree in English with minors in history and religion. Along the way, she'd discovered she was not really fascinated by the actual "insides" of people, but rather by the people themselves and the stories they made of their lives.

She married her high school sweetheart. They had one wonderful son. They moved around the mid-South as her husband's career advanced. She taught at the high school and college level and eventually sold real estate, an interest that resulted from all those early moves. The story of her life has turned out to be a happy one. She is still married to her high school sweetheart. She has four wonderful grandchildren. And she's permanently located in a charming, North Carolina town.

But she'd always enjoyed making up stories about other people's lives in other times and other places, and she finally began writing these tales down. Under another name, she sold over a dozen speculative fiction short stories to major science fiction and fantasy magazines. She's become seduced by the desire for a consistent HEA, however, and now writes historical romance. She currently has four historical romances available: *Kestrel*, *Indentured Hearts*, *Kaleidoscope*, and *A Dangerous Indiscretion*. *The Color of Night*, which is a sequel to *Kaleidoscope*, should be published shortly. Hannah's novellas have also appeared in both *Christmas Revels I* and *Christmas Revels II*.

If you'd like to keep up with Hannah as she examines the human heart (without a scalpel), you can find her at: http://www.hannahmeredith.com and http://www.facebook.com/HannahMeredithAuthor

Our Thanks

Without readers, all authors would simply be talking to themselves. We, therefore, appreciate your choosing *Christmas Revels III* and hope you enjoyed it.

Every year we each try to approach Christmas in Regency England in a slightly different manner. We feel this mimics how individual families still celebrate this wonderful season. We want these tales of the love and hope to speak to people today.

It is always helpful for readers to leave an honest review at any of the purchasing sites, and we hope you will consider doing so.

And please check out our previous anthologies, which are filled with totally different novellas.

Christmas Revels I
Christmas Revels II

We hope Christmas lives in your hearts throughout the year.

Thank you,

Anna   Kate   Hannah

Made in the USA
Middletown, DE
23 October 2017

49886261R00183